WITHDRAWN

THE ACCIDENTAL GUARDIAN

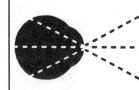

This Large Print Book carries the
Seal of Approval of N.A.V.H.

THE ACCIDENTAL GUARDIAN

MARY CONNEALY

THORNDIKE PRESS

A part of Gale, a Cengage Company

Farmington Hills, Mich • San Francisco • New York • Waterville, Maine
Meriden, Conn • Mason, Ohio • Chicago

Copyright © 2018 by Mary Connealy.
Scripture quotations are from the King James Version of the Bible.
Thorndike Press, a part of Gale, a Cengage Company.

Thorndike Press® Large Print Christian Romance.
The text of this Large Print edition is unabridged.
Other aspects of the book may vary from the original edition.
Set in 16 pt. Plantin.

LIBRARY OF CONGRESS CIP DATA ON FILE.
CATALOGUING IN PUBLICATION FOR THIS BOOK
IS AVAILABLE FROM THE LIBRARY OF CONGRESS.

ISBN-13: 978-1-4328-4933-7 (hardcover)

Published in 2018 by arrangement with Bethany House Publishers, an imprint of Baker Publishing Group

Printed in the United States of America
1 2 3 4 5 6 7 22 21 20 19 18

To My Cowboy. My husband.
My very own romantic cowboy hero.

CHAPTER 1

Southwest of Lake Tahoe, Nevada
October 1867

Deborah Harkness came awake with a snap, her hand already steady on the six-gun under her pillow.

Just as fast, she eased off the tension and the trigger. She knew that sound.

"Deb, I've got to go." Three-year-old Maddie Sue needed to make a predawn run into the tall grass.

It was almost encouraging that, after months of being awakened many mornings in just this way, Deb could still get nervous. A woman needed to be alert on a wagon train heading through the wilderness.

"Shhh, honey. I'll take you. Shhh." The little girl did her best to wait quietly — three-year-olds weren't famous for that — while Deb slipped on the heavy coat she used for a blanket. Not waking up Maddie

Sue's exhausted parents was always Deb's first goal. After that — not waking up Deb's sister Gwen and Maddie Sue's toddler cousin Ronnie ranked very high.

Everyone needed their sleep.

Deb had learned early on during this wagon-train journey to sleep fully dressed, so it took just seconds to put Maddie Sue's little coat on her — it was sharply cold in the peaks of the Sierra Nevada Mountains in October. Deb grabbed her knapsack and shoved her pistol inside. She never, ever left the safety of the wagon train without the bag and the gun. Mr. Scott had stressed this small precaution until it was a reflex. She urged Maddie Sue toward the back of the covered wagon.

A whimper stopped her.

Ronnie. If she left the little boy, he'd be bawling his head off before Deb got back, and it wouldn't just be Mr. and Mrs. Scott who'd be awake — it'd be the whole wagon train. Ronnie could howl something terrible.

"I've got him, Deb." Gwen was awake now, too. "I'll walk out with you."

In the pitch-dark of the wagon, Deb could more hear than see her eighteen-year-old sister donning her own coat.

Deb was tempted to growl with frustration. At this rate, she and Maddie Sue would be leading a parade into the privacy of the grass.

Instead she just whispered, "Thank you."

She and Gwen had teamed up to keep the Scott children tended in return for a ride across the country.

They'd earned every penny of the trip.

Now they walked silently away from the small wagon train. There was not a stir from behind them, so Deb thought they'd left the Scotts still sleeping.

She sincerely hoped so.

The Scotts worked so hard and were so kind to Deb and Gwen. Deb's life hadn't had a whole lot of kindness in it for a long time.

They didn't go far into the grass. Taller than her head, the grass could be disorienting, and in the moonless, starless hours before dawn, fear gnawed at her. If she wasn't careful, she could easily get turned around in her directions and not find her way back to the wagons.

"Hurry up, honey." The chilly air kept everyone moving fast. Gwen had Ronnie quiet, and Deb heard the eighteen-month-old boy sucking at a bottle. Gwen must've had the bottle ready from the night before and thought to grab it as they left the wagon.

9

"Good thinking on the bottle," Deb whispered. The boy was probably too old for the bottle, but in the hectic world of the wagon train they hadn't thought to spend time weaning him, and right now Deb was very glad for that.

Gwen's quiet chuckle was followed by a soft croon as she kept the boy eating. "I'm on to him by now."

They finished their little trip and turned to head back to the wagon when a gunshot cut through the night. Deb grabbed Maddie Sue's arm and dove for the ground. Gwen landed right beside her, then stuck the bottle back in Ronnie's mouth before he could start crying.

A scream ripped through the air.

The gunfire came again and again. More guns, many guns. The shouts, the cries of fear and pain and, to her horror, cries she recognized as people dying.

"Take the children and run." Deb, her heart pounding, her stomach twisting until she feared she'd be sick, drew her gun from the pack and took one step toward the wagon train.

A hard hand slapped her wrist and hung on like a vise. "You're not going back there."

"I have to."

"No, Deb, wait. Listen . . . it's already

over." Sure enough, the hail of bullets had tapered off, followed by a few single but deliberate shots. Another cry of agony. Then the shooting ended as suddenly as it had begun. No more cries of any kind, only harsh laughter and a few last gunshots, aimed into the air maybe, joined by whoops of celebration.

"Let's strip these wagons!" a man shouted in a high-pitched voice. It stopped Deb from trying to pull free from Gwen. Her sister was right. It was too late. There was no one left to save.

The horror shocked her to the marrow.

"We have to go, Deb," Gwen whispered. "In case the children cry out. We have to get out of earshot."

Maddie Sue whimpered.

Though Gwen was right, they didn't *both* have to go. Deb knew full well one adult woman could carry both children.

"You go. I have to at least get a look at them." She turned.

"Deb, stop!" Gwen hissed. "It's too dangerous."

"I know it's too late to save anyone, and I promise you I won't let them see me. But maybe I can see *them.* I can be a witness to this crime and help hunt down a pack of killers."

A crackle sounded, and Deb whirled around toward the noise. Then came the smell of smoke. The outlaws were burning the evidence of their crime.

Gwen was barely visible as a dark shape in the shadows of the tall grass. But Deb sensed her tension. Gwen wanted to tackle her and drag her to safety. Deb's blood almost hummed with energy fueled by fear and anger. If Gwen felt the same, maybe Gwen could carry both children and haul Deb along.

Maddie Sue whimpered again, louder this time. Gwen made a low sound of distress, then caught Maddie Sue's hand. "Let's go, honey. And Deb, I need you."

That was the plain, bald truth, and it affected Deb more than concern for her own safety.

"Be careful. We all need you. I'll be praying every second you're gone."

"Thank you. I'll be praying for all of us." Deb moved away from her sister, feeling as if she were ripping the very fabric of her skin. She glanced back to see Gwen stepping deeper into the grass.

Could they get separated in here forever? Might she be seeing her sister and those two sweet children for the last time? Even though Deb was heading for a group of vicious murderers, she found herself worrying about Gwen as her little sister vanished into a land she knew nothing about. A land where it took strength to survive, and so far in her life, Deb hadn't known a man stronger than Abe Scott, so sometimes even strength wouldn't save you.

Maddie Sue whimpered again, and then there was only silence.

She crept toward the wagon train, the noise of the men a perfect guide. The talking and raucous laughter from the camp grew louder. She saw the flicker of flames and knew the swath of tall grass was thinning.

She breathed as silently as she could, knowing that if she could hear the men, they could likely hear her.

That's when she realized she saw more than the fire. The eastern sky was lightening. In the first blush of dawn, men looted the wagons. She counted three who appeared against the backdrop of flames and tried to judge their height and build.

She edged closer to the trail, praying she wasn't visible.

As she stood straighter, looking for details so she could describe the men's appearance for others, a face appeared in flickering firelight. The face of a killer. She craned her neck for a better look at all three of them. She smelled smoke again . . . and something else. Something she'd never smelled before.

Burning flesh.

Something Trace Riley had smelled before and had hoped and prayed to never smell again.

Wolf snarled and crouched low to the ground, his ears laid back, his teeth bared. Black, Trace's mustang stallion, tossed his head until the bit jingled.

"Easy, boys."

He was worried about Wolf. "Stay with me." He didn't put it past the dog — who looked more wolf than dog, and probably was — to go charging up the trail on the attack. He liked to rip throats out first and think later.

But as was his way, Wolf minded and stayed at his master's side, inching along with Trace, his low growl mingling with the gusting wind and swaying trees, which nearly provided a roof for the high-country trail. Black's muscles bunched, and his ears went back to match Wolf's. Trace wasn't sure if the two critters knew what it was they were smelling or if they just sensed Trace's tension.

Wolf and Black weren't alone in readying

themselves for trouble.

Trace's hands got rock-steady, and his eyes sharpened until every blade of grass, waving in the breeze, became clear. Every puff of wind, and each scent born on it, tested and considered. His rifle filled his hand without a conscious decision to reach for it.

Every one of his senses came alive. He was wide awake to an unseen horror.

He judged every tree and rock along the heavily wooded trail that straddled the spine of the Sierra Nevada Mountains, where California met Nevada right down the middle of Lake Tahoe. Every one of those rocks and trees made a fine hiding place.

Kicking the mustang into a gallop, Wolf loping along at his side, Trace reached the top of the trail, looked down into a hollow that opened to a wide grassy clearing in the forested land, and saw the smoke — a low smudge along the ground. When the smoke rose, the brisk cold wind instantly dispersed it, which was why he hadn't seen it before he could smell it.

And then he recognized what was burning. A wagon train, or what was left of one, in a circle. Except for the flames, the scene was as silent and still as death itself. He wanted to turn away, run. But he could no more run from this massacre than he could run from his own past.

Trace reined in his stallion and waited in a silence broken only by the buffeting wind and Wolf's threatening rumble. Whoever had done this was long gone. The fire was nearly burned down to nothing. But Trace had lived a long time in a hard land and survived against odds so long he'd be the envy of every riverboat gambler in the world.

He studied the trail. He'd been on it awhile now and there'd been no tracks, nor had he met anyone. No sign of anyone traveling his way, not even hours ago. But there were recent tracks headed east; he could see that even from here.

Reluctantly, he kicked his horse down the trail into the hollow. He had to know what happened and see if there was anyone left alive and, failing that, find out who these folks were and then let their families know what had happened.

A chill colder than Lake Tahoe took root in his backbone. Men lay dead, and the fire in his belly for vengeance roared to life. He'd get justice for these poor folks.

He'd done it before.

Breathing hard, fury and grief tearing through his gut, Trace realized his grip on the reins had tightened, causing Black to dance. He forced himself to relax his hands and remembered a time when he'd spent many of his days watching this same trail from a distance, posting himself as a guardian to those hardy few who broke off from the main wagon train and took the little-used trail south.

Back then he'd put a stop to the raiders who preyed on honest folks. Back then he'd known no one, spoken to no one. He'd done his work and slipped away. He'd even chosen not to follow the trail out, find civilization, because the raging need for vengeance kept him here, kept him on guard.

Finally, the trouble had stopped. And he'd stopped standing sentry to those passing by. He'd settled in to a lonely life in the wilderness.

Then Adam had turned up at Trace's property hunting work. His loneliness struck him. He hadn't realized how terrible the isolation had been, with only his anger as a friend.

Trace learned a lot about the outside world from his new friend. He explored more widely and found a few folks lived around him. From them he learned about the ghost who haunted this trail. "The Guardian," they called him.

To his grim amusement, Trace found he'd become a legend. The identity of this ghostly guardian was never known, and Trace sure as certain never told anyone. He'd killed men. Oh, they'd needed killin' real bad, but it was a weight on his soul that he never could shed.

He'd nearly reached the fire circle when a rustling to the north, in the tall grass, jerked him around, his rifle aimed. Wolf whirled to face the noise.

He heard a strange cry that he couldn't identify. It put him in mind of childhood stories among superstitious folks in the mountains of Tennessee, of witches and goblins and banshees. The cry sent a chill up his spine and made the hair on the back of his neck stand up straight.

Trace didn't believe in such things as ghosts, but if ever a place might be haunted, the site of all these murdered souls might be it.

He suppressed the eerie notion. Someone or something was coming and, considering the carnage of the wagon train and the pure fact that someone mighty evil was close by, it looked like, for all his thinking that he was a tough man who survived in the West, he'd walked right into a trap.

He leveled his rifle, ready to fight to the

end. Wolf's ears came forward, and his growl changed to a bark. A mighty friendly bark. It wasn't a sound Wolf used much. In fact, about never. Trace couldn't remember ever hearing it before.

"Stay, boy."

And then he saw . . . something impossible.

With a quick jerk, he pulled his finger away before a twitch could trigger his gun. And how could a man not twitch when he was staring at an absolutely shocking sight?

Wolf took off running. He was just as obedient as he wanted to be and not a speck more.

His pa used to say, *"Believe your own eyes, son. Most of the time."* This might be one of those times Pa was thinking of as an exception.

A woman. He was watching a woman running right toward him.

"Help, don't leave us!" The woman waved her arms, shouted, and generally acted like he was the finest sight short of the Lord returning in triumph.

Which meant she didn't have a lick of sense.

She had no idea who he was, but he had a good notion about her. She was from this wagon train and had somehow survived.

And she needed help. In fact, she should've been sorely afraid that he was one of those who'd attacked and killed her fellow travelers. Instead, she showed herself bold as could be.

"You have to help us, please!"

"Us?" Trace said to Black. And now she was asking a strange rider for help shortly after she'd witnessed a massacre.

On the other hand, she did need his help. He shoved the rifle into the leather scabbard on his saddle and was about to call out . . . something. What?

Relax, I'm not going anywhere.

I'm not a murdering outlaw, and you're shot full of luck.

Please quit screaming — you're scaring my horse.

And then a strange high-pitched squall drew his attention as a second woman emerged from the grass. He noticed the bundle she carried in her arms. It was . . . Trace shook his head with some violence. It was . . . no, it wasn't. Yep, it sure enough was . . . a baby.

Now that he was getting a few more details into his addled brain — and he'd been so proud of what an alert and noticing kind of man he was just a few minutes ago — he noticed the second woman had an older child in her arms, too.

The littler kid just plain howled, which set off the older one — a girl and still mighty young herself — into a fit of wailing tears. The first woman turned away from him and raced toward the second, took the crying older child, then they came at him running, screaming, waving. His mustang just got plain jittery, and maybe Trace was a bit jittery himself.

Banshees were looking mighty good right now.

While they kept running and hollering, he started figuring. He was twenty miles from home. He had one horse to carry five people. He'd been on the trail a long time and had very little food left, and sure as certain no baby's milk. The blustering wind and overcast sky told him snow and cold were on the way and might strike at any time.

He looked down at his black mustang stallion. He'd caught the critter when it was just a foal, standing on wobbling legs behind its dying mama, circled by wolves. Trace had driven the wolves off. The mare died, and Trace had taken the young mustang home and gentled him. He broke it himself and considered the loyal animal one of his few friends. He glanced at Wolf and remembered well that saving the colt had cost the pup its own mama, a dog running with a wolf pack. Between the wolf and the mustang, it was hard to tell which one was his best friend.

"Don't leave us. We need help!" the woman closest to him shrieked again. Hadn't she noticed he wasn't going anywhere? Both kids were caterwaulin' now, both women shouting and waving.

Wolf seemed to have second thoughts and came running back to Trace with his tail between his legs.

Leaning low so he wouldn't be overheard, he rubbed Black's shoulder and said to his friends, "These four aren't the only ones who need help."

CHAPTER 2

"Help, don't leave us!" Deb forced herself to step forward.

As terrified as she had been to show herself, afraid that whoever had attacked the wagon train might've come back, she had to risk it.

She had no idea how to survive out here alone. Besides, she'd seen the filthy villains ride off to the east, and this man had come from the west.

He looked bad. Dirty, his gun drawn, and edgy, like he might shoot first and see who he'd shot later. But what other possible decision could she make than to hope against hope he was a decent man who would help them?

Honestly, they didn't have a thing worth stealing, so unless he was just a pure cold-blooded murderer, he might come to their rescue. Deb had heard that most western men were good to women and children. His dog barked, wagged its tail, and panted. At least the gray dog was willing to be friendly.

"Please, you have to help us!"

With deep prayers for protection from God, she and Gwen rushed forward. Once they'd decided to wave him down, she was terrified the rider might move on before they could gain his attention.

All the prayer and fear and hope brought out the loudest scream yet. "Help us, please. Help!"

The man stared at them. He was still a ways off. She was no judge of distance, but she couldn't see his eyes or the expression on his face. But he did lower his rifle, turn his head . . . maybe looking for danger? And then shoved the rifle down into a scabbard on the side of his saddle.

So that was good. He'd disarmed himself. He looked down for some reason, just sort of hung his head, gave his horse's shoulder a gentle rub, and she thought maybe she saw his lips move. As if he were talking to someone. His horse? His dog? An imaginary friend?

Oh, fine. She'd stumbled on the only help in sight, and he was a madman.

Then his head came up and he reined his horse in their direction and kicked it into a trot. He closed the distance between them and swung to the ground as soon as he was near.

"Are you all right? Are you from the wagon train?" He was tall, taller than Pa, at least six-foot-two. He had a bit of hair showing beneath a sharp-looking black Stetson that must be brand-new. There was a line of white on his neck that told her he'd just had a haircut. His eyes were a darker blue than hers. Concern and confusion shone out of them.

"Yes, we were in the grass when the raiders came and sh-shot everyone." Deb rested her hand on the back of little Maddie Sue's head and urged the little girl, who'd been bounced along as Deb ran, to rest her head. The little sweetie set her cheek on Deb's shoulder and turned to look at the rescuer.

The dog sniffed Deb's skirt and then went to sniff Gwen, then rolled over on his back, legs in the air, panting with his tongue lolling out of his mouth. Not a sign of the killer dog to be seen.

"I'm Deb Harkness, and this is my sister, Gwen. We are caring for these two children, Madeline and Cameron Scott. Their parents were — were —" Deb swallowed hard.

The man nodded. "They weren't with you when the attack came."

Deb shook her head and hugged Maddie

Sue tighter.

"I'm Trace Riley," the man said. "I need to go look at the wagon train. Make sure there are no survivors. My ranch is a long ride from here, and it's the closest shelter around. Give me some time over there, and then we'll be on our way."

Deb didn't want to say it, but she had to. "I think I had better come with you."

"No, I don't want you —"

Since she knew what he would say, and appreciated it, she ignored him while she handed Maddie Sue to Gwen. "Keep the children away."

"Deb, if there is anyone left alive, I can help." Gwen had her arms full, yet Deb knew she was better at doctoring than most.

"I'll come and take over with the children if we need your help. But I don't think they left anyone alive."

Gwen nodded, gave the dog a nervous look, and sank down on the ground. Both little ones had quit their crying and now seemed overly subdued, and Deb worried about that.

The dog turned in a circle three times before lying down at Gwen's side as if to take a nap.

Ronnie was probably asleep, and Maddie Sue looked to be nearly so. They'd usually have gone back to sleep for a bit after the early-morning run into the grass. Since they'd missed that, under the circumstances, this might be a natural nap time. Or maybe the dog was just setting a good example for them.

She looked at Gwen, who met her worried gaze and shrugged. "We'll be fine. Go." Gwen looked past her at the carnage and shuddered.

Maddie Sue huddled even closer.

Deb didn't want to go any more than Gwen did, but she had to find what she knew was hidden in the Scotts' wagon. It might make all the difference to the children's future.

It would also test this man Trace Riley. Because if the thieves and murderers hadn't found and stolen the Scotts' gold, maybe Trace would. Though not a treasure trove, it still had value, and Trace would show himself to be a man of honor . . . or not.

There was only one way to find out. She had to go look at the massacre.

"You can't go look at the massacre." Trace watched her hand off the child just as if he hadn't spoken. He knew the woman wasn't deaf.

She turned to him and, after meeting his

27

eyes and no doubt seeing exactly what he thought, strode right past him toward the circle of burned-out wagons.

Not only was he not stopping her, he couldn't even keep up.

"Miss Harkness," he called to her back as she walked. He hustled to catch up, leading his horse, unsure where to tie the critter in this grassy stretch. He moved along fast. He sure didn't want her getting there first.

As they left the little ears of the kids behind, he leaned close and whispered, "You don't want to see what's in that campsite, miss."

"I know." She gave him a frightened look. "Believe me, I know. But I have to."

Trace didn't know much about women. Practically nothing as a matter of fact. He'd seen a couple just these last few weeks when he'd been near Sacramento on his first cattle drive, but they bothered and confused him to the point they seemed kinda dangerous, so he'd stayed well back.

No chance of staying back now. He caught her arm, lightly, not yanking her around, but just wishing she'd let him get control of her. "It's gonna be so ugly. Please don't walk in there."

She stopped, and his hopes rose. Looking up at him, she met his eyes. She was about four or five inches shorter than him so that her eyes were level with his mouth. He figured himself for around six feet tall — he'd never measured, didn't even own a yardstick — which made her a bit over five and a half feet.

He saw dread and determination in equal parts. Her eyes were a shining bright blue that seemed to be lit from within because of their contrast to her dark brown hair, worn in a single braid down her back. But her hair was all a mess, with long strings of it escaping from both the braid and her bonnet and blowing around her face. Her heavy brown wool coat was buttoned up to her chin, and her bonnet matched the coat. Her skin — what little he could see of it — was deeply tanned, as anybody's would be after long months on the trail.

He'd never been this close to a woman in his life, hardly ever been this close to a person in general, not since the wagon train he'd been on had been attacked all those years back, with him left as the only survivor. Although his hired men rubbed shoulders with him from time to time.

He knew exactly what she was about to see in that camp, and he looked at that pretty face and ached for her because, short of hog-tying her, the unwavering gleam in her eyes said she was going to stay with him.

"Have you seen a-a dead — ?" His throat went bone-dry and he swallowed hard. It was such a terrible thing to be talking about, but seeing it was so much worse than talking of it. He felt a desperate need to stop her. "Have you seen a dead body, miss?"

"My ma and pa are both dead. I saw them."

"Have you seen one that's been burned?"

She flinched, and he felt like a brute. But he went on, trying to sound kind even though he hadn't had much practice at it. A man talked, that was all. He didn't concern himself so much with *how* he sounded to anyone. So he tried hard to wrangle a kindhearted tone to his voice yet wasn't sure he managed at all.

"I would spare you having that vision. Once it's in your head, it's never forgotten."

That got her attention, which had been on him anyway. But by the way her gaze had sharpened, he knew it was more so now.

"You've seen such a thing?"

"Yes." His stomach twisted with the ugly memories that haunted him still, ten years after he'd seen the burned remains of his pa. He'd had to look in order to identify Pa, and it had haunted his nights for years. "I still have nightmares sometimes, and you will, too. Why do that to yourself?"

He realized he still held her arm and let go. "It's nothing a body can forget. Ever."

Her expression of dread deepened, and her eyes looked — were those tears?

Before he could bring himself to ask, she turned to face the wreckage and swiped the back of her wrist across both eyes. "I have no choice. There are things I have to search for. I'm hoping there is some canned milk for Ronnie. The Scotts had other things, including letters, that I hope survived and will tell the address of Maddie Sue's father. He'll need to be contacted. If the fire didn't destroy everything, maybe we can even find diapers."

Trace didn't want to add thinking of diapers to this. "I reckon that sort of thing is all burned away. But I give you my word I'll go through everything, and I'll bring any canned goods that aren't ruined, anything that didn't burn. I'll make a pile out here for you to choose from."

He couldn't bury the bodies, though, and that made him sick with regret. It would take hours, maybe days, to dig a grave for all those people. He had no shovel and doubted there was one with a handle that had survived the fire. The ground was most likely frozen.

And he had these four to take care of. Best to let the bodies rest the way Native folks did. Let nature handle the dead and let the ground reclaim them. He had the living to care for.

"Tell me what to search for and I'll find it. I won't give up until I do or until I'm sure I can't."

He thought he saw her chin quiver a bit, but she didn't admit she was scared. Tough little thing. Poor, tough little thing.

He frowned when she shook her head, squared her shoulders. She stopped and turned toward him. "You say you've seen this before?"

"Yes."

"Then maybe . . ." Her hand tightened on his arm, and her eyes filled with something almost as scary as tears. Was it concern? For him? But when had he ever learned the skill of reading what was in a woman's eyes? Must come natural. "You should stay here," she said. "There's no sense in both of us walking into this, and I have to go. I believe you when you say I shouldn't." Her teeth clenched until her jaw was a rigid line.

Trace shook his head. "I'm not letting you walk in there alone." He made it sound like the circle of burned-out wagons was the gateway to hell. He was sure it wasn't, but then hell must be so vicious . . . well, it'd keep him to his faith just thinking of it.

"Very well." She let go of his arm. "I appreciate your warning and your offer to take this responsibility. I do. But I have to do it myself." She headed out again.

Giving his horse a dismayed look, Trace followed along like a pull toy on wheels — he'd seen such a thing once as a child. Rolling along her trail, he gave up on saving her from the experience. Instead, he caught up and rested his left hand on the small of her back.

She turned slightly, her eyes widening in surprise. Then she laid one hand on his shoulder, nodded, and whispered, "Thanks."

Thanks for what? he wondered. After all, he should be thanking her for going with him. He was probably as sickened to be doing this as she was. Once he thought of it, he knew it was true. He was dreading it more because he'd seen such horror before and understood exactly what lay ahead of them. Her turn was about ten paces away.

They reached the nearest blackened hulk of a wagon, and he tied his mustang to a charred wheel hub. The horse started grazing.

Trace was glad someone's stomach was working.

CHAPTER 3

"Did you find it?" Gwen whispered.

"Yes, I found things hidden in nearly every wagon." Deb had her knapsack, now bulging and heavy, that she'd carried with her when they took the children away from the wagon train before sunup. She had her skirts gathered and full of things too, and Trace carried a load that he was quietly placing into a pack.

Deb handed over all Gwen could carry. Gwen had also taken her small bag this morning. Both of them always kept their guns with them along with a few basic supplies. The Scotts had trained them well to be prepared for trouble.

Gwen filled her own sack while she sat in the grass with Maddie Sue asleep on her lap. Ronnie slept on the ground, on his back. The dog stretched out beside Ronnie like a warm, loyal pillow. It lifted its head and panted while watching Deb as closely as Gwen.

Deb was trying to keep it hidden, but she could tell both sister and dog were noticing how upset she was. She concentrated on the charred cans she'd gathered.

"I found three cans of milk. I don't know how far we have to travel, but we'd best set out soon because this is less than a day's supply." Deb dropped her leather bag on the ground with a dull clank as the cans knocked together.

"Ronnie eats solid food now. He can get by without milk for a while." The words halted, and Gwen gave her a long, searching look. "Are you all right?"

"It was hard to see, but I'm fine." That was just a plain old lie. She wasn't going to be fine for quite a while — maybe never. She had images in her head that would never fade. She did her best to regain her composure after what she'd seen, yet she knew Trace's talk of nightmares would be true for her now, too.

She noticed a gray pallor to Trace's complexion and suspected he was as sick to his stomach as she was. It helped somewhat that a strong man was as affected as she by the ugliness and brutality of what they'd seen.

"Some of us will have to walk. I'm so sorry

we're adding such a burden to your journey, Mr. Riley. Thank you."

"Call me Trace. 'Mister' sounds like an old man to me. Although" — he glanced at the wagon-train ruins — "I'm feeling older by the minute."

"And we are Deb and Gwen. Calling both of us Miss Harkness will be confusing."

Nodding, he said, "Let's get the little ones up on horseback. Black here is strong enough to carry all four of you, but with all these supplies to add, I just don't think you'll all fit."

"That's fine. Gwen and I walk along with the wagon train most days."

"That's what we'll have to do, then. One of you riding and holding the young'uns. Each of you will take a turn walking."

"You'll have a turn riding, too." Deb was determined.

"Let's get moving. We'll worry about who's riding later." The dog, Trace had called it Wolf, or some such odd name, got up and went to his master's side and nosed at his hand. A quiet whine that sounded like sympathy came from the dog, and Trace looked down at it and rested one big hand on his pet's head. Deb could see Trace's very carefully concealed dismay in the gentle way he stroked the dog's gray fur.

His eyes lifted and met hers, and she knew all he felt.

It was a connection between them, a connection Deb prayed that Gwen never shared. Deb had done what had to be done, gone through the wreckage and found what could be salvaged. There was little enough, yet the Scotts weren't the only ones with hidden boxes, and Deb had known where to look. She now carried a small stack of silver and gold coins and some surviving papers, as well as a heavy bag of canned goods. Trace had picked up what he could. The pack he'd formed was tied on his horse behind the saddle.

"Do the little ones need to eat before we set out?" he asked.

Deb was amazed to admit she hadn't thought of it, even with the talk of milk. This whole morning had shaken her right to the ground, and she was a woman who prided herself on being able to handle anything. Though her Heavenly Father knew well that she'd never handled anything close to this.

The dog's head snapped to alert, and without a sound it tore off into the tall grass.

"What happened?" Deb looked to where the dog had disappeared.

"He heard me say *eat*. He hunts his own.

Reckon he'll be back soon."

The children stirred from the sound of voices and sat up.

Maddie Sue rubbed her eyes.

Ronnie woke up crying "Mama." Gwen cradled him, and he leaned against her chest, murmuring "Mama" again through tears.

The children loved Gwen in a special way, as well they should. Gwen did the lion's share of caring for them.

She and Gwen went to work getting a cold breakfast in the youngsters' stomachs. Trace had a tin cup and divided the can of milk between his cup and one Deb produced. One for Maddie, one for Ronnie.

Trace had beef jerky and hard biscuits in his saddlebag, which he shared. Being the first food they'd eaten for the day, and with the morning half gone, the children were mighty hungry.

Deb took a strip of jerky and a biscuit and slipped it into her coat pocket. She couldn't walk all day without food, but she feared she'd empty her stomach if she took a single bite right now.

She noticed Trace did the same.

Gwen ate with little enthusiasm. She was a sympathetic young woman and had to know what they must've seen. None of the adults commented on the eating behavior of the others.

Deb managed a few sips of water from Trace's canteen, and soon they were finished with the simple meal. Little Ronnie started toddling around, heading for the tall grass. Where he'd no doubt vanish, never to be seen again. Gwen made sure to keep up with him.

Maddie Sue said, "Why is your horsie so tall?"

Stumped by the question, Trace looked down at the little girl. "I don't rightly know. That's just how tall he grew."

"Why?"

"Why what?"

"Why did she grow that tall?"

"Uh —" he threw Deb a confused look — "it's a he. And he just did is all?"

"What's a he?"

"The horse is a he, not a she."

"Why?"

"Well, um, I reckon —"

"Why?"

Trace blinked and looked at Deb again.

"She just loves the sound of the word *why.*"

Maddie Sue walked over to him and reached up both arms. "Pick me up."

Trace stepped back so fast he bumped

40

into his horse, who quickly sidestepped. Deb was prepared to save Trace from the little girl, though it was funny to watch him all stirred up. It distracted her from the morning, and she hoped it put Trace's mind on other things, too. Anything but the horror of that wagon train.

"It's time we get going. Which of you wants to ride first?" Trace asked, doing his best to dodge Maddie Sue without letting her get under his horse's hooves.

"Go ahead, Deb." Gwen was as generous as she was pure of heart.

Shaking her head almost violently, Deb said, "I need to walk awhile."

Gwen studied her closely. Whatever she saw must've convinced her because she handed Ronnie to Deb and reached for the saddle horn. She tried to get her foot in the stirrup and missed. The horse tossed its head, and the bridle jingled.

A furrow formed on Gwen's smooth brow as she stepped up to the horse again. She smiled nervously at Trace. "Why is your horse so tall?"

He huffed, almost a chuckle. While it sounded strained to Deb, it was better than his grim silence and few words. "Best to let me help. Black's a good horse, but he ain't used to skirts. In fact, I don't know as

41

anyone's ever ridden him but me. No sense making him jumpy."

Before Gwen could try and climb up into the high saddle, Trace reached for her waist, pulled back before he touched her, then reached again hesitantly. He finally set his hands on her and hoisted her high enough that she could scramble the rest of the way herself. Trace handled her with the finesse he'd have shown for a sack of potatoes.

When Gwen's skirt flapped in his face, he flinched as if it were the tip of a bullwhip.

At least his cheeks were no longer gray. He was blushing. He picked up the reins from where the horse had been ground-hitched and lifted them over the horse's head. Gwen grabbed them tight, maybe too tight because the horse tossed its head.

Deb lifted Ronnie up to Gwen.

"No!" Ronnie's scream nearly peeled the skin off Deb's ears. He kicked his feet as though running in midair, and one of his little-boy shoes hit the horse in the shoulder. The critter shied sideways so fast, Gwen shrieked and threw herself forward to cling to the saddle horn and managed to drop the reins.

That set the horse off even more and it pranced. Gwen clung. She wasn't much of a rider.

Ronnie had been quiet so far this morning. The long walk in the grass and the grim mood coming from Deb and Gwen had weighed on the normally rambunctious toddler. Well, that quiet was over now.

Trace jumped to grab his mount and calm him down while Maddie Sue followed after him demanding to be picked up. After a bit of a tussle, Deb took over holding both children. Finally the horse quit dancing. The wiggling, protesting Ronnie was settled firmly on Gwen's lap, and now the little toddler seemed delighted with his perch. Once up, he quit screaming and pulled on the horse's mane, which the animal didn't seem to mind.

"The voice of one crying in the wilderness," Trace muttered.

"What does that mean?" Deb handed Maddie Sue over.

"Nothing." Trace lifted Maddie Sue up to set her behind Gwen. "The boy crying just reminded me of that verse."

Maddie Sue giggled. "I'm flying!"

The horse lifted its head and looked at Trace. Trace rested a gloved hand on the horse's shoulder and looked back. Deb had a real sense that the two were communicating in some way. Like maybe they couldn't believe what was happening to them.

Well, Deb couldn't either, so they were all in the same fix.

The little girl's laughter helped settle Deb's stomach. She glanced at Trace and said, "There's still laughter in the world."

He nodded solemnly as he made sure Maddie Sue was able to hold on securely to Gwen. There was a good-sized pack behind the saddle, and Maddie Sue fit between it and Gwen to the point she had something to rest her back on, not to mention it pinned her snugly in place.

"Will she be all right back there?" Trace asked.

Deb and Gwen exchanged a look. "I think so," Deb said, "but I'll bring up the rear and keep watch."

"No, you won't. I need to go ahead a bit and study the trail for the tracks of the outlaws. You'd better lead the horse instead."

"You think you can learn about them by studying their horse tracks?"

He paused, a confused look on his face. "Uh, sure I can. I can identify the horses, tell how much the men weigh. Figure where they're headed and who's in charge. I can't recognize faces, but with the trail they're leaving, I can find them without trouble."

"You can do all that from a horse track?"

"You're new to the West, aren't you, Deb?"

This would be when Deb should tell him that she could identify one of the men.

"I think you'd better let Deb lead the horse, Miss Gwen. Unless you think you can handle him."

Deb decided to leave talk of recognizing a murderer until later.

Gwen shrugged and refused to claim a talent she clearly lacked.

"I'll lead it." Deb went over to the horse's neck.

Trace stared his horse in the eye, gave the stallion that shoulder rub, another silent communication.

"Black isn't used to little ones, nor women. But he'll let you lead him."

Had the horse said that? More worrisome, did Trace think the horse had said that?

"I need to get out ahead and read signs before we add any tracks, so if you could lead him that'd help. Be mindful if the kids start crying and such. That might upset Black. If I get ahead tracking, it'll take me a few minutes to get back, so hang on tight to the reins if that happens."

"I'll hang on tight."

"I'll make sure her hands aren't slipping," Gwen added. Ronnie sat on her lap, happily kicking the saddle his short legs straddled.

Again the horse didn't seem to mind. Gwen hugged Maddie Sue's arms where they clung around her stomach from behind and spoke quietly to the little girl.

Maddie Sue rested her face on Gwen's back. "Where Auntie Dee 'n Unca Abe?"

The children had no idea what had happened to the wagon train. Ronnie was too young to speak beyond the most basic words, but included among them were *mama* and *papa.*

But Gwen had cared for him so much that he might not realize exactly who his mama was. Maddie Sue was Abe and Delia Scott's niece, but they'd had her with them all her life. Maddie Sue's real ma had lived with the Scotts while her husband was gone to war, so Maddie Sue thought of them as parents. But Maddie Sue's pa — Cameron Scott, Abe Scott's brother and little Ronnie's namesake — had fought in the Civil War through the time his daughter was born and his wife died.

Cameron had come home briefly after the war ended, and the family made their plans. Cameron would go west ahead of them to serve the army on the western frontier and, while doing that, scout out ranchland for all of them. Cameron, along with his sister Penelope — who had also lived in the tiny attic with Abe and Delia and worked to support the family as much as Abe — had gone. It had taken two years, but finally Cameron had written to them with directions to find him, and they'd set out. And they'd needed help with the two little ones, so they'd allowed the Harkness sisters to ride along and tend the children in exchange for passage.

Cameron Scott was out there somewhere waiting for his family with no idea of the tragedy that had befallen them. Right now the children had no one but Gwen and Deb. And Trace Riley.

The children's lives would go on. Grief and regret weighed on her heart. The Scotts were fine people. Loving, hardworking, with a deeply honorable belief in helping those in need. "The least of these," Delia Scott sometimes called them. That attitude had helped them agree to let Deb and Gwen come along on the trail west.

How could little Ronnie ever know what fine people his parents were? He almost certainly couldn't. But Deb was determined, if she ended up in a position to do so, to help keep memories of the Scotts alive for Ronnie and Maddie Sue.

But how could she do that when they were to meet Maddie's father at the end of this journey? Deb would need to hand the children over to him and ride away forever. And while she was worried about abandoning the children, she wondered how she'd ever make it to Cameron Scott. How could she let anyone know what had become of them?

It was too much to contemplate when she wasn't even sure where they would all sleep tonight. So she shut down her worries and focused on prayers for the children, for Gwen and herself, too. And praise that Trace had come along.

"Hang on tight, Maddie Sue. We're going for a horsie ride."

Bless Gwen, the main weight of caring for the children had always fallen on her. As a mother, she was a natural, while Deb didn't have near the knack for it. The children loved her too, but they just plain preferred Gwen.

Deb was all right with that, because if Gwen did most of the cuddling and rocking, she wasn't doing all the heavier work. Deb wanted to shoulder as much of the burden for Gwen and Mrs. Scott as possible. It was the way she'd done things with her mother, and the way she'd had to do things with her father. It came naturally for her to try to ease the workload of others.

One of the reasons she had convinced

Gwen to come west was Deb's determination to use all her hard work to build something of her own.

Deb didn't pretend that caring for two such young children was a small job, not at all. Gwen worked very hard. And with Mr. Scott leading this splintered-off group of the wagon train, all the driving and much of the horse care fell to Mrs. Scott. Deb always wished she could do more to make the lives of those she loved easier.

"Let's head out." Trace looked at Gwen. "You holdin' on tight up there?"

She smiled and gave a firm nod. "We're ready."

"Give me a few yards' head start so I can study the trail before you walk on it." Trace moved out. As Deb walked along, leading the stallion, she realized she had a thousand questions. Pa had never much cared for a chattering woman. Of course, that's because he was the family's main chatterer.

"Can I ask how far it is to your home?" She winced as she remembered Maddie Sue, who, about two minutes after the wheels had started rolling back at the beginning of the wagon-train journey, asked if they were there yet.

"You see those tracks there?" Trace pointed at the ground.

"I see at least a hundred tracks from wagon wheels. This is the trail we came down yesterday."

Trace shook his head. "Did you notice anything missing from the wagon train?"

Deb stared at him, thinking maybe he'd lost his mind. "Everything was missing, or dead and burned."

"I'm sorry, that was a cruel question. What I mean is, there were a few dead draft animals, probably from stray bullets, but most of the horses and oxen were gone from the traces. They weren't lying there dead."

"I didn't even think of that." How could she when she was busy searching and trying to keep from emptying her stomach after seeing such horror?

"The men who attacked the train stole them, along with everything else they could find."

It wasn't much. It was only five wagons, and Deb had found money caches in nearly every one. Mr. Scott had been the one to devise hidden boxes for any wealth the folks going west hoped to keep for the journey's end.

"There are also tracks from some cattle."

Deb nodded. "There was a small herd being driven along behind the wagon train."

"Those have all been stolen, too."

Deb looked at the trail. "You can see all that on a trail churned up yesterday by the wagon train?"

Trace hunkered down and pointed. "Yep. That track is a horse, a shod horse, and to someone who knows how to read signs, a hoofprint is as good as a man's signature. I'll know every critter with those men if I see them again . . . horses and cattle both. This one has horseshoes with a diamond mark on them, some blacksmith's mark, and it's distinctive."

He moved to another hoofprint. "This is one of the stolen horses. I can tell because it's not as deep as, say, this one." He pointed to another track. "See? It's not carrying a rider."

He indicated yet another track. "This belongs to one of the thieves. It's got a broad pace, and the tracks are deep. Big horse, big man riding it. And the tracks are heading east, when all yesterday's tracks were heading west. This track is distinctive, as are a few of the others, and they're from horses carrying the men who killed your friends. This print here is huge — it must be quite a horse."

"One of the wagons was being pulled by a big Belgian, another by a pair of massive Holstein oxen."

"Those are all unusual animals. That helps. Thanks." Trace glanced sideways at her. "I'm surprised you haven't told me this was done by Indians. Most people blame Native folks for all the trouble out here."

"I heard the attackers yelling, and they were clearly speaking English. Of course, I'm sure some Native people can speak English, but not the way these men did. And . . ." Her voice faltered.

"What?"

"I saw one of them."

Trace surged to his feet and turned to grip her arms. "You saw his face?"

"Yes. In the firelight, just as dawn broke. I would recognize him if I saw him again."

"That puts you in considerable danger." Trace looked and sounded grim.

A shiver raised the hair on her arms and neck. "I suppose it does, but it eliminates all chance that Native folks can be blamed."

Nodding, Trace said, "I'm glad. I could see that by reading the signs, but it was staged, even a few arrows left behind to look as if this was done by Paiutes. But the real killing was done with bullets and, well, there was damage to the bodies that I've seen before. As if someone who doesn't know Indian ways has a twisted belief that there'd be some knife wounds, so they —" Trace stopped and cleared his throat, then gave his head a hard shake, not finishing what he'd started to say.

"The Paiutes are the main tribe around here. And some Washoe. I have friends among 'em, and they're a peaceable people for the most part. I'd hate to see them blamed for this."

"I might recognize the voices of some of the outlaws, too. One — not the one I saw — had a high-pitched voice for a man." She looked sideways at Trace. "I'll testify as a witness if these men are brought to trial later."

"Let's hope it comes to that," Trace said. "For now, we need to get you all to my place. It's a twenty-mile ride. I figured to be home by noon or shortly after. Walking, though — and with three riders and carrying a heavy pack on my horse — I can only guess at how long it's going to take. The whole day and then some for sure. The nearest settlement is over twice as far to the north, and that isn't a fit place for women and children alone. It's still morning, but reading signs will slow me down. I doubt we can make it home until long after dark. We'll have to decide if we want to push on through riding late into the night or if we want to sleep on the trail. If the children can bear it, maybe we can press on."

He opened his mouth to say more, but no words came out. Deb wondered what he'd thought better of saying.

"I've thanked you now several times, but I want to make sure you know we consider that God sent you right to us in our hour of greatest need. Thank you for being an answer to prayer."

She had more questions. She glanced sideways at him and asked, "Do you — ?"

Trace held up his hand as if to halt their progress, yet he kept walking. Deb took that to mean he wanted to halt the talk.

"I mentioned the tracks because I need to study them. I want to be familiar enough with them that if I see one of these horses or oxen or cattle again, I can recognize it. I noticed a few things around the wagon train to give me some idea of the men, but I can learn more. If your questions can wait, I'd prefer to walk out ahead of you and move quiet so I can concentrate."

It struck Deb that she'd never been asked to shut up so politely in her life. "I'll leave you to it, then."

"Obliged." He moved forward at a pace that grew faster until it was the next thing to a run, but not a run, just the next thing to it.

Twenty miles he'd said.
It was going to be a long, quiet day.

CHAPTER 4

Deb dropped back until Trace was about thirty paces ahead. She kept that distance, vowing silently never to slow him down.

She held the horse's reins, though the animal seemed content to traipse after its master. The dog came back, apparently its hunger sated, woofed at them in a friendly way, and trotted ahead toward Trace. It ranged off the trail in both directions, sniffing the ground, studying the trail as closely as Trace was doing.

Because leading the horse wasn't a real job, beyond hanging on tightly to the reins, she dropped back to walk beside the horse's shoulder, alongside Gwen. The two talked quietly as they followed Trace. The grassland was swallowed up as the trail narrowed and slanted up a mountainside. The woods came in closer.

They were retracing their steps from yesterday. Deb remembered her relief when they'd emerged from these thick woods, and now here she was reentering them. Only now they climbed instead of descended. Yesterday had been all downward, winding around boulders and ravines, downed logs and washed-out ruts big enough to swallow a wagon whole.

After an entire day following a trail so narrow the trees brushed the wagons in places, they'd found that big swath of prairie grass. Deb had been able to take a deep breath for the first time in hours. It had a nice level stretch where the wagons could form a circle, with plenty of grazing for the horses and a spring to water them.

It had seemed so safe and comfortable. Little had she known.

As they rode back into this mountainous woodland, that weight returned to her. Only now it felt as if there were eyes on them. Guns on them. As if the men who'd done such evil to her wagon train lingered in the woods, watching, waiting to kill again. Her breath shortened, and sweat broke out on her forehead as her eyes darted from tree to tree, boulder to boulder, looking for guns.

"He's a barely grown boy." Gwen's quiet comment tore Deb out of her frightening thoughts, and she was grateful for it. Trace knew far more about the wilderness than she did. If he was worried, he'd say something.

But Gwen's words had caught Deb by surprise. She narrowed her eyes to look at Trace's back. He was tall and broad shouldered and carried himself with such confidence. He seemed like a full-grown man to her, not old but certainly not a boy anymore.

"Do you think so?"

They kept their voices low, not to be secretive but because both children had fallen asleep, and it was much easier to travel with them this way. And Deb didn't want to distract Trace. Although to her it looked a lot like he was just walking.

"Oh yes. I wonder if he's much more than twenty."

Little Ronnie whimpered and tossed his head, his eyes fluttering open. He'd slept a long time, yet it couldn't last the whole trip.

"Well, he seems at home in this country." Deb walked along easily. In fact, this was the easiest traveling she'd had in a long while. Usually she walked all day with a child in her arms.

The wagon had been heavily loaded and the team gaunted up, so they'd walked to lighten the load as much as possible. Deb carried one of the children for long stretches, with Gwen carrying the other.

Mrs. Scott drove. Working the reins and the wagon brakes was exhausting — even worse on a downhill slope like yesterday. Mr. Scott spent the day on horseback. He moved tirelessly, helping anyone who needed a hand, scouting the trail ahead or hunting food.

Today, Deb walked the same as always, but she was empty-handed. She could keep walking too, probably for twenty miles, if Trace did decide to go the whole way without sleeping.

All things considered, she thought going on was the best idea.

"There's a fork in the trail ahead," Gwen said from her higher perch.

At that same moment, Trace turned to them. "I need to study this for a bit. Take a break. Eat. Let the youngsters stretch their legs. There's a spring drizzling out of that rock on the right side of the trail. Refill the canteens and let the horse have a drink."

"That's a good idea," Gwen said. "My legs could use a stretch, too."

Trace went on studying. Deb had her hands full getting Maddie Sue down off the horse, pinned as she was between Gwen and the large pack. But it helped Deb feel better about how secure the girl was up there.

The dog came up and stood beside Maddie Sue, so close that she leaned on him and hugged his neck.

Deb remembered how the dog had growled at first. A dangerous creature, but now it acted friendly as could be. Deb hoped the dog's behavior was sincere because she could see no way to keep Maddie Sue and the dog apart. They appeared to have bonded, and as Gwen passed Ronnie down, Deb's hands were too busy to keep Maddie Sue up off the ground.

Gwen climbed down from the horse, mostly in a controlled fall. But she clung to the saddle horn, then the stirrup, and ended up standing, so Deb counted it as a successful dismount.

"There are some flat boulders over there we can sit on when we eat. We can take turns watching the horse while we let the children move around."

"If we need to, we can use that boulder to stand on to get back into the saddle." Deb smiled. "You think that will make Trace proud of us?"

Gwen chuckled. She produced her bag and Deb's, which had been hanging from the saddle horn rather than stowed in the pack on the horse. She also brought two canteens down with her. They tended themselves and the children, including a dry diaper for Ronnie, and a quick trip into the privacy of the woods for the rest of them. They let the horse drink, its reins tied to a low shrub so it could graze.

They took out some beef jerky and more biscuits. Gwen also had an apple in her bag, which she cut into five pieces.

"Look at him." Gwen nodded toward Trace as they stood eating.

Deb would've preferred to sit since she'd walked all morning, but it turned out it took both women to keep the little ones from harm. Ronnie wanted to stand under the horse and splash in the spring. Maddie Sue wanted to pull the wolf-dog's hair and look at its teeth while standing on the poor animal's toes.

Finally, Deb convinced Ronnie to toddle toward Trace, who was a good fifty feet away. Deb thought to fetch the little boy before he got close enough to mess up any tracks.

Trace crouched down by the trail to study the ground. Then he stood, moved left, right, looked down again, then side to side.

"I don't know what he's doing, but there's something to interest him." Gwen chased after Ronnie, plucked him up, and kept a watchful eye on Maddie Sue. The girl chased after the dog, which seemed to have made a game out of staying just out of reach

61

of her fur-tugging fingers.

"I wish I'd had the courage to shoot those men." Deb's conscience struck. "All I could think of was to stay hidden and protect myself. I saw one, heard their voices, and I can bear witness to their crimes. But I should have fought."

She clenched her fists and felt the anger and guilt mix into something ugly. "My gun is a revolver, six shots. I could have at least tried to get them all. I didn't even have the courage to pull the trigger once."

"Stop, Deb. You did the right thing, and you know it. It was before the sun was fully up, you've not done much shooting in your life, and you'd only have missed them and brought the men right toward you." Gwen let Ronnie go, and the boy aimed for Trace again.

"But I could have sneaked closer. In that terrible firelight I might have been able to get close enough to hit them all. I could've at least gotten a look at them all." Deb looked down, ashamed of herself. "The truth is, all I could think of was myself, my own survival. Almost the first thing Trace spoke of was reading the tracks so he could recognize those men later and bring them to justice. That's a noble way to behave."

"Deb, we'd never been in a wagon-train

attack before." Gwen sounded dry, slightly teasing. "I'm sure with practice you'll get better at handling such a thing."

A smile quirked Deb's lips. "I hope to have no more such practice, for heaven's sake." Her chin came up. "But I am going to change, Gwen. I am. The West is different than where we came from. It's a land that demands strength of people. A land that tests courage. With the muscles in our backs and the brains in our heads, we can do whatever we want out here, and I intend to accept that challenge and grow strong enough to belong in this wild and rich land."

"Rich?" Gwen asked.

"Yes, look around. The beauty of these mountains, the wealth in lumber, the food to be had from hunting and trapping. Mr. Scott fed our whole wagon train with the use of his rifle. We couldn't do that in a city back east. And women aren't allowed to be more than wives and mothers, or spinster teachers."

"You ran Pa's newspaper single-handedly, Deb."

The spark of anger flared in Deb until she felt almost big enough for the frontier. "Yes, I did. I gathered the news, wrote the stories, set up the printing press, sold the ads, kept the accounts and paid the bills. And no one gave me credit for it."

"You mean *Pa* never gave you credit for it. I always knew who ran things."

"And Ma did the job before me. She's the one who taught me what it took to run a newspaper while Pa was busy being a showman. He talked in the diner and on the boardwalk and in the taverns while he smoked cigars and played cards. He ate at the restaurants while we scrambled for enough to feed ourselves at home. He led parades and visited with the mayor and spoke up at community events." Deb darted after Ronnie again when he got too far away and carried him back.

"While you took notes and wrote the stories later." Gwen took Ronnie from Deb and stood him on his little feet. The boy squealed in pleasure and immediately headed for the horse. Sighing, Gwen directed him elsewhere as the little tyke protested.

"It wasn't just Pa who never gave me credit. Not one man in that whole town ever did. Including the ones who knew I was interviewing them for a story or making purchases and paying bills for the paper and convincing them to buy ads for it. They saw me as an errand girl for our great and wise father."

"Who spent every cent we couldn't hide from him on poker." Gwen shook her head in disgust. There was no sense saying more; it was a simple fact. They'd worked their hearts out for a man who did nothing and took everything.

When he died, the paper had closed because no one did business with or bought ads or subscriptions from a paper whose editor was no longer there, even though nothing had changed.

Deb had tried to keep it all going for a few months, but finally she faced reality and sold the printing press, moved out of their rented house, and headed west, determined to find a place they could work for themselves for the first time in their lives.

They had dreams of making it in California, and they still would someday. Deb's jaw firmed as she vowed to herself and to God that she'd find a way to head west. She'd carve out a life for herself and Gwen.

She'd do it. She was capable. She'd fight for justice for folks like Ronnie's parents. And she'd run a newspaper again — she had years of experience as proof she could do it.

She was out here in a land where anyone could succeed if they were bold enough, if they were smart and strong enough. And she was all of those things.

Before she'd done it for Pa. Now she'd do it for herself. And somehow watching Trace, and knowing he thought first of justice, made something grow inside her. It gave her the strength to do anything she put her mind to. She trusted herself enough to believe.

Chapter 5

He didn't trust himself.

He was too filled with fury, too hungry for revenge.

Finding these men and punishing them threatened to take him over and send him galloping down the trail — the fork that led him away from home — with murder in his heart.

The men who did that to the wagon train were filthy, brutal murderers. They needed to die. Just as the men who'd done the same to his father's wagon train needed to die.

Worse yet, from what he'd seen in that wagon circle, he knew these were the same men. The knife wounds, the scattered arrows made to look like the Paiutes had attacked. But the arrows weren't right. And the little things they'd done wrong were the exact things the men who'd killed his father had done.

He could catch them. They had a few

hours' start, but driving a herd was slow and his horse would close the distance fast. Knowing they were within his reach added to Trace's desire for revenge.

They needed to die for the multiple murders they'd committed today.

But of course he couldn't go after them.

God had given over to him the care of four helpless people, and he had to get them home.

His throat felt thick with the two tearing needs — to chase these men and to protect this brood.

Seeing those women come running out of the grass, well, nothing had ever hit him that hard. Not since he'd been left completely alone, a fifteen-year-old who'd considered himself a full-grown man, until he had to be. The aloneness on this high mountain trail had threatened to break him.

There was never any question that he'd help four stranded travelers. Any decent man would help, and there were plenty of men who'd be described as less than decent who'd've helped them, too. Not the marauders who'd killed men and women in that wagon train, but most men in the West treated women with almost reverent respect. There were just too few women. They were rare and precious and to be protected above all.

But beyond that simple right and wrong — beyond what any man would do — came a blow to Trace's gut at seeing that these folks had survived the same thing he had.

And God had allowed him to come along and help them. Trace considered that a great honor. Which didn't mean that watching a baby get its diaper changed wasn't enough to set off a deep panic in his gut. What if he was asked to help?

That alone gave him a powerful incentive to keep the women happy and healthy. But caring for all of them ran directly at odds with what he wanted to do, which was ignore the trail that led home and keep after those vicious outlaws.

Trace hadn't been able to do anything when his wagon train was attacked. Survival took every ounce of his strength, and even then the winter in the High Sierra had almost killed him.

Things were different now. He was fully capable of fighting back. And the desire to do it was so strong, to take on three men by himself, that he had to call it bloodlust.

He was on his way home from his first cattle drive. He'd just run his cows to market in Sacramento. Because he'd never been away from his ranch, not in all these years. He'd sent his cowhands on home days ahead of him and then set out to wander. They were there now, he was sure, caring for the good-sized herd he had left, which were on rich winter grazing land so they needed only minimal care.

He had nothing but time.

The little boy giggled and pulled his thoughts back to the present.

He needed to get these folks to shelter. It was October in the peaks of the Sierra Nevada. October was a serious month up here in the thin chilled air of this stretch of the mountains. It was a man's last chance to get everything ready for the long, hard months of cold. His ranch was at a lower elevation, but they had to ride a trail that climbed to the highlands, then wound down to get home.

Even at home, lower wasn't low enough to stop winter from hitting hard. The snow came in feet instead of inches. The wind howled, and the trails locked up deep and tight.

This wagon train had been traveling dangerously late in the season. Though it could hold off for a month, Trace knew at any minute winter could land flat on their heads, and the twenty miles they needed to travel today would become impossible.

There'd be no vengeance today. He needed to tend babies and women and dodge diaper-changing duty with every ounce of his cunning. That'd keep him mighty busy for who could say how long.

Trace straightened from the tracks and turned to see Maddie Sue yanking on Wolf's tail.

Swallowing a gasp, Trace fought down the reflex to shout a warning and sprint. At any second Wolf could revert to form. He was friendly to Trace, and he'd accepted the hired hands, but that had been slow in coming and the men were mighty careful.

They sure as certain hadn't yanked on his tail on the first day.

For the most part Wolf was a bad-tempered critter who bared his teeth and growled at most anything new — and a lot that wasn't new. He was the best protection Trace had at the ranch, and Trace loved him. But that didn't mean he didn't recognize the wolfish half of the beast and respect it.

Maddie Sue wasn't showing one bit of respect.

Trace flinched when Maddie Sue dove at Wolf and tackled him to the ground. Wolf wagged his tail and panted while the child wriggled on top of him and stomped on his legs. Wolf licked the little girl's face, and she giggled and hugged him tight.

It was just plain odd.

Trace got to the women and children and, acting as casual as a man could, he picked Maddie Sue up and held her against him. It was awkward because the little girl smiled at him and kicked him at the same time. She reached down and yelled, "Doggie!"

Trace figured he was holding her wrong somehow. Then he had an old memory from his pa and hefted the child higher and set her on his shoulders with her legs around his neck. Now he could hold her feet. And when his hat went flying and she used his hair as a handhold, well, it hurt, but it beat having her chewed up by the dog.

"The men I was tracking all followed the north trail. But we need to head south to reach my ranch. It's the closest shelter."

The pretty, dark-haired one, Deb, with those shining blue, intelligent eyes that made her seem smarter than Trace probably was, smiled. "So we'll be putting some space between us and them?"

As if that were a good thing.

"Yep. Are you ready to move on? I've been going slow, holding us back, but now we need to push hard."

"Let's go."

"It's your turn to ride, Deb." Gwen, the blonde, pretty as a picture and with a sweetness about her that seemed to draw the children, finished with the diaper and quickly dressed the little boy. She seemed to do more of the care of the children while Deb did everything else. And looking at Gwen and those young'uns, a body'd be excused for thinking she was their ma. They all had nearly white blond hair. The two little ones had blue eyes, and Gwen's were a different shade, more greenish, yet the three looked like a matched set.

"I want to walk a little farther, Gwen."

"You've been walking all morning." Gwen scowled.

Deb smiled and slid an arm around Gwen's waist. Sisters. For the first time Trace could see the resemblance when they stood close. The dark hair against the light fooled a man, but they had those same bright eyes and pretty oval faces.

"You know the children behave better for you, and they've just had a long nap. Ride with them for an hour or so more, then I'll take a turn with them when they're sleepy. You'll be working harder on that horse than I will walking."

Gwen's eyes narrowed. "Deb, I'm not riding all day while you walk."

Trace could tell these two had similar battles often as they tried to share the work.

Deb laughed and it was such a sweet sound, Trace found himself leaning closer to her. He straightened away as soon as he noticed what he was doing.

"I've walked all the way across this huge country, Gwen, and done it mostly carrying a chubby little boy. Walking all day isn't much of a problem."

"I know." Gwen smiled.

Ronnie said, "Mama? Where Mama?"

The smiles on both sisters faded.

Ronnie started crying and clung to Gwen's neck and repeated "Mama" against it in a muffled voice.

"Where Auntie Dee 'n Unca Abe?" Maddie Sue asked from her perch on Trace's shoulders.

Trace's big hands on those little-girl legs tightened slightly. He knew about a parent dying. Knew too much about it. He thought again of *The voice of one crying in the wilderness.* It reminded him of some crying he'd done years ago when he was alone in the wilderness.

Gwen held Ronnie tight and rocked him. Deb didn't try to explain it.

Trace's mom had died when he was about

Maddie Sue's age, and he had no memories of her at all. If no one ever spoke of the Scotts again, would these children soon forget they'd ever existed? Ronnie would for sure, while Maddie Sue might hold on to dim memories.

Gwen and Deb shared a somber, worried moment. None of them knew what to say. Try and explain death? Distract the young'uns and move on? Which was right?

Gwen said quietly, "I'll ride with the children. At least for now."

Nodding, Deb stepped up to Trace and reached for him in a way that made his heart start pounding. Deb reached on higher and lifted Maddie Sue off his shoulders.

He felt a little dizzy once he realized she hadn't been reaching for him; his mind had just gone wild.

He helped transfer Maddie Sue and got everyone mounted up on Black, hunted up his hat, and they set out.

"I'm going to walk just as fast as we can, Deb. Let me know when you need to slow down, but by my figuring we've only come about five miles up that trail, and with my tracking we made mighty slow work of it. We have to cover a lot of ground. The temperature out here drops at night, and we'll be walking well after dark even if we make good time and don't stop very often. We'll be sorry to be caught out."

"As I said, Trace, I've walked across the bulk of this whole country. Let's move fast and try to beat as much of the cold as we can."

CHAPTER 6

They turned south at the fork in the trail and walked along in silence for a time, Trace setting a fast pace with his long legs and Deb keeping up without a word of protest.

She didn't want to make this one bit harder on him than it already was. The man was saving their lives plain and simple, and she'd do her best to make that as easy as possible. He was already taking a twenty-mile walk when he could be riding.

Trace led the horse. Deb listened to Gwen and the children's lighthearted chatter about everything — the trees, the horse, the dog, the sky. No such simple conversation sprung up between Deb and Trace.

It reached a point, though, when they'd settled into a comfortable walk and had put an hour of the trail behind them that the silence began to bother Deb. And it didn't look like he was ever going to break it.

"Tell me about your ranch, Trace."

"Uh . . . well, it's a ranch." He lapsed back into silence. It was possible he was walking faster, too. "With cows and such."

Cows and such? Well, Deb had interviewed people for her newspaper and heaven knew they weren't all eager to talk.

"You're back from a cattle drive? Didn't you say that? Where'd you take the herd?"

"Sacramento."

Silence again. Taking the direct approach, she said, "Don't you want to talk to me? Is that it?" She couldn't see why he wouldn't, but then her father had been a talker of the highest order. In fact, the man never shut up. And he'd talked himself into a heap of trouble, so Deb couldn't fault a quiet man. She saw a faint blush on Trace's cheeks. "I'm sorry. I don't mean to embarrass you or make you uncomfortable."

He shrugged. "I-I've . . ." His cheeks got purely pink now. Well, not pink exactly because he was so tan, but it was undeniable that under the dirt of a deeply tan cowboy who'd been on the trail for days, he was blushing.

She waited. Wolf ran back and forth across the trail, sniffing and studying everything in complete, almost eerie silence. The horse quick-stepped along, led by Trace. The children chattered quietly, and Gwen spoke as if she didn't want any loud voices to disturb the horse, so Deb didn't try and listen to them.

"I've . . . that is, you're the f-first woman I've . . . I've practically ev-ever talked to. Ever. In my whole life." His eyes narrowed thoughtfully. "There was a woman who brought me food in the diner in Sacramento. And one behind the counter in the general store where I bought some new trousers and shirts and a new hat. I said what I wanted to eat, later 'thank you' to the waitress, and she said I was welcome. And at the store, the woman behind the counter asked me if I had a list and I said —"

"You are speaking literally? With those two exceptions, you have never spoken to a woman?"

"There was one or two on the wagon train when I came out. But I fought shy of them." He looked up at the riders. She didn't think he was trying to evade her question, he was just a watchful man.

"I have no memories of my ma. Pa said she died when I was near three years old. Pa and I lived on a farm in the hills of Tennessee, and we were a long ways out. There were other men there but no women. My grandpappy lived with us and betwixt him and Pa, if someone needed to head for town, leaving me behind was always simple. I preferred it anyway. A town sounded like a strange place to me."

"Towns aren't strange. Well, not exactly."

"Sacramento was big, though we stayed at the edge of town with the herd, and I didn't go in and explore much. And no one seemed to like Wolf, nor my horse. I'd call it strange."

"There isn't a town around here anywhere?"

"Dismal is about thirty miles past my place. It's a frontier town with some of the men who got fed up with mining the Comstock Lode. It's mostly men. There's some law there, but it's no place for women and children alone. I can't take you there and leave you. It wouldn't be fitting."

"Well, if you start doing a cattle drive every year to Sacramento, there are lots of women there, so you'll get some practice talking to them over time."

"I reckon."

"So how'd you end up out here from Tennessee?"

"Grandpappy died the year I was ten. It was a hardscrabble life on a piece of poor dirt that stood more on its side than laid flat." He paused and looked around as if maybe he realized he hadn't changed things much because these mountains didn't have much flat about them.

"Pa thought we could do better and we headed west." He quit talking as if that were the whole story.

Deb was struck again by the quietness of the man. Her father never had a quiet moment in his life. The quiet was comfortable, and yet at the same time she wanted to know more. "So you came out here when you were ten?"

"Nope, just to Missouri."

More silence. "When did you come out here?"

"The Missouri land was in the Ozarks and no better'n what we'd left. I think Pa stopped there because one of our horses came up lame and the huntin' and fishin' was good, so he stayed. I liked it and figured I could live there happy enough forever, and Pa was mighty good in the woods and taught me everything he knew."

He was actually talking now. Deb didn't say a word that might make him notice what he was doing.

"But Pa wanted farmland, and it was true enough that he spent all his time trying to carve himself out a few acres, cutting down trees, grubbing out trunks and roots, picking up rocks, and fighting the woods that wanted to swallow up the little land he could tear open. So after a few years there, we headed farther west and caught up with a wagon train that'd come out of Saint Louis." He fell silent again, only this time it was as if he was exhausted from that long spate of words.

Deb didn't push. She figured she'd hounded the poor man enough for now.

He surprised her by taking up his story again. "We weren't really with the wagon train. We were on horseback, and we caught up to it. Pa signed on as a scout, and he did a lot of hunting to keep fresh meat around for all the travelers and checked the trail ahead for trouble. I stuck by his side and helped out plenty. Learned even more about life in the wilderness on that trip. Good thing I did."

Trace fell silent once more, though it had a different quality to it now. She had to work up the nerve to breach it, but before she could, a sharp yip from Wolf cut the air.

Trace whipped out a gun so fast it shocked her. He shoved the reins in her hand.

"Get off the trail." He jabbed a finger to his right at a pile of boulders that would easily hide riders on horseback. "Take everyone behind that jumble of rocks over there. Stay quiet. Keep watch." He took off running after his dog.

Head spinning at the suddenness of the change in Trace and the possible danger, Deb didn't think of disobeying. She turned off the trail toward the rocks.

"What's happening, Deb?" Gwen asked.

"Shh! Keep the little ones quiet if you can." Deb led them behind the boulders, then peeked out. Trace had sprinted away, vanished.

If it weren't for the horse, it would have been easy to believe he'd never been here. A ghost she'd made up in her fear at being stranded in the mountains. She saw both children were asleep again. How long had they been walking since the last break — several hours possibly?

It was her turn to ride, but she wasn't the least bit tired and wanted to talk more with Trace.

"I'll stay up here until he comes back so as not to wake the little ones," Gwen whispered.

Deb was impressed with her sister for not asking questions. Of course, there were no answers Deb could provide, and maybe that was what held Gwen back.

Deb tied the tall black mustang to a stout limb that somehow grew right out of the middle of the pile of boulders. She pulled her gun out of the pack she'd been carrying since they left the wagon train this morning and checked to make sure it was loaded.

"I'm going to see if I can tell what's going on."

"Be careful," Gwen whispered. "And don't shoot Trace by accident."

Nodding at the excellent advice, Deb cocked the gun, aimed it at the sky, and edged forward to peer out from the rocks. She'd taken very little with her west. The Scotts' wagon was already full to bursting when Deb and Gwen got included. But this gun had come along and plenty of bullets. She was heading into a wild place, and there'd be no sheriff to summon for help.

She studied the trail Trace had run down. Nothing. No one. Where had he gone?

What if he never came back?

The thought was as wrenching as how she'd felt this morning when she realized the wagon train was destroyed and all those with it were dead. Once again she was with her sister and the little ones, in the wilderness, completely and utterly alone.

Trace was completely alone.

Alone not counting his dog. And the dog counted for a lot. He trusted Wolf more than he trusted himself, and it was the critter that'd warned him there was something, or someone, out here. Trace would put that dog up against any tracker or mountain man or Indian scout he'd ever met, and he'd met a few.

Wolf wheeled and darted into the underbrush along the trail, silent as a ghost.

Sprinting to the spot Wolf had entered the woods, Trace slipped in. He knew how to be quiet himself. It wasn't a skill just for dogs.

He couldn't hear a sound out of his dog, and he hadn't expected to. But there were tracks, stretched out, the dog moving with speed and ease in this rugged stretch of woods. Trace was on an uphill slope, and the way got more treacherous. It took him a while to notice, but Wolf was following a whisper of a game trail so faint that Trace would've never seen it himself.

Trace moved as fast as the dense woods and rocky climb would allow. He was mindful of the trail, the woods that were around him, and what lay behind. Though he trusted Wolf, Trace knew his own skill in the woods and he used his own eyes and ears and nose.

No one was lurking along the trail.

Suddenly, Wolf appeared ahead of him, coming back down the trail, trotting, tongue lolling, calm as could be.

"What is it, boy? What did you smell?" A distant rumble distracted Trace from talking to his dog. He looked up and saw on the far western horizon the first glimpse of a gray cloud. A barely visible bolt of lightning reached for the ground.

It was miles away, probably not coming right at them, but they had one more high peak to get over before they started the long downhill slope to Trace's cabin. He was way too high. Lightning up in the peaks was a terrible, violent thing. He had to get moving or they might all be caught in it.

The dog took one more long look in the direction he'd come from, then turned and went on past Trace, heading back for the women. Trace looked in the direction Wolf had come from and itched to go on, to investigate. But Trace didn't do it, not with lightning on the way. He'd left the women and children behind, and he had to get back to them and lead them out of here. He picked up his pace, running with an ease that was second nature to him.

"Deb, I'm back," he called and then emerged from the woods. He didn't want to sneak up on her.

She stepped out from behind the boulder pile, gun lowering. She returned it to the bag she carried with her. It lifted his spirits to think she'd been ready to fight.

He reached the trail just as she did, leading Gwen and the children.

"We've got to move fast, Deb. There's a storm coming, and up this high it could get fierce." Trace looked at the horse, then down at her. With sudden moves, he reached up, unstrapped the pack on his stallion's back, and strapped it onto his own. It was everything he'd carried from his travels, besides all they'd scavenged from the wagon train. The pack weighed a hundred pounds or more, but he needed to set a faster pace, and to do that he needed everyone else to ride.

"Black can carry all four of you at least until we get over the next peak. He's a strong animal, and we're going to let him do more of the work now."

Deb sputtered, "I can walk. I'm not tired."

"I'm going to run."

That quieted her down.

"I do plenty of running on these trails and can keep it up a long time, and I want to get us off this trail. Whatever bothered Wolf must've moved on, but that storm isn't moving anywhere but right at us. I don't want to be out here when the sky opens up." He thought of those tracks he'd wanted to follow north and almost growled with frustration. This could be snow, but the lightning meant it was probably rain. Those tracks were going to wash out. He had plans to hunt those men down, and if rain passed over, Trace would have a harder time finding them.

He heard a distant crack of thunder and quit talking. He didn't wait to ask for permission from Deb. That was time he didn't want to waste. He caught Deb around her trim middle and swung her awkwardly up onto the mustang's back behind Maddie Sue. Black stepped around a little.

Deb squeaked and grabbed around Gwen with Maddie Sue asleep between them. She was sitting too far back on the horse, and the poor critter wasn't used to any of this.

But Trace had a firm grip on the reins and controlled Black until he calmed down.

"Hang on. I'll start out walking, then trotting and that'll jiggle you all up some. But I'll try to move fast enough we can get Black into a slow canter."

Trace moved out, silently apologizing to his overburdened horse. But even all four of them up there weren't too heavy of a load, and the pack Trace had put on his back had been most of Deb's weight, so Black could keep this up if he didn't get cranky. Trace gave the threatening sky a hard look and hoped he could keep it up, too.

It didn't take long for the trot. Trace hoped he'd be in time to catch anyone who fell off. Yet they hung on, and finally Black broke into a canter so slow he was surprised the horse could manage it. Maybe Black was getting tired of bouncing around with all that weight on his back — the riders certainly were.

Trace'd lived awhile out here with only the old horse he'd been riding on the day Pa was killed. He'd learned to travel well on his own and could run for hours at a decent speed. Now he was going to test his endurance.

And to make himself go on, all he had to do was imagine someone in those woods, maybe someone evil enough to kill a wagon train full of people, maybe someone with a rifle scope pointed right at them.

Because someone was out there. Or had been. Trace couldn't read Wolf's actions any other way.

Thunder rumbled, and Trace pushed himself harder, driven by the lighting coming and others watching them, others with reasons for not showing themselves.

That could only be bad.

CHAPTER 7

Trace didn't know much about women and less than nothing about children, except he'd been one himself. But these four seemed like a decent bunch.

Through sheer effort, he kept himself from saying so.

He didn't want to start the women talking again, even worse the children crying again, because how quiet they all were was a big part of what he admired.

They rode along in silence. Not a word of complaint from any of them. He'd settled into a steady run, up and up and up, and thought he could probably keep going almost forever.

Back in the very beginning he'd had an old plow horse, the one he'd been riding the day of the wagon massacre. The horse hadn't survived the first winter. Trace had learned to use his feet. And though these days he wasn't forced to run everywhere he went, he still did a fair amount of it when the distance wasn't too far. He could keep going for miles. But he didn't usually go for one of his long runs with a hundred-pound pack on his back.

He reached the mountaintop and felt the coldness of a nasty storm breathing down his neck. He passed over the heights and began miles of descent. But once the worst of the danger had passed, it was as if the storm decided that if it couldn't stab him with a lightning bolt, it wasn't interested at all. It headed toward the east, rushing on, leaving them dry.

Trace saw the sheeting rain. It drenched the trail he'd wanted to come back and follow to get the men who'd massacred the wagon train.

Oh, he'd find them. The determination burned in him like the flaming sword of justice. But the rain made it harder.

He settled into the rhythm of the run as time and territory passed. If he could keep going — well, he was still going to reach home long after dark — the sun was setting earlier every day. There'd be no camping on the trail. Whatever was out in those woods made him want to make it home as soon as he could.

■ ■ ■ ■

"Wake up!" Trace hadn't meant to yell, but it'd come out mighty loud when he was jumping to catch Deb as she came sliding off his stallion's back.

He caught her. He'd touched both her and Gwen when he was helping them get on and off his horse, but he was struck now by this live wiggling woman. Something about the weight of her in his arms struck him as the best thing he'd ever felt.

Of course, he was half asleep with exhaustion himself, so he could be imagining things.

She jerked awake. He grabbed the reins with his teeth so he could hold her with both arms. The horse shied, and he decided, though he'd've liked to hang on to her longer, that he should act in the best interests of his teeth.

He eased her to the ground but she didn't stand. Her legs buckled, so he guided her all the way to the ground to keep her from plunking down hard. It was cold. Past midnight and the ground was white with the flurries of snow that'd begun about two hours ago. Black danced sideways, and Trace caught Maddie Sue falling next.

Trace spit out the reins and shouted, "Deb, Gwen, wake up! I need some help out here!"

Deb stirred from the cold more than from his words. Trace hated to jar them like this. They'd hung on to the horse with the grit and courage of warriors all day, but they had to help him for just a few more seconds.

Deb pulled Maddie Sue onto her lap as Trace lifted Ronnie, deeply asleep and limp as a rag doll.

A lantern came on in the house, and the front door swung open. Utah Smith, a cowpoke who'd come wandering through right around the time Trace was starting the cattle drive, came rushing out, pulling on his thick winter coat.

"Boss, we were fixin' to come huntin' you."

Trace had tarried so long he was two weeks behind his men.

"I need more hands, Utah. Quick." The pack on Trace's back felt like the earth had grown claws that were trying to drag him right underground. His hands were too busy to shed it. Ronnie hung, fast asleep, in one arm. He grabbed Gwen in the other and eased her down, her eyes blinking up at him owlishly. Unlike Deb, she managed to stay on her feet.

Utah caught Black and led him aside. "What in tarnation ya got here, boss?"

He was too tired to smile, but he didn't blame Utah for being surprised. Adam Thayne was a pace behind.

"Put the horse up, Utah. Adam, help me get them inside. And grab this pack I'm carrying. I'm about all in." Which reminded him he didn't have a bed to sleep in, and neither did his hired men. They'd realize that soon enough. Still, they were tough western men — they'd slept on a hard patch of dirt many a time.

Utah headed for the stable with the mustang.

Adam got Trace's pack. "You want this inside?"

"Yep, and the women and children. All of the menfolk are sleeping in the stable."

It didn't matter too much. The house was so poorly built, it wasn't much better than the barn. Utah had seen the place when he signed on for the cattle drive and told Trace he was a handy carpenter, offering to build a new house and stable in the spring.

Trace was all for it, yet it was only talk at this point. And talk didn't put a roof over their heads tonight.

The house's one advantage was that it had a fireplace — and that was a big advantage.

"Adam," Trace said when his hired man rushed back outside, "take the little boy. He's fast asleep. Just get him inside and put him in any bed."

Adam gathered up the boy and cradled him awkwardly.

"I'll help settle him." Gwen went after the boy.

Deb had gotten off the horse several times throughout the day and run along to lighten the stallion's load. The mustang was mountain born and bred and a strong tall animal, but four riders, even with two of them little, was a heavy load over long hours.

Trace figured Deb's willingness to walk was the difference between their making it or not. It also explained her deeper exhaustion than Gwen's.

Trace was about used up, but he dug deep and found the strength to pick Deb up, with Maddie Sue asleep in her lap. He adjusted the load to keep from dropping the child and headed for the house with both of them.

"No," Deb muttered, her words slurred, her voice groggy with sleep. "Give me a few minutes to gather my wits and I'll walk."

Since Trace sincerely hoped to be asleep in a few minutes, he just carried her on in. And tired as he was, he enjoyed every second of it. In fact, it struck him that if he hadn't been quite so close to insensible with exhaustion, he might've had a little more self-control and not enjoyed a woman in his arms nearly so much.

He came inside to see Gwen collapse on one of the bunks. Adam handed Ronnie to her, and she wrapped up in the blanket and was asleep instantly.

There were three hard little beds. One brand-new, probably built for Utah. It had an old blanket sewn up and stuffed with what smelled like dry meadow grass. That's the bed Adam had picked for Gwen, and Trace was glad there was clean straw for her.

Adam built up the fire.

Trace lay Deb down on his bed, and Maddie Sue just snuggled up right in her arms. He paused a second at the wonder of having a woman in his bed. It wasn't quite how it sounded, but that didn't keep the thought from bouncing around in his head like some kind of mountain echo.

Trace covered Deb and Maddie Sue with his only blanket, then forced himself to look away from her.

He said to Adam, "We're evicted from the house, I reckon."

"I reckon." Adam plucked his blanket off his own bed. Beyond that he didn't speak as he headed outside. Trace wore his heavy coat, and it looked like that was all he was getting.

He left, pulling the door shut behind him and saw Adam give Utah the news.

"They took all the blankets, too?"

"Nope, we got one, but they took yours and mine," Trace said. "There was one in my bedroll on Black — did you get that?"

"Yep. We've got two, one short."

"You take it. My coat is plenty warm."

"They get the fire and the blankets?" Utah sounded resigned, and why not? No one was going back in there to tear a blanket off those women and children.

"It don't seem right, does it?" Trace chuckled, surprised he had the strength.

The other two added their own quiet mirth.

Utah spoke with laughter in his voice. "I been around women some. It's probably right." He turned and headed for the stable with the rest of them.

"Where'd you find two women and two little'uns?" Adam was close enough that, as he held the door for Trace to go into the stable, he could see the man's brow, furrowed with confusion.

"It's a family? Did you bring them from

Sacramento? Why did you have only one horse?"

The stable was no great structure. Trace had hoped he could keep Utah on for a long time, as he seemed like a man looking for home. If he'd stay until they'd built a new house and stable, Trace would finally have a real ranch going.

But even if he could see stars through the gaps in the roof, and snow silted down here and there, Trace had straw aplenty, just dried meadow grass but as soft as the beds in the house. The wind was cut by the walls, mostly, and with Trace's good coat and complete exhaustion helping him along, he was asleep before he could relax into the straw.

If the men asked any more questions, Trace was beyond answering.

CHAPTER 8

A scream jerked Trace awake.

He charged out the door, glad he'd slept in his boots and coat.

The scream echoed again, shrill and terrible. He sprinted toward the house and heard feet pounding behind him.

Had the outlaws come for the women? Had they found out someone from the wagon train survived? Had they — ?

"Potty!" The scream was a word this time.

Trace skidded to a halt, and Utah slammed into him and sent him staggering forward. Adam ran on past, then stumbled and fell to his hands and knees.

From behind him, Trace heard Utah mutter, "Potty?"

Adam leapt to his feet and charged right straight back to the stable as fast as he'd run out. Adam was young, but he'd been with Trace four years and was already a tough, seasoned cowhand when Trace hired him. Mr. Tough Man Adam had finally heard something that scared him.

"I gotta go potty!" Maddie Sue was up.

The sun was just showing itself over the snowcapped mountains to the east. Trace pivoted and headed straight back to the stable. He didn't see getting any more sleep, but he wasn't going in that house for nuthin'. He finally had time to notice that every bone and muscle in his body burned like he was on fire. He'd taken a beating yesterday with the long, hard run carrying that heavy pack.

As he headed for the stable, Utah fell in beside him and started chuckling, Adam laughing out loud.

Trace felt his cheeks heating up. "This is the strangest situation of my life." Well, no. Not in his life. Being stranded on the frontier, completely alone with winter coming on, was stranger.

"Potty!" This time little Maddie Sue just plain yowled like a wounded raccoon. What was going on in there? Trace hadn't thought to point to the outhouse last night. But it was right out back, and the women struck him as bright little things. Maybe . . . he shook his head and refused to think about going in there now and pointing. Instead, he started laughing. Surviving out here was a serious business, so he'd take his laughter where he could get it.

They all laughed so hard, Trace wondered if one or the other of 'em were near to collapsing. They settled down after a bit, but after yesterday and what Trace had seen, it felt good to laugh. Thinking of yesterday sobered him.

"What's going on, Trace?" Utah broke the friendly silence.

Utah didn't quite count as an old-timer, though he was the oldest of the three of them and the newest on Trace's ranch. From working alongside him, Trace knew Utah was a man in his prime. But life out here put lines in a man's face. If he owned a mirror — and where would he get one of those? — Trace would probably see a few lines in his own face.

Back in Sacramento, before they'd split up, he'd heard Utah mention growing a beard to keep the winter from freezing his face. He'd started it on the ride home, so he had about two weeks' growth, and the beard was salted heavily with gray. That aged him, too.

There hadn't been two minutes last night for them to talk. Now it was time. "They survived a wagon train massacre."

"Paiutes? Never heard much trouble coming from them." Adam had been with Trace the longest. Adam said he was on the run from a shrewish wife. Trace had needed help, and Adam said he'd stay for a while. That was four years ago.

Adam was short and stocky, solid muscle. No man carried fat out in this land. The work was too hard and the food too hard to come by. Adam was a Swede with white-blond hair and skin that burned in the sun rather than turn brown. He didn't mind the heat in the summer nor the cold in the winter. He said the cold reminded him of his folks talking of home back in Sweden. The high-up mountains, too. Adam was born in Denver, and he'd been wandering for a time before he settled in with Trace's HS Ranch.

HS . . . Trace still felt a sweep of pride when he thought of his High Sierra Ranch. He'd made his own branding iron, an *HS* inside a circle. He'd registered the brand a few years back, but long before he registered it, he'd been slapping the brand on cattle he rounded up that he'd found running wild in the mountains.

Both of these men had considerable cow-hand skills — most of them equal to or better than Trace's. The only thing that made Trace the boss was that he'd managed to claim a homestead the fifth year he'd been out here alone — they'd finally passed that law. That was the year he finally found a town, and Adam. He was still working out the homestead years, but while he did, he bought up more land every time he gathered enough money to do it. He'd bought land for pennies an acre that had high mountain valleys full of lush grass and year-round water. Once, he swapped three cows for three hundred acres, and the folks in the land office had laughed at him and called him a fool. He let them laugh just as he'd done the same several years running, cornering water rights and buying grassland no one knew was up here.

It was as close as he could get to making his pa's dream of farming come true. No corn grew up here, but the tough, wild cattle were mountain born and bred, and they thrived through the harsh winters.

And Trace's land, here where his cabin stood, wasn't in the highest peaks. This was his homestead land, and it was lower, in a nice grassy valley.

The three of them — Trace, Adam, and Utah — had worked well together through the roundup and cattle drive. Trace respected each of them, and he thought they returned that respect.

"Nope, it was made to look like an Indian attack, a few arrows and such, and . . . and some . . ." Trace shook his head, sickened by it. "Some scalping . . . d-damage to the bodies before they were burned, but it was white men who done it. I could read the signs everywhere."

Utah flinched just a bit, enough that Trace suspected Utah had seen such things before.

"And the ladies confirmed it." Trace didn't like that.

"They saw their attackers?" Utah looked sickened that the women had witnessed such a thing.

Trace hesitated over this. If the knowledge fell into the wrong hands, Deb would be in danger. "One of the ladies saw a man in the firelight after they started the wagons burning. I haven't even asked her to describe him — we were on a fast march to get to shelter last night. She also heard a high-pitched man's voice, not the man she saw. And they definitely spoke English. She says it wasn't Indians."

Both of his friends heaved a sigh of relief. Trace understood it. The Native folks in the area were a decent bunch, and any trouble blamed on them could bring big trouble. He was glad he'd seen enough to be sure it wasn't Paiutes, but he wished like the dickens he hadn't seen any of what he had, and he regretted to the marrow of his bones that Deb had walked through that burned-out circle of wagons with him.

"The women and children walked away from the train into some tall grass before sunup. They were well hidden when the gunfire and screaming started." Trace stopped talking for a moment. He could well imagine their horror. When it happened to him, when Pa had died, he hadn't heard a thing. He'd been off hunting meat before the sunrise and only knew what had happened when he rode back to the wagon train . . . and smelled the burning flesh.

"It's a long ride to a town, and I'm not sure what two young women and two little'uns would do if they got taken there. Dismal is closest, but it's not a fit place for women and children alone. Bodie's no better. To get her . . . uh, *them* to Carson City, well, we could do that, but they'd still be alone unless they hitched a ride on a late wagon train. They can't stay the winter alone in Dismal. Where do they stay? Who would protect them?"

There was a stunned silence, until Adam asked hesitantly, "You're fixin' to keep 'em on the HS through the winter, boss?"

Trace hadn't really put it into words; he'd

only thought of all they couldn't do. "What choice do we have?"

The men were silent.

"I need to talk to them. They weren't headed toward Sacramento. They'd taken the south fork of the California Trail that stays up in the high country. The baby boy had folks killed in the massacre. The girl is his cousin, and she's got a father building a house and getting ready for them. We need to find out who that is and get a letter to him. We can make a run to Dismal to send a letter, but it might not get out till spring. Nothing gets through once the passes close up for the winter. The Donner Party cured most folks of trying to make a late-season passage. There are always a few, though."

"I can make a run to Dismal," Adam offered. "I ride a fast critter. I can go out and back today. I'll leave as soon as we fetch a letter around and find out where to send it."

Nodding, Trace admitted Adam's horse could beat every other animal on the place and it had endurance, too. Adam could get to the rugged frontier town and back in half a day if he pushed hard. "I appreciate that. No matter where our company ends up traveling on to, they look to be spending the winter in my house."

"Which means we get to spend the winter in the stable, Trace?" Utah looked straight up.

Trace's gaze followed. Snow was sifting in through the roof. And this light snow was nothing to what was coming.

"Truth is," Adam added, "the house lets the snow in almost as bad as the stable."

Utah sounded glum. "Cabin's got a fire-place, though."

"So . . . Utah, I said I'd like you to build a house come spring." Trace crossed his arms, knowing he was asking a lot. "And I wanted to take our time so I could learn some building skills from you."

Utah nodded. "We're going to start building right now, today, aren't we? And build as fast as we know how. And it'd better be two houses if we can find the time. Because I've stayed a few days in that cabin of yours and I don't know how you've survived all these years. We'll build a cabin for the winter, and a bunkhouse for us to sleep in for now, and then next spring you can have your own house."

"And I'm not going to be all that much help to you building it."

"Why not?" Utah asked. "I can teach you some of the ways of building."

"I'll learn all I can, but I'm going to be

busy on something else."

There was a stretch of silence that Trace hated to break.

"Something else?" Finally Adam couldn't control his curiosity. "Like what?"

Trace felt that grim rage take hold of his heart again. "I'm going to be hunting the men who massacred the folks on that wagon train. And I'll ride as far and as hard and as often as I need to. Those men are vicious killers. They're going to pay for their crimes. It rained on the trail behind us, on the north side of the peak. So the tracks will be washed away. But I'll find them. I'm planning to ride out every morning, ride to the north and find the men selling stolen cattle and horses. I'm going to see them hanged. I'll try and help with the building, and I'll stay and see things settled in for today, but starting tomorrow, I'm going hunting."

That caused another uncomfortable silence, broken when Utah said, "If they stole cattle and horses, they'd lay up a while and work over the brands. Some animals coming from the east aren't branded, so they'll be easier than altering brands. New brands take time to heal. They might hide out for a while until the brands look right."

"I can wait a few days maybe, figuring they're not moving and their tracks are gone." Trace considered this for a moment. "But bad weather is coming. If it settles down on us, I won't be going anywhere. By spring these men will be long gone."

Adam shrugged. "They think they got away clean, killed every witness, so why would they be long gone?"

That pulled Trace up short. "They might haunt the trails awhile longer. There are usually a few late trains going through."

"Maybe instead of hunting the men," Adam said, "you hunt the next wagon train. Nothing much easier to find than a whole great big string of wagons."

Adam had known him longest and had some idea of Trace's past, though none of his time spent guarding travelers. He'd told no one about that.

"And then I am there to protect the train the next time there's an attack." Trace knew how to do that. He'd been that trail's guardian for years. It was the same men. Or remnants of that old gang. The predawn attack, the falsely laid Indian signs, the same mistakes made copying the Paiute arrows, the fire, and the mutilated bodies done in just the way Trace remembered. That thirst for revenge woke up hard and vicious, and he fought it down and thought of his Bible reading.

"Go when you've a need of going. While you're here, help build the cabin." Utah grunted as if things were settled, then headed for a big wooden tool bin in the corner of the stable. He swung the lid open on squeaking hinges and pulled an ax out of the box. "This is mine. Do you have another?"

"Yep." Trace followed Utah and dug through the tools until he found his pa's heavy old ax. He had a newer one, too. "Adam, fetch the one by the chopping block."

"Good. We can have three men felling trees." Utah reached for Trace's ax. "Give it here. I can get an edge on all these that'll whistle through those trees like wind through their branches. I can probably fell a tree or two before breakfast. You men do the morning chores, rustle up some grub, and get those women to writing a letter. We can chop while Adam rides to Dismal. Before you leave to hunt down those yellow-belly varmints, you can help frame up the house."

Adam said with an odd, nervous note in his voice, "Maybe the women will cook."

All three of them pivoted to look in the direction of the cabin.

Adam smiled like a sunny day. Utah quit

talking about building and just stared through the barn wall as if he could see right into the cabin to the women cooking up a storm.

Trace said, "I don't see how it can hurt to ask." He started for the house, and the men fell in behind him.

"Turn 'em east, Meeks!" Raddo Landauer hollered to Bud Meeks, his saddle partner who rode out front leading this small herd.

Meeks reined in his horse to block the trail and turn the oxen and cattle, ten critters in all, off the main trail. They'd hold 'em until Raddo found a buyer, then turn this lot into cash.

It was a poor return on their work. A few dollars taken out of pockets, nothing much else except the cattle and horses, and a few of the herd had been lost in the attack.

They had no choice but to strike somewhere again soon. Times were bad and money was tight. But this had been a wasted effort. An early morning, a long ride, a lot of hot lead. And all for this sad lot.

He'd hoped this hit would set him up for the winter at least.

Raddo had done honest work for a stretch of years. He'd never struck it big like his outlaw pard, Luth, but he'd seen enough

111

color to keep himself fed and warm . . . and then his mine played out.

Didn't matter. Honest work hadn't paid as well as thieving, anyway. And it hadn't been a fraction of the fun.

The cattle turned. There just weren't enough of 'em, blast it. He and Dalt Callow brought up the rear, then Dalt pushed through the herd to lead and Meeks fell in beside Raddo.

"See if you can conceal the tracks from where we turned, Meeks."

"Why? No one alive to tell the tale of what we done."

Raddo glared at Meeks, who shrugged. "Fine, I'll do it, but it looks like rain's a-comin'. That's gonna do my work for me."

"The trees are so tight." Raddo looked overhead and saw that the trees spread across the faint trail. No sky visible. "I can't get a look at the sky."

"But listen." A rumble of distant thunder sounded.

"It could come as snow. We'll watch, and if the sky opens up on this stretch, then hunt around for any sign you don't think'll wash away and deal with that first. Then leave the rest to the rain."

Meeks nodded. "I'll go back where I can get a clear look at the clouds." He reined his horse and headed for the turnoff.

Raddo spent long minutes riding, listening. Finally a low, distant rumble told him rain was on the way for sure. The storms here most often came from the west, heading east, and when they hit the peaks, it was like the clouds couldn't climb with the weight of the water and they emptied out. Happened a lot up here.

With grim satisfaction, Raddo knew his tracks would be covered and there'd be no need for anyone to bother with 'em. He turned around to tell Meeks to put aside cleaning up. No sign of him.

Well, Raddo wouldn't go hunt him down. Meeks was a lazy lout. He wouldn't mind staying back when there was work to be done. And with this narrow trail and the cattle and horses following placidly after Dalt, there was no need for a third man to handle the drive.

He'd let Meeks have a break.

They'd lay low awhile. Rework the brands. Then Raddo would ride out and find a cattle buyer who didn't ask a lot of fool questions. They'd get rid of the herd and decide where their next money would be coming from.

Wherever that was, it had to be soon.

The thunder rumbled, louder this time.

Almost sure to hit them, though it'd be a while. The distant storm echoed in Raddo's chest like the rumble of wagon wheels coming down the trail, bringing him his next big strike.

Gold found the easy way, with a six-gun instead of a pickax.

Raddo was already looking forward to it.

CHAPTER 9

A knock on the door made Gwen jump.
Then she looked over at Deb and shrugged
sheepishly at her own taut nerves.

Deb shook her head, rushed to the door,
and swung it open to the chilly October
morning.

Trace stood there, tall and strong and
heroic. It did something to her heart. She
wanted to thank him again, for the one
hundredth time.

"Come in."

Trace looked over his shoulder.

Deb looked past him and saw the other
men who'd been here last night.

"All of you, please, come in."

Trace looked at Gwen, who had Ronnie
on one of the beds, changing his wet
britches. Maddie Sue lay across Ronnie's
wriggling body to hold him down. Gwen
had made it seem like a game, but that was
the way they tended the little cyclone most

of the time. The boy didn't seem to mind and was kicking for all he was worth while Gwen tried to wrestle him into a diaper without sticking him with a pin.

Maddie Sue looked over her shoulder at Trace. "Where's Wolf?"

The dog barked and dashed past Trace's legs to rush to the bedside.

"Wolf never comes inside." Trace sounded baffled. "Not even on bitter cold nights. Not since he was a pup. I used to drag him in when it was so cold that the inside of the cabin was almost too harsh to stand. He ran back outside. Once, I managed to keep him in for almost an hour, though he howled at the door the whole time. When I finally opened the door, he threw himself into a snowdrift as if he was burning up."

With a shrug, Trace added, "I've decided his fur is made to withstand winter. But it looks like he can't withstand not being with Maddie Sue."

Deb thought Trace looked a little . . . betrayed. Like a kid who found out his best friend was playing with someone else.

Then she remembered her manners. "Thank you all for giving up your beds last night." She looked back at Trace. "Would you like me to get a meal on for all of you?"

Trace froze for a minute, as if her words

had overwhelmed him, then perked up at the offer. And what man didn't perk up for food? "None of us is a hand at cooking, Deb. We get by eatin' mighty plain. You cooking would be a fine thing."

The men all crowded in and pushed Trace over the doorstep. "I'd be pleased to get a meal on if you'll tell me what food supplies you have and where I can get wood to build up the fire."

There had been a small stack of wood by the fireplace, but she'd used it up trying to keep the little cabin warm. It was impossible with the wind whistling straight through the many cracks in the walls.

One of the men stepped back so fast he bumped into someone else, then almost shouted, "I'll get wood." He then vanished around the side of the cabin.

Well, she couldn't really say he vanished because she saw him through the wall. The logs were so uneven, and so poorly chinked, she could see right through.

"We have chickens, ma'am. I'll fetch eggs," a gray-haired man offered with a grin. "The cow needs milking before we can eat." The man was far enough inside he caught sight of a bucket sitting by the wall near the front door. He grabbed it and rushed off.

Gwen finished. Maddie Sue hopped off

Ronnie and dove at the dog.

Ronnie burst into loud wailing tears and cried, "Want my mama!"

Cooing and whispering, Gwen picked up Ronnie, who kicked and thrashed in her arms. Gwen held him close, trying to comfort him.

"Mama, Mama."

Maddie Sue had heard the little one cry plenty of times, it seemed, because she ignored him and tugged on the dog's ears.

Ronnie's crying got even louder. "Mama!"

"Poor little guy." Trace brushed past Deb.

She'd expected him to run off with the other men. But now that the diapering was finished, he might stay. She swung the door shut.

"Mama!"

Trace reached for the toddler and pulled him into his arms.

"Papa?" Ronnie broke off the crying.

"Hush, little one, don't cry. I lost my papa and mama, too." Trace held him and, for no reason Deb could understand, the struggling and kicking stopped. The boy wrapped his chubby arms around Trace's neck and cried softly now. Trace held him and patted him, murmuring things she couldn't quite make out. Deb did hear Trace say, "The voice of one crying in the wilderness."

He'd said that yesterday, and she'd been amused by it because it really fit Ronnie, and yet it missed the meaning of the Bible verse completely. As she was sure Trace knew.

Anything else Trace said was too softly spoken and meant only for Ronnie's ears. The two swayed slowly, gently side to side.

Maddie Sue happily tormented the poor, patient wolf-dog. While the dog seemed to be content, Deb intervened to protect the poor critter and sat on the floor with Maddie Sue on her lap.

"Gentle touches, Maddie Sue. Be gentle with the nice dog." She tried to teach the girl.

The crying eased until finally Ronnie lifted his face from Trace's chest and looked down at the floor. Ronnie pointed down and said, "Dog."

The storm had passed.

Trace lowered him to where Maddie Sue sat on the floor. Ronnie dropped down beside her, and Maddie Sue made a very precious effort to teach Ronnie how to be gentle with a wolf.

Gwen moved to block the fireplace. The boy tended to toddle straight toward whatever was most dangerous.

"I'll go get some bacon and flour," Trace

said. "There are plenty of supplies in the root cellar. If one of you comes along, I can show you the place so you can help yourselves. I really appreciate that you're cooking for us."

Deb took a second to try to remember her pa ever once thanking her for anything.

"Deb, you go. I'll watch the youngsters."

Deb wondered at Trace's courage when the others had run. She didn't really blame them — they weren't used to children, but neither was Trace as far as she knew.

As they walked outside, the sun was just barely easing the sky from black to gray. Deb looked around. Neither of the hired hands was in sight, although she did hear wood being chopped. She was tempted to shout that Ronnie was all done being diapered. But she figured the men would risk returning eventually. In the meantime, she followed Trace to a door covering a hole in the ground.

Trace held open the door and let Deb walk down the stone steps to his cellar. At the bottom he lit a lantern that he kept down here.

"There's milk and eggs. The men could've waited until after breakfast to do chores." She gave Trace a grin.

"That diaperin' is enough to run off a man." Trace smiled back. "What all do you need? I've got flour and a side of bacon. Sourdough starter that Adam knew how to make."

He started picking up whatever he thought they'd need. "Utah and Adam haven't been around little ones much. Sorry they ran off. But I don't blame them one speck."

"Let me help." Deb reached out, and Trace handed her some of the supplies he carried. "I don't blame them, either. But you're made of sterner stuff, aren't you?"

"Yesterday helped break me in." Trace shrugged, not mentioning how it affected him to hear that little boy cry for his mama. No sense going over all of his own history, being stranded, losing his pa. That terrible loneliness. It'd all happened a long time ago.

"What makes you say *'A voice of one crying in the wilderness'*? That's a Bible verse about John the Baptist."

"Yep, and little Ronnie's no preacher, least ways he's not shown signs of it yet." Trace finished gathering and walked to the stairs. "Go on up ahead. The steps are steep, and I can stop you if you start tumbling."

"I appreciate that." She passed him and headed up, not a bit unsteady.

"My men brought supplies of all kinds

back from Sacramento, on a string of pack-horses. I made good money on my beeves and had it to spend and paid them their time, so they added a few things they wanted. We've plenty to get through winter."

"Even with four extra mouths to feed?" Deb asked.

He hesitated. Not so sure. "I'll do some hunting. I've got a herd . . . so we've got food on the hoof. There are some chickens. I'll keep us fed."

Utah was visible by the chopping block, nearly behind the cabin, stacking wood at the speed of molasses in January. The sky was lighter from the approaching dawn.

Trace called to him. "Hurry up, the baby is dressed again."

Utah shuddered, grabbed the wood, and followed Trace in. He seemed to be using Trace to block his view of the cabin until he was sure it was safe.

"Wolf's gonna chew one of those kids up," Utah muttered from behind Trace.

"He seems to love them. Strangest thing I've ever seen."

"I'm pretty sure I saw a *Ts'emekwe* when I lived with the Cayuse Indians, so I'm not saying this is the *strangest,* but it's strange all right."

Trace turned to look at Utah. "A what?"

122

"It's kinda a wild man covered with hair. Heard it called Sasquatch. Bigfoot. A wild man. I described it to the tribe, and the Cayuse called it *Ts'emekwe.* They said they lived in the highest hills and fought shy of people. Pretty sure I saw one. And I once shot a buffalo, cut it open, and slept inside it to survive a blizzard. That was almighty strange." Utah passed Trace and went to build up the fire.

Trace shook his head to knock loose the image of a wild man covered with hair living inside a buffalo, then set the flour and other supplies on the small table beside the things Deb had carried.

From where he knelt by the fire, Utah said, "I'll start building a new house today."

Deb gasped and turned from Utah to Trace. "You don't have to do that. Not for us. Trace, you and your men have already done so much."

"We were planning on building in the spring, miss," Utah said. "But now that you're here, we decided to get on with it and hope the weather holds until we can get the roof on. When I got back from the drive, I decided to talk Trace into building now anyway. I didn't want to sleep in here all winter. So I reckon we'll build two houses if we get the time."

Deb looked bewildered. "Two houses?"

Trace nodded. "And I need you to write a letter."

He saw Deb's eyes light up. "To Maddie Sue's pa, you mean? You can mail a letter?"

"Yep, Adam'll make a trip to Dismal, the nearest post office. Three hours on a fast horse, one way. So he wants to get moving."

"That's wonderful. Where can I find paper and a pencil?"

Trace stopped in his tracks. "Uh, don't you have that?"

CHAPTER 10

Deb had spent her whole life writing. Well, about all of it she could remember, anyway. She'd started fetching and carrying for Ma at the newspaper since before she went to school.

Then she got a few years in school until Pa saw she was writing and reading well, and he brought her home to help Ma with the paper. She still studied at home some, using Gwen's books, and managed to get to school enough to keep passing through the grades, but mostly she'd worked at the newspaper. With the writing and the bill paying it'd been a fine education of reading and writing and arithmetic. But never before in her life had she wondered how to find a piece of paper.

"No, I don't have any." She thought of the bag she carried with so many supplies in it. She'd never considered adding paper and a pencil. "There was paper and such in the wagon, but it all went up in flames."

Trace's brow furrowed, and he snapped his fingers. "I know where I have a piece of paper. No pencil, but maybe one of my men has one." He turned to the fireplace. "Utah, have you got such as a pencil or a pen and ink among your things?"

"I can't read nor write, Trace. I have no need to carry those around."

"Well, can you go ask Adam? Though I doubt he has any. He's been here four years, and I've never seen such things."

"Maybe you can write with a bit of charcoal," Utah said. "I seen it done once."

"Or we could burn a pointed stick and use that. Okay. Go check with Adam just in case."

Utah headed outside.

"I'll get breakfast started," Gwen said. She began bustling around the table, taking steady glances at the children.

Trace went to a corner in the cabin, a square space formed where the head of one bed touched the foot of another. There was a gap, and Deb saw there was a trunk of some kind back there hidden in the shadows cast by the cabin's single lantern.

Trace bent down and lifted the whole box. Not that big, a couple of feet high and deep and wide, but Trace's muscles bulged as if it was heavy. He set it on the bed, flipped a latch, and swung the lid open with a rusty squeak.

Deb saw the trunk was full of . . . "Books. Is that full of books?"

"Yep. I've hung on to every one I've ever gotten hold of."

There was a Bible on top. A strangely battered Bible that looked as if it'd been burned around the edges. Deb frowned. She hated to see a Bible treated so poorly.

Trace pulled out one book after another. She saw a thick book of Shakespeare's plays. A book by Plutarch and another by Plato. Charles Dickens and, of all things, a copy of her favorite book ever, *Robinson Crusoe.*

"Have you read them?"

"Yep, over and over. Adam too. I'll get Utah to readin' by the time winter is over. It helps pass long days when we can barely move in the snow." Trace turned a copy of Ben Franklin's autobiography over in his hands.

Deb had never in her life had time to just sit and read. Oh, she'd done it some — she'd managed to finish *Robinson Crusoe,* and she knew the Bible pretty well, which Ma had read to them every night. Deb had loved it, but there was always work. Long hours, all spent writing her own words and setting up the press and cranking out copies and selling them on the street, then writing out bills and collecting payments. All she knew of words was work. But how she'd dreamed of long stretches of time and a book in her hand.

"If we are to stay here all winter, do you think I might be able to read some of your books?"

Trace smiled as he continued to empty the box. "I'd be proud to share them with you, Deb. Gwen too, and you can read to the children."

He turned to the back of the book, to the last page. "It's blank." He held it up for her. "We can use this for paper."

"You know all these books well enough to know one of them has one blank page in the back?"

Trace's hand tightened on the book. "It feels wrong to tear it up. But this page serves no purpose, does it?"

He looked hopefully at her, as if asking her to approve of what he wanted to do.

"It does seem wrong to tear up a book. You're sure there's no paper?"

Trace's eyes fixed on something, as if sorting through everything he owned. "Wait, I think some of the supplies from Sacramento were wrapped in paper." His whole face lit up.

"I'll go search the cellar." He set the book down and ran out. A man eager to protect a book. How had the Bible been so badly abused, then?

Deb ran one finger over the last book he'd held, the one with a single blank page. "*Robinson Crusoe.* Can you imagine finding a copy here in the high-up mountains between Nevada and California?"

"I've never had time for much reading," Gwen said. "But I would purely love a chance at a book and some stretch of quiet to linger over it."

Maddie Sue shrieked and wrestled with poor, patient Wolf. Deb wondered if quiet would ever really exist.

"Maybe we can spend this winter reading aloud to each other, taking turns." Gwen rescued the dog and set Maddie Sue to playing with Ronnie. "We can rock the children to sleep and read a chapter each night. And add a bit of Bible reading, too. Maybe we can work our way through a lot of them."

"It sounds blissful." Deb looked around the tiny cabin. "And keeping this place tidy shouldn't take up much time, now, should it?"

"I hope they don't build us a big house." Gwen went to work on breakfast. Back east she'd done most of the household chores while Deb ran the paper, and she was a fine cook. "We'll have to clean it."

"Let's make sure they don't think we need a lot of space. Of course, the cabin is for Trace and his men, so maybe they want more room."

"Not if they've been putting up with this little wreck of a cabin for years. I don't think we need to worry on that score." Gwen stirred up pancake batter.

"But two houses? One for us, one for them?"

"They don't want to spend the winter in here, either."

"Even though they've lived here a long time?" With a shrug, Deb found a skillet among the supplies she'd scavenged from the wagon train. Trace had one too, but this one was bigger, and they had a lot of food to make. She got to work on the bacon, and soon they had a meal cooking along.

Trace came back with a small can wrapped in paper. "You can write your letter on this, and Adam said he's got a pencil. He went to fetch it."

He sniffed. "That smells great."

"Pancakes and bacon. And there'll be

130

fried eggs in a few minutes. Grab a plate and start eating. We found four plates, so you men eat and we'll feed the little ones, and then we'll wash up a couple of the plates and eat ourselves."

Utah came in the door with a milk pail. Deb had him figured out: the man planning to lead the building. Next came Adam, the stub of a pencil in his hand. He had the fast horse, and he carried a tin basin full of eggs. Deb needed to get that pencil and unwrap the canister, then figure out where to send this letter. She'd looked through the papers she saved and hadn't found much.

"Maddie Sue, what's your pa's name?" Abe had talked of his brother a lot. Abe was proud of him for fighting in the war and heading west and finding them land. But his name . . . Deb was having trouble remembering it right now.

"It's Pa." Maddie Sue blinked her eyes at Deb as if the question scared her.

"It's Cameron, remember, Deb?" Gwen said. "Ronnie is named for him. Cameron Scott."

"That's right. And what town would you say he lives in?" Deb searched her mind.

Gwen stopped, and Deb could actually see her thinking.

"We were to ride about another ten days

on that highland trail." Gwen looked at Trace. "What town would you say that leads to?"

Trace shrugged. "Sacramento is more straight west, not sure what's to the south."

"It was definitely in California. The town was named Fern, I think," Gwen said. "No, that doesn't sound quite right. Abe said his brother Cameron had a nice payout when he left the cavalry, and his sister earned good money too and had saved it faithfully. They homesteaded some farmland with plans for Abe to get more."

Trace said, "Never heard of Fern, California. But then I've hardly left this area before our cattle drive to Sacramento."

"I think it was Fen, not Fern. Fen Canyon," Deb said uncertainly.

Gwen brightened. "Fen Canyon. That sounds more like it."

Utah said, "I heard tell of a Fenler Canyon. Could that be it?"

Deb and Gwen looked at each other.

Finally Gwen said, "I think that's right. I remember. I saw it on an envelope. I think that's the only time I even heard the Scotts speak of the town. But then we'd never planned to stay with them so maybe I just didn't listen. They mentioned grandparents, too. I'll send two letters. Deb and I were heading on to San Francisco to start a newspaper."

"A newspaper? Two women?" Utah sounded well and truly shocked.

Deb rather enjoyed surprising people.

"I worked at my pa's newspaper back east, and by the time he died, I was running it myself." Truth was, she'd run it herself ever since Ma died, but she wouldn't bother to talk about that right now.

"I don't have a printing press. We sold everything when we headed west." For no money, because Pa had creditors who took nearly every penny. Another thing Deb didn't bother to mention.

"But I hope to get a job working at a newspaper and save up until I can afford to start my own," Deb said. "Can Adam buy more paper when he's in Dismal? I have a few coins, so I can pay for it."

The Scotts had a cache of money, but that belonged to the children. "I should write letters to the families of all the people who died. I know their names and where they're from. I'm not sure if they had kin back home, but I found a few things among the wagons that can be sent back if we can find out where to send them. And there are some salvaged papers I have only flipped through while looking for Cameron Scott's address.

Even if the letters don't go out until spring, they need to be mailed at some point."

"I'll pick up paper and another pencil, Miss Deb." Adam ate his pancake, sitting on the side of a bed. There was a table in the little cabin, but Gwen had used it for a work place, and a bowl of pancake batter sat there as she poured new cakes onto the skillet, red hot in the fireplace, flipped them, and then served them. The men had been roughing it here. Deb wondered if Utah knew how to build furniture as well as houses. She'd certainly appreciate a chair to go with the table.

She decided to wait and ask after the house was done for fear she'd sound unappreciative, when in fact she was anything but. She knew full well she owed these men her very life.

Deb wrote the letter to Cameron Scott, hopefully in Fenler Canyon, California, with as much compassion as she could muster. She hated to put the words on paper telling of Abe and Delia's deaths. She'd worked with words all her life and did her best to be as kind as possible in her limited space. Trace got a second piece of paper he'd found in his cellar, to send a letter to Edmond and Florence Chilton, Ronnie's grandparents. She hoped telling the man and the grandparents that the two children had survived would soften the blow.

She handed the letter to Adam, with Cameron Scott's name and Fenler Canyon as an address. But since the mountain trails were about to snow closed, it wouldn't matter if the letters got out or not. No one was getting in here to collect the children before spring.

With a pang, Deb looked at the little ones and knew that if it didn't work out for Cameron Scott or the Chiltons to come, she'd gladly take the children. She and Gwen could raise them as their own.

Deb got to work feeding the men. As she fried and served, she was reminded that one thing she vowed to herself when she'd come west was that she was going to work for herself. After years of working for Pa, she had promised herself that she'd work to build something for her and Gwen rather than serving an ungrateful man. It bothered her a bit to be right back to serving.

"Miss Deb, Miss Gwen," Adam said, handing Deb his plate, "I will try and buy more plates while I'm in town, too. It ain't right for you to work so hard feeding us and then have to wait until we're finished to eat yourself. I thank you for your gracious patience. You're fine women. And it was as fine a meal as I've had since I sat at my ma's table and that's near ten years ago."

His voice almost throbbed with sincerity, and his eyes shone with gratitude. "Now I'd best get on the trail."

The kind words were so sweet to her ears, Deb took a moment to fight down tears. When she was able, she found the money in her bag. "Can you buy some fabric too, Adam? I think this is enough money. We don't have a stitch of clothing beyond what's on our backs, though there might be a piece or two of clothing in my bag for Ronnie, and there was one spare diaper. We'll need the diaper cloth more than anything else. Flannel if at all possible."

Adam froze, his hand extended for the money. "Diaper flannel?"

Her tears forgotten, Deb bit back a smile as she dropped the coins in his hand. "Yes, please. And probably as much as they've got, considering the state of most small-town general stores. If you get too much, I can sew up shirts for you men so you'll have spares. Then I can do the washing for you."

"You're going to make our shirts with the same cloth you're making diapers?" Adam looked at his hand as if she'd dropped a rattlesnake in his palm. He gave his head a violent shake as if he'd been dunked in water, whirled around, and ran out of the house.

These men certainly did like to dive into their work. Especially when it meant putting space between themselves and anything to do with a diaper.

Trace and Utah handed over their cleaned-up plates with polite words. Utah found his hat on a nail in the house and tipped it as he thanked them both.

It was so flattering, so touching, Deb could only nod.

"We'd best get to chopping wood so these women have a snug, warm place for the winter." Trace followed Utah out. Wolf looked back and forth between Maddie Sue and Trace and appeared just plain torn about what to do, but finally he went along with his master.

It soothed her soul to be told "thank you" by a man, possibly for the first time in her life.

No, goodness gracious, she'd be honored to cook for these fine gentlemen for the winter. Trace saved them. And these men gave up their cabin for them and now planned to build, so they all could have a warmer home.

Whatever they needed — mending, washing, cooking, cleaning — she'd do. The men would never lack for thanks, either.

Hooves pounded away. Adam on his way.

Deb washed up two plates. She and Gwen had their breakfast and planned the next meal while they ate this one.

The rhythmic ring of hewing axes set their work to a kind of rough music.

CHAPTER 11

Adam took a packhorse. Trace had heard Deb ask for flannel, but that didn't require a spare horse. And taking the packhorse slowed him down because no critter on this property was as fast as Adam's stallion. But without the load of a rider it could keep up. Because of the early morning wake-up, thanks to Maddie Sue's hollering, it was only just past sunup. Trace hoped Adam could get back not too far past midday.

Trace worried about him because the sky was overcast. There'd been heavy snow all day up in the peaks. Only a little fell down here on lower ground, but more would come, and soon.

He hated any man being on the trail this late in the season, and Trace's turn was coming. He had some hunting to do.

"We're going to be lucky to get a roof over the women's heads," Trace said to Utah as they passed each other. They'd chopped down trees all morning, and now Trace and Utah used the horses to drag logs up to the building site. They had enough to start the walls, and Utah wanted to get the framing done.

"Why here?" Trace asked. He knew nothing about building except some real basic things he'd learned as a youngster working with his pa.

His cabin stood as proof of that.

Utah started in talking about the direction of the wind in winter and how the rain came in during spring storms. He seemed stuck on morning sunlight as opposed to afternoon and pointed to trees that lost their leaves and compared them to pines that didn't — as if that meant something important.

A spring bubbled out of a rock in one spot and created a little stream. He said a man who fights water always loses.

Trace heard every word, though it didn't make a lot of sense. That's why he'd wanted to wait until spring, so he could learn all this.

And then they started building and he did learn. He found out that if a man chinked out the corner of a log a hundred times, he started to get good at it. And Utah wouldn't do it for him and wouldn't put up with a poorly done corner. It wasn't as if Utah was sitting around idle; he was working on the sides of the trees, getting rid of knots and branches, picking out logs straight as a lance, rejecting bent and warped trees. He said they'd be used for something else.

Trace saw the sun high in the sky and wondered where the morning had gone. But sure enough, his stomach told him it was mealtime and beyond.

Deb wanted neither to interrupt the commotion outside nor to run afoul of it. Add in the image of a tree falling on one of the children and she was firm in her course that all of them should stay to the house as much as possible.

The only times they dared go outside were for a few minutes to the privy, and a quick run Deb made to Trace's root cellar.

"He's got so much food, Gwen." Deb heard the hungry excitement in her voice.

Gwen laughed. "Better than on the wagon train?"

"Well, considering we've had little but venison roasted in strips over a fire and hard biscuits for months, yes, better than the wagon train. By about a thousand miles."

She lifted up one arm to present a ham.

Gwen's gasp of excitement made Deb take

her turn laughing. "I see you're a bit tired of tough deer meat too, sister."

"And you've got potatoes. When is the last time we ate a vegetable?" Gwen moved to the cupboard under the sink and swung open a door. "There is plenty of flour down here, and I added to the sourdough starter."

"I found two bushels of apples, Gwen. We've got plenty of time to make pie."

Gwen was the better baker of the two of them, though Deb wouldn't be ashamed of what she could produce.

"I'll make two of them," Gwen declared. "We'll have three hungry men to feed, and two pies will give everyone a generous slice for dinner and supper."

The chopping had gone on steadily since it had begun.

"There was also yeast in the cellar. A cake of it that looks as if it's never been touched. We can get a rising of bread started for the evening meal. I'll put the ham on to boil, then get to the pies. I'll stew potatoes to mash and make redeye gravy."

The menu made Deb's mouth water.

"The only thing he's short on is pans." Gwen's brow furrowed, and she turned to study the meager contents of the cupboard.

"Wait." Deb looked around and saw the pack she'd gathered from the wagon train.

"I got a pan out for breakfast, one I salvaged from the wagon train. But there were others I didn't get out earlier. No amount of burning is going to damage a cast-iron skillet, and the murdering thieves didn't bother themselves with stealing such practical items."

Ronnie was on his back, trying to put his toes in his mouth, with considerable success. Maddie Sue sat beside him, chattering away. Ronnie could say quite a few words back, though he wasn't much fun to talk to, especially considering where his toes were. Fortunately, Maddie Sue preferred it if no one interrupted her, so they were getting along well.

Gwen whispered, "You found the Scotts' gold?"

Deb nodded. "And some from the other four wagons. Abe was the one who told them how to conceal their coins, so I knew right where to look. There were a few more things I wished later I'd picked up. More pans. The hardware from the harnesses. Even the hubs from the wagons — they'd be a good start for someone wanting to build another wagon or a wheel for any use. They're too thick to burn all the way through. But how was I to carry all that?"

"You should suggest going back for them

to Trace and his men. Maybe they'd want some of those things enough to fetch them. It's not that far a distance on a fast horse. Look at the way they sent Adam to a town far away with plans for him to be home soon."

With a hard swallow, Deb said, "The money I sent with Adam this morning was the last I had. If there are other things to buy, I'll have to use the Scotts' money. I don't feel right about spending other folks' coins. I plan to find their families, their heirs, and send that money to them. I have the names of those who died, but I don't know who to write to. For now, I won't worry about it, but I do want to hold back the money. I'll not steal from those who died being robbed just because the robbers weren't thorough."

"I agree completely. But using the Scotts' money is different. We need to care for the children. And if there is some left, we can send it along with Cameron when he arrives to claim his daughter. I suppose he'll want Ronnie, too." Gwen gave the little ones a wistful look. She'd fallen very much in love with them during their journey.

Ronnie pulled his toes out of his mouth, jumped up, and rushed the fireplace. For no possible reason on the earth, he seemed fascinated by the deadly flames.

With quick, practiced skill, Gwen inter-
cepted him and picked him up to tickle his
tummy. She was very good at diverting the
little ones.

"You watch them while I get on with the
meal. The bread first, then the ham. I'll let
you make the piecrust — you do it in half
the time I can. You keep Maddie Sue and
Ronnie out of trouble. I'll handle the food."

Cooking in Trace's fireplace was so much
like what Deb had been doing for the wagon
train that it wasn't much trouble.

Gwen helped when she could, but the
children kept her running.

A gust of wind blew through the cracks in
the house walls.

Looking worried, Deb asked, "Does this
cabin wobble a bit in the wind or am I
imagining it?"

Looking around her, Gwen said, "I'm not
sure, but I hope those men get a cabin built
fast, and a second one for themselves."

"I certainly hope we're not too much
trouble," Deb said dryly.

Gwen snorted. Deb couldn't help but
laugh.

"Can you imagine three men living in
here?" Gwen shook her head. "So small and
so cold. I can't see how they stood it."

Deb worked and talked with Gwen and the children. She raked the burning wood forward in the fireplace and carefully nestled two pies into the back corners to bake. The ham was soon boiling in the covered Dutch oven. Deb put biscuits on to bake, along with another pan of water for the potatoes. There wasn't room in Trace's small hearth for everything, but soon the biscuits were done and set aside. She prepared a small mountain of potatoes and set them to cooking. They'd be done in time to give her space to make the gravy at the last minute.

She and Gwen were very busy seeing over the pans to keep everything from burning while keeping the children out of harm's way.

"Call them in, Deb." Back home, Gwen had run the household while Deb ran the newspaper. That arrangement kept Gwen in school, even though Pa thought it was a waste of time to educate girls.

As Gwen whipped the gravy into perfect smoothness, Deb took her turn corralling the children and knew they both had their hands very full.

"I'll take the gravy up in a few minutes. By the time they wash and get in here, dinner will be ready."

Deb went to the door, a child in each arm,

and did some fumbling to get hold of the knob and swing the door open.

In her clear, pretty voice, she yelled, "Dinnertime!"

CHAPTER 12

Trace jerked his head up so fast he almost embedded the ax in his foot.

Utah laughed from where he was digging a trench in which to set the foundation logs. "Reckon I haven't heard a sound that pretty in many a day, Trace. And two meals in a row cooked by a woman's hand."

"You ate woman-cooked food at the end of the cattle drive." Trace didn't know why he was correcting Utah. He agreed. It was a mighty fine sound.

They were hustling when they walked into the house and smelled heaven.

Utah poked Trace in the back so hard he almost stumbled forward. But no words or pokes were needed, at least not between the men.

But words were definitely needed for the women.

"You made ham and potatoes." Trace could barely hold himself back from diving into the food. "This looks delicious. Better than any food that has ever appeared on this ranch."

Which wasn't much of a compliment considering Trace's cooking skills. He needed a better compliment.

He washed up, then was afraid his dash toward the food was flat-out embarrassing, but he couldn't stop himself.

Gwen set the biscuits on the small table. Everyone would need to take a plate and sit on the beds. Trace figured he'd better give Gwen and Deb and the little ones his bed to sit on. They needed to build furniture. Funny, he'd never had such a thought until now.

Hoofbeats thundered outside. Adam was back. It'd taken him just over six hours and that was close to a record.

Trace should have gone out to help, but he had a plateful of food and honestly he just could not make himself put it down. And the flattery from Utah, not to mention from him, almost drowned out the sound of a rider, so he decided to pretend like he hadn't heard anything.

He and Utah all sat on the bed farthest from the women. It seemed proper. He really did need more furniture. Of course, the cabin he was building needed walls and a roof even more, so he had to get that finished first.

Trace saw one plate left, and Gwen was chopping food up on it in such small bites he figured it was for the children. No plate for Adam, then, and none for the women who'd made the feast.

Eating fast, and he didn't mind doing that one bit, Trace cleared his plate and went to the sink to wash it up for Adam.

"I'll do the dishes." Deb came and for a second looked to be preparing to wrestle him for the plate. He kinda hoped she would.

But she saw him smile at her, and he had no idea what was in that smile, but she backed up and crossed her arms, tapping her toe. Then she sniffed at him and turned back to the hearth, dropped to her knees, and started working over the fire.

Adam swung the door open. Trace saw his horse and the packhorse just outside the door. Both had a full load on their backs. They didn't need many supplies; they'd just stocked up in Sacramento.

"Help me unpack the —" He froze like he was underwater in January in Lake Tahoe as Deb rose from the fireplace. "Is . . . is that . . . ? Ma'am . . . Miss Deb, is that . . . pie?"

Deb turned, pie in hand — absolutely a pie.

Trace gripped his clean dripping-wet plate, unwilling now to let Adam use it for his meal.

"I'd say the meal was a success." Gwen chuckled a bit, then broke out laughing.

"I'm glad Adam had the sense to mention he bought a few more plates. I thought there might be a fistfight." Deb looked at Gwen's pink cheeks and suspected hers were a match. She and Gwen didn't look much alike, but they both blushed at similar things.

And this wasn't even a blush — it was delight. "Feeding those men made me feel better than anything I've ever done. Far better than the time I wrote that story about the burned-down general store, and folks came in and there was a building day and money donated to restock their shelves. And that made me feel very good."

"And look at the fabric." Gwen nodded at the stack in all colors and fabrics teetering on one of the beds. "We need to hem some flannel for diapers as soon as we can."

Gwen rocked Ronnie by standing up and swaying. There was certainly no such thing as a rocking chair. Deb worked quietly shaping bread loaves so that Gwen could get the boy settled. Maddie Sue had crawled into bed and gone to sleep without a fuss. The children were exhausted after yesterday's long ride. They'd slept well through the night and looked to be settling in for a good nap.

Deb finished with the loaves as Gwen lay Ronnie down to sleep in his own bed. The boy tended to kick in his sleep, and both children slept better if they were apart.

The chopping went on. Gwen went to the door and opened it a few inches. "They've started on the walls, Deb. I can see where the cabin will be. I can't believe they're building a cabin for us."

Deb washed the flour off her hands and took the towel with her to the door to peek out. She enjoyed the sight of hardworking men for a few more minutes. There was a nice stack of logs, but more trees were being felled. Adam was out of sight, his ax ringing out at a steady pace.

"Let's get the supplies Adam bought stowed and see about more diapers, then turn our attention to supper."

"I'm going to have to make both of us a dress," Gwen said. "We have to have at least one change of clothes. We honestly need nightgowns, too."

"I sent enough money along to pay for this cloth, though I didn't expect to get quite so much. We can use it for ourselves. I had one extra dress for Maddie Sue and a pair of overalls for Ronnie, but they need more than that."

"Where'd you get them?" Gwen asked.

"I'd stuck them in my satchel earlier when we were walking through those woods. I often keep a change of clothes for them. And they never needed them, and there they still were when I grabbed the satchel to carry along into the tall grass."

"Mr. Scott was always reminding us not to go out unprepared. I'd say you learned that lesson."

"We'll have to find time when the children are napping to see about new dresses." Deb looked down at her faded blue gingham dress. She'd worn it most days, with only one other dress to change into when this one was getting the rare washing.

"Adam went overboard with the fabric." Gwen looked at the stack of bolts and giggled.

"I must have scared him with my talk of diapers." Deb grinned at her sister. "He certainly didn't want to be caught short. What are we going to do with all this?"

"The men left here quickly last night and

I've looked around. I've found a second shirt for each of them, and they are mighty threadbare. We can make shirts for the men, maybe trousers, too. Unless they're stored somewhere I can't see, none of them have much to spare."

"You've had to drag Ronnie out from under every bed. There's no corner of this cabin you haven't seen."

"Let's get to work. We need to try and outdo ourselves for supper."

Shaking her head, Gwen said, "I'm not sure we do. I get the feeling it will take only very simple good food to keep the men happy. Plenty of it, of course, as hard as they're working."

Midafternoon on the fifth day since the wagon train massacre, Trace came in alone, smiling. "It's done. There's finishing work to do, but the roof's on, the chimney is solid and ready for a fire. Utah built a couple of cots in the bedrooms. So you can sleep in the new cabin tonight. The men are chopping down a few more trees, younger ones so Utah can build a few chairs and make a table tomorrow, and there's work to do on cupboards and such. He says he can figure out how to make a crib for Ronnie, Maddie Sue too, if you think she needs one."

"You've worked fast." Deb was near him, just pulling a cover up over Ronnie. Both children slept soundly at nap time. Deb and Gwen didn't worry about talking while they slept, and neither child had noticed the door open or the gust of cold wind that came in or Trace talking.

Going the few steps to Trace, Deb rested a hand on his arm. She was so delighted she had to make sure he knew it. "Thank you for all the hard work. For all you've done and keep doing for us, Trace. As for the cribs, we didn't have any on the wagon train, so we can get by without them."

She looked at Gwen, who smiled at Trace from where she kneaded bread at the table. "I don't think you need to build a crib, either. Maybe instead you should build a couple more cots, if the house is going to be for you and your men once we're gone."

"We aim to put up a bunkhouse after you get moved in. We'll live in here until it's done, then tear down this house," Trace said. "We're going to keep chopping down trees as long as the weather holds. If we can't build now, and I hope we can, we'll do it in the spring. But we'll have a jump on it by having the trees ready. Utah's determined to get on with it."

"I'm so impressed with how hard you're

all working. You're wonderful, decent men."

Trace looked down to where her hand rested on his arm. She had since taken a nice firm grip. Deb realized she had a tight hold and let go. She stepped back so fast she almost stumbled.

Trace opened his mouth, then cleared his throat awkwardly. "Uh, the house, it's mighty raw, there's no floor . . . but then there isn't one here, either. Utah says that's a winter job. And we need to seal up some holes, yet it's a mighty fine house, especially compared to this one." He gave the sleeping little ones a nervous look. "Can you come out and see it? Will Maddie Sue and Ronnie be all right in here alone for a few minutes? I'd like to show you. I appreciate how you've kept to the house. I worried that the children could come to grief with all the axes swinging and such — and there's gonna be more of it."

"Can we wait until they wake up?" Deb asked.

"No, you go ahead, Deb." Gwen cut the dough in three pieces. "My hands are already in the dough. I need to shape this into loaves, and I don't want to leave the children sleeping. They would probably sleep through our absence, but if they did wake up, I'm afraid they might wander too close to the fire."

Deb smiled at Trace. "I'd really love to see. Maybe we could go take a look, and then I can get back so Gwen could go?"

Trace nodded. "Sounds fine to me. Grab your coat."

Deb was already shrugging it on.

She dressed as warmly as possible all the time. The house was chilly. She and Gwen had made heavy shawls and wore them around the house, and they'd used wool Adam had brought to sew stockings for themselves and the children.

Deb wished she'd asked for yarn to knit mittens and scarves, but she didn't mention it because she was sorely afraid Adam would just jump on his fast horse and run the hours to town. They were all trying to take such good care of the women and children in their midst that Deb found herself more than willing, in fact eager, to take care of meals, mend and wash their clothing, do anything she could to ease the burden on the men.

She remembered her promise to herself to quit working for men and mentally stiffened her backbone. She'd keep helping here and enjoy doing it, but come spring, she and Gwen were heading for San Francisco and a new life.

Deb walked beside Trace toward the house. They were nearly there when she noticed something. "The wind died."

She had her chin tucked into the collar of her coat, but now she relaxed and straightened her neck.

"It didn't die. Utah picked this spot behind what he called a windbreak. It makes sense just hearing it, but I never thought of that when I built the cabin. Utah's teaching me a lot." Trace led her to the door on the west side of the cabin.

She'd expected it to be on the north, where you could step out and see the old cabin. He opened the door, using a wooden latch.

"Look at this. We can latch the door from the inside at night." Trace grinned. "Not that we have a real big problem with intruders."

"Utah says he'll add on an entry room when he's got time. It'll cut the wind if we shut one door before opening another. It'll keep the cabin warmer."

"That's so obviously a good idea, but I'd have never thought of it." She went on into the cabin.

His smile was so friendly, and so happy about this cabin, Deb couldn't help but return it. Then she stepped inside to a hallway.

"There are two bedrooms, one on each side of the hallway. Then on through is the main room."

"It's four times bigger than the old cabin. It's so nice." She walked slowly to the middle of one large room. Fireplace right beyond the hall to the north, another door that must lead outside straight ahead.

"It is, isn't it? Utah did a good job of picking straight logs and knew how to shave the branches off smooth. He's going to do something more to stop the wind, chink every gap, I don't know what all, but even without that it's so much better than the old one, I can't quite believe it. And the fireplace is tight and big enough to be more convenient for cooking. Utah left a couple of logs out up high on the inside walls."

Deb looked at the oddly placed open strips on the walls that separated the big front room from the bedrooms.

"He said those will let warm air into the bedrooms and keep it decently comfortable. Utah's got plans for a table and chairs, too. He says he knows how to make sturdy things but not too fancy. I told him it sounded like he was describing me."

"Me too." Deb turned in a circle, taking

in everything. The front door faced the east. A window with a shutter was on either side of it — no glass of course. There was a window to the south, the fireplace taking up the west wall. The north wall had a countertop and what looked like a cupboard for a kitchen.

"You're pretty fancy, I'd say." Trace had wandered to the fireplace and was feeding logs into it. There was a roughly built woodbox nearby. "He's going to spend time this winter adding more cupboards. We'll move the beds from the cabin in here for tonight, and he'll get on to building one more cot so you'll have four. The little ones can each have their own. You and Gwen can decide how to divide the bedrooms up with the little ones. He's got lots of winter projects planned — a dry sink and a split-log floor. He said things I didn't understand about finishing. Well, he's got lots of good ideas."

Deb quit her quiet circling. "This is so nice of you, Trace. But you and your men should sleep in here. Gwen and I are getting by in the old cabin. And this has so much more room, a much better place for three adult men."

"Utah said if the weather holds, he'll get up the other house. I reckon I won't stop him, but he seems to think the hired men should have a separate house from me. I mean, he's thinking to the future when you're not here anymore." He swallowed as if his throat had gone bone-dry.

Deb, for some reason, found his sudden awkwardness endearing. Almost as if he didn't look forward to that day.

She opened her mouth to thank him again, but she'd already thanked him so often she was afraid he might find it annoying. But didn't it have to be said, anyway?

"Trace, the lengths you've gone to in taking care of us is nothing short of heroic. You are a blessed miracle from God, you and your men. You saved us and now you care for us. It's the Bible's very definition of a Christian."

Smiling, his cheeks a bit pink, he said, "That's not how it seems, Deb. Having you here, well, I don't feel like we've thanked you enough. The food has been like a dream come true. We really rough it out here. Now to have good food, clean clothes, our mending done. It's an honor to provide you with a roof . . . one I was going to build anyway, and a warm fire and the goods so you can cook and sew."

Unsteadily, Deb reached for Trace's arm. "You can't know how hard I worked back east, for the paper and at home, and for

161

nothing like the thanks you're giving me. I can hardly believe a man can speak so kindly."

"I thought you wrote for a paper with your pa?"

"I did."

"And he never said *thank you*?"

Deb laughed with an edge of anger she instantly regretted showing. That shook loose more of the truth than was usual when talking with anyone but Gwen. "I didn't just *write* for the paper. I went out and gathered the news stories. I ran the printing press. I sold advertisements and collected the payments for them. I did all the bookkeeping and paid our bills. I had a paper route, and I'd go around town delivering the papers, sell a few more on the street, and we had a paper out five days a week."

"And your ma?"

"Ma died a few years back, but she's the one who taught me everything. She ran the paper before me."

"But your father was there."

"Pa was an important man in town." She fought to keep her voice calm. "He was friends with the mayor and the sheriff, the banker and the only lawyer in the small town near Philadelphia. He was the friendly face of a very well-respected paper. He took all the credit and never did a lick of the work."

Trace was silent for a long moment. Then he caught Deb's hand and turned her to face him. His touch was so warm and strong, it stopped her from her embarrassing talk of her father.

Thank heavens, something stopped her.

CHAPTER 13

"You were on your own at a very young age," Trace commented. "Just like me."

Deb looked at their entwined hands. Trace waited for her to pull away. He had no business holding her hand.

And then she tightened her grip on him, and the relief of it washed over him like a spring rain.

"What do you mean, 'just like me'?" she asked.

She'd tried to get him to talk on their walk home, and he hadn't said much. Now he found the words rushing out. "My pa died in a wagon train massacre just like the one you were in. I was away from the wagons, hunting. I came back and it was all over. I was alone in the wilderness with an old plow horse and my rifle with not that many bullets and winter coming on."

On a little gasp, Deb said, "Even worse than me. I wasn't alone. Oh, Trace, I'm so sorry. How old were you?"

"Maybe not worse. You had children to protect and no horse, and honestly it was a terrible situation, I know that. But . . . well, there's nothing like being completely alone." Trace shook his head, looking back into the past. "That trail you were on wasn't nearly as well traveled back then. A better trail heads for Sacramento, but the one you were on veers almost straight south and you still had some rugged country to cross. My pa and I were with a split-off group from a bigger wagon train that went its own way."

"That's exactly what we did. We'd only been with the smaller group for a few days."

Trace held on tight, so tight he was afraid he'd hurt her. But she didn't protest, so he didn't let go. "When we took it, well, especially back then, it was a poor trail. When I found everyone dead, I wasn't even sure where to go. I headed on south since that was Pa's plan, but the trail as good as disappeared in spots. I've found out since then I went the wrong way and twisted around in the mountains. I ended up in a thick forest that was endless. On cloudy days, I couldn't even see where the sun rose. I was all right in the woods — Pa had taught me a lot — but I just got so turned around." He shook his head.

"I finally stopped moving just because I had no idea which direction to go next. West, right? It should've been simple. But there were cliffs and streams and trails that just ended or curved so slightly I'd be way off course and not realize it for hours. Before I could figure out where I was headed, the snow started falling. Snow like I'd never seen before. Feet of snow would fall overnight. I had to find shelter."

"How long ago?"

"I've been out here nearly ten years now. I was alone for four or maybe five winters — I lost count — before Adam hired on. By then I was past the worst of it. My old horse didn't survive the first winter, and it was so harsh and food so scarce, I reckon dying was a mercy for him."

Trace didn't say it, but he'd suffered, too. He hadn't known where to find food on a mountaintop. "Old Rex was my only —" Trace realized he was embarrassing himself, so he finished with a shrug — "my only friend."

Deb's free hand touched his arm. The touch was so nice, Trace felt a little addled, and it helped him pass through the strange confession of his animal being his friend. It was true, of course, but saying it out loud sounded foolish.

"I'd been here for a stretch when I found Black and Wolf. Both real young, and we were sort of a . . . family."

He shut up again. Good grief. A family.

He decided to talk about something less foolish. "By spring I couldn't figure out why I should go on west. There was nothing there for me. Pa talked of homesteading. It wasn't legal yet, but he said it was coming, and he'd be right there to grab up some land. But I was so lost I couldn't even find my way back to the trail the wagon trains traveled on. And if I had gotten to a town, I wasn't old enough to file a claim."

He had found the wagon train trail eventually. He'd come upon it because of the smell of burning flesh from a new massacre. Not a single person left alive. And he could've found his way out then, but instead the sight of those murdered people had awakened a rage within him, a hunger for revenge. Instead of seeking out a town and people, he'd stayed. And he'd guarded that trail.

It was his ugliest sin, and he didn't want Deb to know what festered in his heart.

"I found broad meadows and rich grassland and decided to stay. I found a water hole in a box canyon where some wild longhorns came to drink. I put up a fence across the mouth of the canyon, left the gate wide open, waited until the cows walked in for a drink, then swung the gate shut and called them mine. They got used to me and had some calves, and my little herd grew. I'd find a few more cows that wanted in the canyon, probably for the water. The herd grew more until I found a place to sell them. I even had some cash money because Pa split what little we had. I had it in my saddlebags the day everyone died. And there sure as certain wasn't anywhere to spend it. Besides that, I found a few stashes in the wagons, and a few other supplies, including another gun and a mold to make bullets. That's where most of those books came from, too. I survived the first winter through pure stubbornness. Reading the days away. That case full of books, by now I might've read each of them ten times, the Bible twenty times. All by firelight in a dark cave."

"You were all alone out here through the winter?"

"With my stack of books, so not all alone." He'd been so alone it had nearly broken him. He didn't admit it, but the ache of that loneliness had carved itself into Trace's soul. He wondered if he'd have survived the weight of it if not for those precious books. He wondered if he'd been a little bit crazed

168

and that had prompted him to be guardian of that trail and keep himself secret even when he saved a wagon train. He could have gone down. He could have ridden on with the survivors.

"And then more years?"

Trace nodded. "I reckon I'd turned half wild by the time Adam came along. My clothes were rags. I'd trapped some furs and brought down deer for food and the hides, built that ramshackle cabin and the barn and made some furniture. With no horse at first, and then I got Black when he was a youngster. I took to running the hills to check snares I'd set, and while I did I learned the land."

"Running the hills?" She made it sound like maybe he was an animal. And maybe he was. Living in a cave, dressed in fur. The books separated him from being pure beast, he hoped.

"Yep. Found some likely places. No one else knew about them, and after I'd staked my homestead, I ended up owning a lot of high valleys."

"That's how you could run almost all day, leading us on your horse?"

"I still do a lot of running. I like the land and — strange, I reckon, but I like the feel of my feet pounding on it. That first winter, in a cave, well, I'd lived in the wilderness all my life, in Tennessee, then Missouri, now here. So I knew how to start a fire." That fire had in some ways been his friend, too. He worked hard to keep it alive. He'd talked to it. He didn't admit any of that; he'd said enough about his strange loneliness and what he claimed for friends and family.

"Before the worst of the snow slammed down, I found some roots and dried berries, pine nuts. I had to fight a bear that tried to use my cave for a winter den — it was probably *his* cave. It was a fight I won just by, honestly, the miraculous hand of God. I skinned him out and had a bearskin blanket, and the bear meat kept me going when the snow was so deep I had to dig a tunnel to get out of the cave. And when I did dig out, I found nothing I wanted to see. The whole world was eyeball-deep in snow. The cave was big enough for me and not much else. I stored the bear meat in the snowdrift clogging the cave entrance and concentrated on not freezing to death. I lived like that until spring."

Deb made a little sound of distress.

Trace quit fussing about his lonely years to reassure her he'd been fine, though at the time he was about the furthest thing from *fine* a man could be. He considered telling her about his guardian duties and how he planned to ride out and hunt the men who'd hit her wagon train. But then he hesitated when his gaze caught on hers. Foolish though it was, he believed that if he looked deep enough, long enough, he'd see something that would answer a lot of questions he'd never thought to ask. Questions that, when answered, would explain his whole life.

"After all that, here you are. With land and a home and a ranch. Good friends. And with the heart of a true hero."

She was going to thank him again. She'd done it so many times it was making him squirm. He'd helped her, sure. But any decent man would've done the same. Any one of his hired men. In fact, the ones who would not have helped her were few and far between and the lowest type of scum. Which perfectly described the men who'd attacked her wagon train.

He was tired of being thanked. He couldn't stand it anymore. He wanted almost desperately to stop words he didn't deserve. And that was the only reason he could imagine when he leaned down, then stopped, realizing he was about to kiss her.

He barely even knew what a kiss was. There'd been mention of it in the books he read, but he'd almost never spoken to a woman or been around one. Still, the whole notion of it came real natural to him.

She pulled back, then stared at him while he braced himself to get slapped. Then she brought both hands up to his face and laid them gently on his cheeks, possibly the nicest, sweetest moment of his life.

The moment stretched and grew and filled his head with all sorts of notions, then as suddenly as it had started, it ended. Deb stumbled back from him so fast he rushed forward and kept her from falling, then let go before she could run straight out the door.

"What were you doing?" She pressed both hands to her mouth, which only drew his attention to what they'd almost done . . . well, as if he could forget, so it didn't matter.

"I — I don't know. I just . . . I was . . . I don't . . . know." Dismay swamped him. He'd just ruined his chance to be friends with the nicest woman he'd ever known.

Pretty much the only woman he'd ever known, but that was beside the point.

"I have to leave, Trace. I . . . well, I don't want to give you the idea I'm going to stay."

He hadn't asked her to stay, but when a man went holding a woman and almost kissing her that might be asking her to do *something,* and he was pretty sure staying was part of that something.

Nodding, because words were beyond him, he stood there silent.

"All my life I was . . . was . . ." Deb shrugged and seemed to rush through the next words. "I was little better than a servant to my pa. After Ma died, I did everything to take care of his business while Gwen ran our home." She pursed her lips as if she wanted them to stop moving. Then she forced herself to go on, or it looked that way from where Trace was standing. "And now here I am, right back to serving someone else."

Did that mean she didn't want to help? He'd said it before, but he rushed to say it again. "We really appreciate all you do, Deb."

"You've said so and thanked me."

"And I appreciate all the times you've said thank you," Trace went on. "But I probably haven't said so because thanking you for thanking me seems stupid."

Her smile cut through some of the thick tension between them. "My goal, and Gwen's, is to reach California. After years and years of working for someone else, letting someone else take all the credit — and mostly all the money — for our hard work, we plan to work for ourselves. We aren't going to tend men anymore like we did for our father. And here we are caring for you and your men. And we are willing, even eager, to do it because that's fair. You're working as hard, no . . . even harder than we are. Of course we want to help and will work just as hard as we need to. While we're here, we are happy to do our part. But we aren't going to do it forever. In the end we'll find Maddie Sue's father, leave the children in his care, and head on west. And . . . and well, I can't be kissing a man. That's a good way to get tangled up in . . . in forever."

Which must mean, Trace decided, that when a man kissed a woman, it was the next thing to a marriage proposal. And he sure didn't think that was what he'd meant when he leaned toward her.

Of course, he hadn't been thinking at all. Or yep, he'd been thinking, but his head was all over in a wrong and confusing and fascinating place and stuck there solid as ice . . . only not cold at all.

"This is probably why it's a good thing I've never been around women. I don't know what I'm doing." He threw his arms wide. "I don't know how to act right, how to treat a woman right. Prob'ly won't never figure it out, neither. I remember my pa saying females could be notional, but I never really understood what that meant."

Deb shrugged. "I don't know what it means, either. But men and women not understanding each other is a mighty common thing, I'd say."

"It's a wonder they don't do a better job of avoiding each other." Trace would do his best to avoid Deb from now on, or at least avoid being alone with her. Because being so close to her, having her touch him the way she'd done, was one of the sweetest things he'd ever been part of, and if he had his say, he'd probably want to fetch himself that kiss he'd just been denied.

And despite her words, he had a sneaking feeling she might just cooperate. In fact, it was all he could do not to test out that idea right here and now.

"Time to go back," he said too loud and fast. "We can see if Gwen is ready for a tour of the house." Trace turned to the door, and Deb grabbed his wrist and sunk her nails in.

"Ouch, let go." Trace pulled against her grip, but she hung on and glared at him.

"What's the matter?" Trace rubbed at the little grooves where her fingernails were decorating his wrist.

175

"I just, well, you won't . . . won't take . . . that is . . . Gwen is young. She's mighty young."

Trace wondered if Deb had taken leave of her senses. "She's not all that young."

Deb's hand shot out again, but Trace dodged her this time. She might draw blood if he wasn't careful.

"She's only eighteen."

"Well, that seems grown up to me. I was on my own in the wilderness at fifteen. Talk about 'a voice crying in the wilderness.' "

Deb's expression changed then. He wasn't sure what it had been before, something mighty strange. She'd seemed upset, angry, maybe her feelings hurt. That all made no sense. Now her eyes went wide and she reached for his wrist again. He didn't jump back, just because her expression had become so kind. She caught his arm much more gently.

"Did you cry out, Trace?" Her eyes got wider, and her bottom lip trembled. "Or did you just cry?"

"Men don't cry!" Trace was horrified. How had she known? "It means like hollering. The voice of one *hollering* in the wilderness. I'd rewrite that part of the Bible if I could. I think of that because once in a while I'd do some yelling, wishing someone would hear me."

Nodding, Deb said quietly, "I can't imagine how lonely you must've been."

Her eyes fell shut as if the weight of the lids was beyond her. "I know I was always around people, Trace. I'm sure I can't compare it, but running the newspaper, with no respect or thanks from my father, a woman doing a man's job while the man got all the credit for it, I had days I felt so lonely I could've cried in the wilderness, too. Only I'd cry real tears."

Trace stood listening to her, the pain of that loneliness etching lines in her forehead. "I can see you're a real smart woman, Deb, educated and a writer. So I may not understand words to mean just what you're saying, but I don't exactly think those are the same. My loneliness out here and yours in a city full of people. Maybe both things feel bad, though they seem mighty different to me."

Nodding silently for a time, finally Deb opened her eyes and lifted her chin. "Of course it's different. Let's go on in now. And my very much younger little sister, Gwen, a girl still, not a woman yet, can come out here and see the house with you. So long as you remember how young she is."

"You mentioned she's eighteen. How old

are you? Nineteen?" Trace decided maybe she *had* taken leave of her senses, so it'd be best to get her back to the house before she said something else crazy.

"I'm twenty." She said it with her spine straight and a glint in her eyes.

"When is Gwen nineteen?"

"Not for . . . for a few weeks yet."

Trace rolled his eyes, and they walked back. He was careful not to get too close — he didn't want to set her off again.

Or maybe he was just afraid that if he touched her right now, he just might haul her into his arms and kiss her.

CHAPTER 14

"I'll miss the noon meal today." Trace headed for the cabin door after breakfast. "I should be back in time for supper. But don't worry if I don't make it. I might be out overnight."

Utah said, "The weather's holding, Trace. I'll push hard and get the second cabin done, then ride to catch up with you. It's safer with a saddle partner."

Trace nodded but didn't speak.

Miss the meal . . . why? Out overnight . . . where? Safer from . . . whom? Deb struggled to follow the conversation.

Utah and Adam headed for the door right after him. They either knew where he was going or they just didn't care.

"Wait!" Surprise made Deb's voice louder than she'd planned.

All three men wheeled around as if she'd cried out for help.

"Why won't you be here?" Honest to

goodness, she shouldn't have to ask that question. And yet it appeared she did have to. "Where will you be? When *should* we start worrying?"

Trace tilted his head a little as if the world was lopsided — or rather as if her questions made no sense. "You shouldn't *ever* start worrying. The Bible says clear as can be that we're not supposed to worry. In Matthew, Jesus says, 'Don't be anxious about tomorrow, for —' "

"Trace." She cut him off with a near shout. "You're missing the point." She decided to use straight, simple questions that required brief answers. She'd interviewed a few reluctant witnesses in her day.

"Where are you going that will take you away all day?" There, how could he dodge that?

The men sidled past Trace and closed the door. Better than leaving it gaped open in this weather.

"I'm going to hunt the outlaws who attacked you." He didn't sound as if he was reluctant but rather that she was wasting his time.

"No!" Her heart lurched, and she rushed to him and clutched his wrist. "They're dangerous. If they get their hands on you, they will kill you with no remorse. You saw what they did to the folks in that wagon train."

Trace leaned down a bit, and his eyes held an intensity that kept her silent. She thought of him as young, but right now he had all the authority of a much older man.

"There is nothing to discuss. I have no choice but to go after those men."

"But how can you do so by yourself? You can't hope to handle so many."

"How many do you think?"

With a weak shrug, Deb said, "It seemed like a lot."

"The tracks I followed said three. Three men. All cowards who attacked innocent people while they were sleeping. My trouble won't be fighting them off; my trouble will be catching that pack of yellowbelly vermin. I don't want to shoot someone in the back, and you can bet they'll run before they face an armed man who's wide awake."

"But this isn't your fight."

Trace narrowed his eyes, furrows appearing on his brow. "Deb, justice is every man's fight. To right a terrible wrong and make evil men pay for their crimes is part of why I'm going, but there's more. It's not just about punishing the men who attacked your wagon train. These men are dangerous. They'll hurt more folks if they aren't stopped."

"You're right. Of course they need to be stopped, and I admire that you are willing to take that job on your shoulders. But, Trace, even if they are cowards, if you corner them, they'll fight back. Can you just track them down, then go fetch the sheriff?"

Trace held silent for a moment. "It may sound boastful, but I'm as good as anyone at following a trail or slipping up quiet on a man. So I'm not taking that big a risk. And I take no great pride in saying I'm lightning fast with my six-gun and a dead aim with a rifle. It comes very naturally to pull the trigger and hit what I'm aimin' at. I've learned to be cautious and think twice when it comes to shootin' because it's a little too easy for me. My horse is strong, mountain born and bred. And if I have to leave the horse, you saw that I can run for miles, lope along with Wolf, and be just as quiet. I'll take these men to the sheriff if I can, but I won't sit safe at home while they plot another attack. It's late in the year for another train to go through, but there are always a reckless few who try and make it, and usually they manage it. And if they try, these men might attack. Someone needs to be their guardian on that trail. I'm taking that job."

Deb held his wrist the whole time he talked. She looked into his deep blue eyes, until it seemed as if they were the only two people in the world. Finally, she said, "Please be careful, Trace. I would miss you terribly if harm came to you. I hate that you're going alone." Then she straightened her spine, and her face lit up. "I saw that man. I can recognize him. I should go with you."

"What? After what you just said about the danger? You can't go."

Her hand closed on his wrist once more with a firm grip. "But don't you see it will make you safer. You'll be busy protecting me, and because of that, you'll take far fewer risks."

Trace looked down at her, his head shaking. "I won't let you take such a chance."

"Then I won't let *you* take such a chance."

"You can't stop me, Deb. But I can stop you. You have no horse, and no man here will share his with you for such a harebrained idea."

Deb frowned. "You could be standing right next to the killers. They could be sitting at the table in some diner while you ask questions. They'll know you're after them, but you won't realize you've warned them. They could lie in wait. They could bushwhack you."

"I'm not that easy to bushwhack. I'm good in the woods, and you're right, I don't know what these men look like. It's a good reminder, so I'll be mighty cautious. I promise you, I'll be careful. And I don't plan to stay on the hunt for days. I'm going to ride to the nearest towns to the north, on the west side of Lake Tahoe, on the trail those men took. Then I'll see if any wagon trains are coming through. If so, I'll warn them and offer an escort. Please, trust me to be careful."

"I do trust you, Trace. But you should consider letting me come. I'm the only person alive who got a look at those killers, the only one who heard their voices. I could help you. I want them caught just as badly as you do." She let go and straightened away from him. She hadn't realized just how close she'd gotten.

"I'll check with cattle buyers and see if anyone's tried to sell stock with altered brands. Mostly I'll ride to the small settlements along the north fork of the trail we were on. That's the trail you came down before the massacre. If I have to, I'll ride all the way to Virginia City and Carson City. I won't get that far today, though, and I hope I don't need to go that far. I plan to ride hard and check as many places as I can, then come home for the night. I prefer it to sleeping on the trail, and I'm hopeful I can find evidence of these men fast. And checking for new wagon trains will be easy."

"Well, then, there'll be food . . ." Her voice faltered, and she lifted her chin. "There'll be food waiting for you when you get back. Make sure and knock on the door — no matter how late — and we'll see you're fed."

She missed touching him. She was leaving for California and knew that when she traveled on, she'd miss him for the rest of her life.

"I'll come for the food."

Deb nodded silently. The silence had an intensity that stirred him.

"Goodbye, Deb." He turned and left — almost fled. And she was glad because she was suddenly afraid that if he didn't leave now, she might never want him to . . . ever.

Steaming mad, Raddo stormed out of the Stoney Point Diner, slapping the bag of coins and itching to grab his gun and take every cent that cattle buyer had on him.

"What'sa matter, Raddo?" Meeks asked.

"The buyer just cheated me on the cattle. I couldn't get him to pay a fair price." Truth was, Raddo didn't know what the going price was for the animals he'd driven in. Oxen, draft horses, some cattle. Ten animals in all. But it had to be more than ten dollars a head. Split three ways, this lousy hundred dollars wasn't even enough for a man to have a good time in the saloon, let alone pay his old gambling debts.

"Lousy, rotten, dirt-poor movers. Shouldn't have come west if they didn't have a better stake." Raddo scowled at the money and hated to share it.

Meeks and Dalt closed in around him, and Raddo handed each an equal share. These two were loyal as long as the cash flowed. Raddo had to respect that, as he felt the same.

"The buyer didn't ask no questions, did he, Raddo?" Meeks asked.

"Nope, just took a look and made his best offer." Though Raddo had wondered if that city slicker suspected the herd might've been stolen. Raddo had picked him because he had a reputation for not asking blamed-fool questions. But then he didn't offer top dollar, either.

Meeks looked at the pathetic stack of coins and shook his head. "We need more money, and the wagon trains are done for the winter."

Dalt made a sound that drew Raddo's attention. A man was wise to listen carefully when Dalt talked.

Once they were both listening, Dalt said, "I heard there are a couple more. They're traveling late, but they're pushing on, trying to make California before the snows close the trail. And the ones coming on are bigger than five wagons."

"We followed the longer train and decided we couldn't take 'em," Meeks said sullenly. "We were lucky that smaller group split off."

"We couldn't handle a train with fifty wagons." Dalt gave him a murderous look. "But these aren't that big . . . a whole lot bigger'n five, though. No one even got his gun into play on that small train. We can handle a larger group. We have to unless we aim to starve this winter."

He threw his coins up in the air and caught them with a wicked swipe of his hand. "If we want more, we're going to have to take more." Dalt turned his black eyes on Raddo. "We can slip in and slit a few throats, kill as many in their sleep as we can before we open fire. Think we can handle a big wagon train that way, boss?"

He said the word *boss* with a tone of mockery, and Raddo wasn't about to push back. That was a good way of getting shot. Raddo had never killed a man with a knife, and it wasn't something he looked forward to. A sleeping man at that. He wondered how he'd gotten so low and felt a pang of shame, then quickly stifled it.

"Dalt's right. We couldn't take a train of fifty, but we can sure as certain handle a bigger train than five. I can't live on this scrap of money. We'll take on a bigger train this time. Each of us can quietly handle a few wagons apiece. Even the odds. We'll thin the herd of fighting men until someone sets up an alarm. Then we open fire, shooting with both hands."

CHAPTER 15

The tracks were gone. Trace knew they would be, but he'd hoped to find something, some proof that a small herd had passed through.

Even though there hadn't been a wagon train since the one with Deb on it, there had been much travel on this same route throughout the summer. So there were plenty of signs to read. Like a broken wagon wheel, or a discarded pot with a hole rusted through tossed to the side of the trail — these could easily be from some other train. In fact, they almost certainly were.

He watched the trail carefully but kept riding, stopping at small settlements, asking questions. Learning nothing. The one encouraging thing he heard was that no more wagon trains had passed by. He thought he'd've been able to see those tracks, unless there'd been more rain. But he was glad to have it confirmed.

No one had word that more were coming. But wagon trains didn't always pass word forward along the trail. They rolled through when they rolled through, and you knew they were coming when they came.

Everyone Trace talked to agreed there ought to be at least another one or two before the trail closed for the season. There often were a hardy — some might say foolish — few who risked a late crossing. And if they stayed on the main trail they could make it, for it was a heavily traveled road these days thanks to the California gold strikes and the Comstock Lode. They still snowed shut, but until they did, they were wide and well-traveled trails and didn't snow shut as early, what with the trees cleared back from the trail and with men willing to dig through any drifts.

So more wagon trains were expected, and it had to be soon or not at all.

Trace wanted to stay on the trail, riding around the lake where a train might even now be heading toward him on its way to the Sierra Nevada crossing, with Sacramento or San Francisco as their final destination.

The small group Deb traveled with had split off from the larger wagon train, heading south, the Scotts' wagon aiming for the land Maddie Sue's pa had claimed.

Trace found no one who'd seen a small herd of mixed animals, including a pair of Holstein oxen. A big black-and-white team like that ought to be mighty noticeable. And the big Belgian draft horse — gray with a black mane and tail — was an unusual animal. Neither the Holsteins nor the Belgian horse had been killed during the massacre. They were out here somewhere. And if anyone saw those animals, they'd remember.

Trace had studied the tracks enough he knew just which ones belonged to the Belgian and which ones the Holsteins. The other animals were less distinctive, but he'd recognize them too probably.

Yet no one admitted to seeing them. A few folks Trace questioned had a sharp look about them, enough to make Trace wonder if they'd spoken the truth. A man in the West who bought stolen stock would be quiet about it. And to a knowing western man, this group of critters would have the look of a stolen herd — right down to the altered brands, which many a man would note instantly.

He couldn't help but be wary about his questions, thinking of what Deb had said about his sitting right next to a killer and

191

letting the man know he was being pursued. It was madness, but he wished now she was with him. He'd have the courage to ask questions a bit more insistently if he could be sure none of the men nearby were the killers he hunted.

Trace stopped in five settlements along the way without gathering even a snippet of information. Of course, three of these so-called settlements were little more than a general store. One was a single house standing alongside the trail, offering weary travelers a place to sit a spell, eat a meal cooked by someone else, even sleep on a straw-tick mattress.

Calling these places "settlements" was a long stretch of the word, but Trace stopped in all of them regardless.

He put in a full day, pushing hard but, he hoped, not so hard he missed any useful information. Finally he rode for the ranch. A long day wasted. He itched to ride on, even reined in his horse and hesitated, not sure if he was making the right decision to go all the way back home. He'd be two or three days on the trail if he rode the rest of the way to the north shore of Tahoe, rounded it, rode through Carson City, and then back home. He needed to visit all those places, and soon. At last, though, he decided to ride for his High Sierra Ranch.

Was he doing the right thing? Should he stand as guardian over the trail west, because he meant to see that no more harm came to wagon trains. But it was too early to stand watch over the trail since no more wagon trains were passing through.

No, he'd best get home, which was to the far south shore of Tahoe, and then ride up the east side of the lake tomorrow. This time he'd ride as far as he needed to, even if it meant he had to be gone overnight.

And he hated that. His home, with the fine meals, the fresh laundry, and now a new cabin for the women and children, with another one in the process of being built for the men, had never been a more welcoming place.

As he rode toward home, he let Black stretch out in a ground-eating gallop and pondered the wisdom of having an eyewitness at hand the next time he went hunting. If it were anyone but a fragile woman, he knew he wouldn't hesitate. But it went against all he considered right. At the same time his common sense said it made no sense to leave her behind.

He had to decide before he got back.

"He's back," Gwen whispered from where

she was peeking out the little hole in the front shutters — the little slit worked as a peephole and a gun sight — without swinging the shutters wide and letting in the cold. The shutters were tight; the whole cabin was well built, warm, and had a safe, almost fortress-like quality to it.

Deb's heart sped up, and her breath caught a bit. He was much earlier than she'd expected. She steadied herself and whispered back, "Get away from that window and help me get a meal on. We finally have enough space we can all sit in a chair."

"Enough space and enough chairs." Gwen hooked the peephole closed and came back, grinning. "I can't believe the men built a cabin for us and enough furniture for us all to sit on, and a table to sit at."

They could have a meal together and it'd be all three men, because Utah and Adam had worked through supper on the bunkhouse.

Shaking her head, Deb forced her thoughts away from the window. "It makes me think of Pa and how he was always so busy, too busy to take care of us or Ma or our house. He couldn't even find time to repair a wobbly step or a broken railing. And yet these men built a whole cabin in a few days."

As she talked, Deb sliced a tender venison roast. Adam had brought in a deer and butchered it right after the noon meal. He left most of it hanging to freeze but brought in a good-sized roast, almost apologetically, wondering if they'd like to cook it for supper. Like maybe he was ruining some plan already made.

"I've spent too much time believing all men are like Pa, just because he was the only one I was really around in a personal way. The only one who was supposed to take care of his family that I knew. But men can work hard and be depended on to keep their word and think to the comfort of others."

Gwen stirred the roast drippings into a thick gravy, while Deb set the platter of sliced roast to the back of the fire to keep warm and lifted the pot of boiling potatoes off its hook to mash. The whole cabin was warm and secure.

She felt safe, Deb realized. Yes, even with those evil men running loose. And then she realized the feeling had sprung up when Trace had returned. Until now, Trace hadn't been safe. Here she'd stood with plentiful food in warmth and safety, but with a heart aching to think of him on that cold trail. And now he was home and, at least for tonight, she felt safe.

Gwen set a smaller pan near Deb. "Pour the potato water into this. I need it to thin the gravy."

Adam had come in today excited because he'd found an old apple tree with slightly withered apples. It was far past the proper harvest time, but still, he'd brought in a bushel of them. They were indeed sad old apples, not in good enough shape to store. But carefully peeled, they cooked up into two bubbling apple pies baking at the back of the new, bigger fireplace. They'd have to cook the apples up fast before they spoiled. Utah gave them some advice about using honey rather than sugar — Trace had a good supply of it. Deb realized they didn't need to constantly use Trace's flour and sugar for a delicious apple dessert, although they'd made crusts today.

The whole place smelled of savory and sweet food and newly sawn wood. And Deb was almost embarrassed to realize just how much she wanted to impress Trace.

They kept busy, with Deb listening for the sound of the men coming in to eat — and one particular set of feet.

When at last she heard boots, she waited, silly of her, until they came in and shed their coats. Then once they were watching, she fetched the apple pies out of the fireplace.

She carried them to the table and managed a quick inspection of Trace. He was just fine. The men gave her a very gratifying gasp of excitement. Compliments flowed.

Deb couldn't help but smile as she set the pies down. This was much more fun than writing for a newspaper.

"And today," she said and swept a hand at the chairs, "we have enough places at the table so you can each have a seat. All of us can eat together."

The children were long asleep, but there was a chair for Maddie Sue if she'd use it. Ronnie was still going to be on someone's lap for a while.

Utah was the first to slide into a chair. "I made the table and chairs just for this purpose, Miss Deb."

"We appreciate this house and the furniture so much. We pray for God's blessing on you many times a day. And the food you're so kind about is here because you all provide it so we can cook a good meal." Deb and Gwen hurried to set the food on the table. The men were always starving by the time they came in to eat, and tonight, being late, they were more so than usual. Deb and Gwen were good and hungry, too.

"You used my apples," Adam said. "Sure glad I found that tree. Trace, next year we need to go back earlier and pick the whole thing clean."

"I didn't even know there was an apple tree near here. After all these years I haven't explored all this land yet."

"And you cooked this venison tender as I've ever tasted." Adam took a big bite and chewed for a while before he went on. "I might've shot it, but you ladies turned it into something special. You are fine cooks."

The meal was a cheerful one. Trace told about his futile search but with firm determination that he would search until he found the men he sought. Deb thought he gave her a considering look that made her wonder what he was thinking.

Utah and Adam talked about building and discussed what else they needed to add to the bunkhouse.

"I'm mighty glad you're putting up that bunkhouse," Trace said. "But if Deb, Gwen, and the youngsters leave, I'm not going to want to live in this house by myself. I've had enough of being alone."

Utah laughed. Adam, who sat next to Trace, slapped him on the back.

"If?" Deb repeated.

All the men fell silent and chewed as if that was the reason for the silence, even though two of them stuffed food into their mouths after Deb had spoken.

"I mean . . . when," Trace said quietly. "I reckon it's just been so nice to have you here, I can't help but wish you'd . . . you'd stay."

The other men nodded, still chewing.

Deb didn't know how to respond. Of course they were leaving. Even though these men had just built her a house, the nicest thing a man had ever done for her. She hadn't known men like these existed, and here were three of them.

She finished her meal quickly and dished up the pie, still mulling over the right thing to say, especially since being wanted, and yes, needed, was a fine feeling.

When the meal was done, Deb asked Trace, "I know you've had a long hard day, but would you mind going for a short walk?"

The other men rose from the table. Wolf was sleeping in front of the door, and he jumped up and stood aside. Deb thought Wolf was guarding them, but Trace said the dog liked the cold and had picked that spot because a winter breeze tended to slip under the door.

Utah said, "I'm gonna get a few more licks in on the new cabin. It's late, and the sun is gone, but we are moving faster. I reckon it's due to practice. I think we can get the walls up past the window level if we work awhile tonight. Who knows, but at this rate, if the weather holds we might get a new barn up, as well."

He led Adam outside so fast it looked like they were running away.

Trace sat there looking trapped. "Uh . . . a walk would be a good idea. You and me. Us." He cleared his throat, and his eyes shifted to Gwen. "But maybe we should stay and help clean the supper dishes?"

Gwen smiled. "The youngsters are asleep. I can tidy up in peace. You two go on."

Trace rose from the table, fetched his hat and coat. He waited while Deb found her bonnet and her own coat, and they walked outside together, Wolf on their heels.

The air was cold but not bitterly so.

Trace said, "Let's take the trail behind the barn. If it gets too cold, we've got the fire lit in the old cabin — we can go in there to have our talk."

"Let's walk at least for a while." Deb reached down and patted Wolf on the head. "Is this really a wolf or a dog?"

CHAPTER 16

Well, Trace would surely prefer talking about his dog to whatever else Deb had on her mind.

"His mama was a dog. No doubt about it. I —" he broke off. Why in tarnation had he thought this was a good idea? "I k-killed her."

Deb's head whipped around. "I suppose she was dangerous."

He could tell she didn't mean it. She'd just decided he was a low-down, mother-killing sidewinder. It was nice of her to pretend she wasn't horrified.

"It was late in the spring, winter still hard upon me, and I found a pack of six wolves pulling down a wild mustang mare. She was standing in front of a spring colt that was maybe a couple months old, not a newborn thing. The mare was fighting for her baby's life, but she was losing. She looked like an old one, tough but at the end of her years.

At least I like to hope so."

They walked past the barn. The trail here led all the way to Dismal, but they sure enough weren't going that far.

"I jumped into the fight with a pistol and a rifle." Trace was silent a moment, remembering the terrible sight.

Deb nodded. "And you saved the mare?"

"Nope. Each of my guns was a one-shot. I managed to finish four of the wolves, because twice I was able to put a bullet through one and it passed through and killed the wolf behind it. I had my knife in hand, ready to wade in and fight the last two, but they ran off yelping. The mare was bleeding bad from her throat. She was barely on her feet. She turned, saw me, and tried to charge, still fighting for her baby. But she was used up, and I got far enough away she didn't have the strength to catch me. She circled back to her baby, and just as she reached him, she stumbled to her knees and then rolled to her side. She just lay there, breathing hard. I reloaded my guns, thinking of the wolves and wondering if I oughta put the horse out of its misery. I hated the idea of shooting the old girl. Before I'd worked up the nerve to do what I knew was the right thing, she died. Her poor baby just lay down beside her, shivering, as if it had no plans to go anywhere."

Deb's hand reached for Trace's arm. "That's so sad."

Fine snow drifted down on their heads. The wind was quiet tonight, and Trace heard an owl hoot in the woods that grew out of the mountain that rose up on the west side of the trail to Dismal.

"I saw that colt planning to stay put, probably until more wolves came, maybe until it just starved to death. I pulled a lasso off my waist and roped him. I didn't try to move him or lead him anywhere. I just secured him to a tree. Then a glint of light from one of the wolves drew my eye. I realized as I looked at her that she was no wolf. Some wolves can be black, but she had a white stripe down the middle of her face and the glint of light was an old collar. She was someone's dog, gone back to being a wild critter. I was curious so I went to look closer at the collar, and when I did, I realized she was a nursing mother. She had pups somewhere. Pups I'd just consigned to a slow death from starvation."

Her hand tightened on his arm. She was trying to comfort him. He was supposed to be a tough man, but he'd been touched so little for so long that he couldn't help but enjoy it. Then he thought of how she'd react if he told her of the three years he'd been The Guardian of that trail, how he'd killed and done it so well that after a couple of years the outlaws — those who were still alive — went on their way out of fear. But the killing had stained his soul to the point that when he looked down on people in that first wagon train he'd guarded — the only people he'd seen for a year, people whose lives he'd just saved — he hadn't gone down to talk to them. He'd done his work from the hilltop, then kept away from the wagon train and the decent folks riding in it. And because he'd kept to himself, he'd become a mystery, a ghost, a legend. He'd become The Guardian, when all he really was, was a half-rabid fool driven by vengeance and hate.

"The strangeness of me saving a baby who'd just lost its mother, by killing another mother and leaving another baby to die, was a weight on me that I didn't want to bear. So I started back tracking the wolves. I led the foal along. That little colt didn't like leaving its mama, but he was too little to resist and before long he'd started following willingly. He was old enough to graze on winter grass and drink from a stream. I was afraid the colt was too young to survive without its mother's milk.

"I'd already caught my first few cows and managed to gentle three of them to be milkers, so there was cow's milk once I got Black home. I was relieved when he ate and seemed to befriend me. I was three days hunting when finally I found the den. In it was one surly little pup that looked half-starved, his legs weak and wobbly. He still wanted to chew me up when he saw me. But he was still just a baby, so I handled him." Trace nodded toward Wolf. "I wrapped him up in the blanket from my bedroll to keep him from biting me, and we set out for home."

Deb smiled. "So Wolf is that pup, and the horse you ride is the colt?"

"Yep. And Wolf and I and Black lived alone out here for another two years." Trace thought of it and how much more bearable the loneliness had been with his two new companions with him. God had truly been looking out for him, because he wasn't sure he'd've been able to hold on to his senses if he'd been completely alone all that time. "It was two years before the colt was tall enough to ride. Heaven knows he ain't well trained because I knew nothing of properly training a horse. But these two and me got to be mighty good friends."

He led her along, her hand settled into

the crook of his elbow, the moon peeking between fast-moving clouds. A gap in the mountain ahead was his destination. He turned off the trail and led her to a gate built of lodgepole pine that closed the gap in the canyon.

"My herd is in there." He pointed through the heavy gate. "Mostly all longhorns I caught wild in these mountains, though there are a few other breeds too — five years' worth of young stuff mostly all born on my property. I had near two hundred cows and sold off one hundred of them on the drive. I think I'm finally established enough I can live on the cows I raise, hold a cattle drive every year, and make enough money to support myself and maybe buy a few nicer cattle. Herefords, I reckon. They're gentler and gain weight faster."

Her breath caught. "I can see them. They're mostly white against the brown grass. With the snow drifted around, I couldn't tell the cows from the snow at first."

"Once the snow covers the ground they almost vanish, even though they're speckled. But the snow doesn't get too deep because it's really protected, so the grass stays uncovered for a long time, and these are mountain-bred cattle that know how to dig for food. I came upon this canyon while I was scouting the first summer, and there was a small herd of longhorns grazing in there."

Trace smiled. "It's got one other way out. I tossed up a gate right quick, here and on the other end, and slick as that I had started in the ranching business."

He leaned his arms across the top railing and enjoyed the clouds skimming by overhead, hiding and revealing the moon. Then he asked the question he really didn't want to know the answer to. "What made you ask me to come out here?"

Deb rested her arms on the gate and, because she was shorter, it was the perfect height for her to rest her chin. "What made you say 'if'?"

"If? What?" He couldn't remember.

"You said, 'If Deb, Gwen, and the youngsters leave, I'm not going to want to live in this house by myself.' Are you thinking we might stay?" She turned to face him. "Is it something that's . . . well, you didn't say it as if you were dreading it."

Oh, yep, he remembered that. Trace looked down at her. "I reckon it was my own hope talking when I said *if.* We had a moment together when I was giving you the tour of the new house. A moment when I came close to . . . to kissing you."

Deb's eyes dropped, and even in the dark he saw a blush on her cheeks. She remembered that just fine.

"Yes, you did," she said.

"And since then I've had it in my head more than once." He reached out for her hands. She took them and held on tight. "That we might . . . might spend this winter seeing if we suit each other. What I said to my men about living alone, I've been mighty lonely for a long old time. Adam's who I hired first, and I'd been here alone for years. I hired Utah just a couple of months ago for the cattle drive. My hired men have made my life better. And then you came along. Are you helping because of the simple knowledge that we need help, or is there more? *Could* there be more?"

Deb's heart pounded until she felt it in her ears. She certainly hoped he couldn't hear it!

She swallowed. Then, because her throat was still bone-dry, she swallowed again. He looked at their clasped hands, very bold. She'd never held a man's hand before, not really, and certainly never kissed one. Truth be told, it wasn't that she was so upright and moral — something she might have believed once. Now she knew she'd never *wanted* to do such a thing. No man had ever compelled her this way.

"I've given very little time to thinking about marriage. For the last few years, since my mother died, I've been running the newspaper, and that's long hours that never let up. As soon as one newspaper gets printed and spread around, I'm right back to work on the next edition."

His fingers tightened on hers. "A hard job for a woman."

That irked her a little. "It's a hard job for anyone."

"It sure as certain is." He pulled her close and wrapped his arms around her. "I haven't been around women much, so if I say something that hurts you, I swear it's out of clumsiness. I might be saying rude things to everyone I meet, my hired men, the folks in the general store in Dismal. I had a . . . a rough spell when I was left out here, and whatever civilized manners I had, and living mostly alone with Pa, I'm sure they were mighty scarce . . . well, I lost them."

"It's not you, Trace. Not exactly, anyway. I'm just so tired of working so hard for my pa and for the men of businesses who bought ads from my paper, and getting no respect from them. I'm a little sensitive on the subject."

"Sensitive?"

"Okay, I want to crack someone over the head."

Trace laughed. "That's a little more than sensitive."

She scowled at him, but there was a twinkle in his eye and it lifted her spirits. "I'll try to be less sensitive — also less furious — at least to you."

"I hope you can, because I have nothing but respect for the strong and steady hand it took to run that newspaper every day. And I'm so blessed by all the help you've given me, all while caring for two children. I can see how you try to lift burdens off Gwen's shoulders."

"She does the same for me."

"You are wonderful, loyal sisters. You're never alone so long as you have her."

It was almost impossible to resist Trace's kindness; she'd had so little of it from a man. But how did she dare go from service to her father to another man who, she sadly feared, was interested in her mainly because she could cook and he was lonely?

"Trace, thank you so much for saying such kind things to me. I am sure we will spend the winter getting to know each other better, but I want you to think about a question I have. Are you really interested in me? Or are you interested in *any* woman's company?"

Frowning, Trace said, "I'm not planning to wait until you say no and then toss the idea at Gwen, if that's what you mean. I never gave a moment's thought to a woman before I met you." A light blush appeared on Trace's cheeks. "Well, I mean, sure I've given women a few thoughts, but never a specific woman — not until you. Gwen is a wonderful woman, but something in you . . ." His blush deepened and he shrugged.

For a time Deb didn't think he'd go on. "Something in you draws me. I suppose that sounds stupid, but it's true. It's you I want to take walks with. It's you I want to talk to. I know we'll get to know each other over the winter, so you can just forget what I said about thinking of me in a special way."

She seriously doubted she could.

"We'll just let things —" he stopped, swallowed hard — "go along however they will."

For a moment, something flared in his eyes. He was going to kiss her, and Deb wasn't sure if she wanted that or not. But then he let go of one of her hands and turned her so they were walking back toward the cabin.

"Anytime you want to go out and have a private talk with me, just know that I will for sure say yes."

"I enjoyed our walk, Trace. I would like to take another one sometime."

"That would be my pleasure." Trace smiled so wide his teeth gleamed in the dark.

She liked the warmth and strength of his hand. As they walked, the only noise that broke the silence was the whack of a hammer near the bunkhouse. It was full dark, but the moon and stars above the scudding clouds lit the yard up almost as bright as day.

More building. More planning. Deb knew now that some of this planning had to do with her. She tightened her grip on his hand.

Wolf growled low in his throat. He whirled to face the woods and raced away.

Trace took two running steps, then turned back to Deb. "We've come too far from the house. I can't leave you alone here and I left my gun behind." He grabbed her hand. "Let's get you back and I'll alert my men."

"What is it, Trace?"

"I have a notion, including why Wolf broke off the chase last time — when we were walking home. Let's hurry."

They ran toward the ranch yard. As they

came close enough, Trace yelled, "Someone come and get Deb! Wolf smelled trouble."

The hammering stopped. Boiling motion in the night made Deb feel safer, even safer than she'd felt with Trace.

Adam appeared out of the dark. Armed. "Which way?"

Trace pointed and said a few quick, harsh words.

Adam vanished in the direction Wolf had run. Trace kept her moving. Utah was a few paces behind. He'd probably been on the roof.

Trace shouted, "Take her and guard the women."

Deb saw Trace run off toward the old cabin where he'd been staying since the new cabin was done. Utah hustled her toward the new one. An instant later, Trace was outside, gun in hand, sprinting after Wolf, hard on Adam's heels.

Utah escorted her inside. He must have thought of the sleeping children in the back room because he didn't speak, and he shut the door quietly and threw a heavy beam across it to bar the entrance.

Gwen shot up from her rocking chair. She looked from Deb to Utah and whispered urgently, "What happened?"

"I don't know." Utah spoke quietly, but

he managed to scare Deb to the bone. "The boss said I'm to guard you."

"Wolf growled and ran into the woods," Deb said. "Just like what happened on the trail home. Trace and Adam went after him."

CHAPTER 17

Trace caught up with Adam and rushed on past. He recognized the trail Wolf was on and knew where he was going so he could run flat-out.

This time he'd keep going. He thought he knew who was out there and why Wolf had broken off the chase before. And Trace hadn't been able to keep up the pursuit before with the women and children left defenseless behind him.

The growling ended, and Wolf was back, wagging his tail. Trace ran on. "Dumb dog."

Yet if Trace was right about things, the dog was smart to end the chase.

It was almost pure dark in the woods, and Trace knew he couldn't follow his prey if they got off the trail. But it was such a narrow trail. The woods on both sides were near to impenetrable. He also thought the one he pursued had probably calmed Wolf down to make him turn back. Suddenly he ran head on into a man, and the two of them went flying to the ground.

Trace recognized him the minute he quit tumbling and his head cleared. "Tavibo?"

"Yes, Guardian, it is me," said Tavibo, a Paiute Indian who had befriended Trace shortly after Adam had come.

"Don't call me that. My name's Trace and you know it. Why are you upsetting Wolf? Why didn't you just come to the door?" Trace heard someone coming. "That's Adam. No need to worry. He's a good man."

Tavibo caught Trace's arm and dragged him off the trail.

Trace could have called out, but he wanted to hear what Tavibo had to say and he wasn't a man to stick around when he didn't want to. So he let Tavibo lead him about twenty paces off the trail before they stopped. He heard Adam run past, and Tavibo stood in utter silence until they were out of earshot.

"I tossed your fearsome wolf a hunk of venison, patted him on the head, and sent him back to you."

"He is fearsome when he needs to be. When he came back so calm, both times, I decided whoever was out there wasn't too dangerous."

"Not to him, I'm not. Not to you. But

trust me, Guardian, I can be dangerous."

"Don't call me —"

"I have great worry about that wagon train that burned," Tavibo said, cutting him off.

"You worry that the Paiutes will be blamed?" A cold wind wasn't enough to explain the chill of dread that raced up Trace's spine.

"Yes. My people are peaceful and have done nothing to deserve soldiers."

The trees swayed so thick, even with their leaves shed, Trace couldn't see a single star.

"I'm working on finding the men who attacked the wagon train," Trace said. "I've been to a few settlements on the west side of Tahoe, but I haven't spoken of the attack. I'd know the stolen horses and cattle if I saw them. But I don't want to warn the outlaws so I'm not just yelling questions at everyone I see. They left their slaughter behind not knowing they left witnesses. I saw what they did. They used arrows similar to what the Paiute use. They left behind a hatchet carved with Paiute symbols. I know they are hoping someone will blame you and not search for the true killers. But I wasn't fooled. And what these outlaws don't know is that there were four survivors."

"I saw you traveling home with two women and two children."

"One of the women was close enough to hear voices, one unusually high-pitched, and see a face. She says it was done by white men."

Trace heard Adam heading back down the trail.

"I go. I do not want to see more white men."

"No, wait, you should meet him, and you should feel free to come to the ranch." Trace looked in the direction Adam walked. "We could —" He looked back. Tavibo was gone, slipped away into the night.

Trace walked back to the trail and whistled. No sense making an armed man nervous. Adam came back from where he'd passed Trace on the trail. Adam was a good tracker, but in the dark he'd never seen Trace turn off.

"What's going on?" Adam asked.

"I found out who Wolf went after. It's a Paiute named Tavibo."

"I've heard you talk of him, but he's never wanted to meet me."

"He fights shy of white folks, and Native folks too if they're not of his tribe. I have known him since about the time you hired on, Adam. I've done some trading with his village. He told me he saw the wagon massacre site and wanted to make sure I knew

218

it wasn't his people who did that."

"The varmints who done it wanted Paiutes to be blamed?"

"Yep." That was one of the reasons Trace had immediately suspected the same men who'd killed his pa. They'd done the same.

They headed down the mountainside together, single file because the trail they followed was so narrow that branches brushed at their shoulders and tore at their pants.

"I knew those killers had left false signs. But others might read it different. Tavibo doesn't want the cavalry to decide they need to force Native people out of the area."

Adam said, "You sure enough run like the wind, Trace."

"I learned to be fast and how to run a long time."

"We need to clean up a little at the bunkhouse," Adam said. "But that's all we'll do for the night. We got a good day in and helped the women settle in a bit more to the new cabin."

"The women! We'd better hustle back. They might be scared. I'm gonna run to cut their worryin' time short."

"You'd best do that. Deb sure does seem to enjoy fretting over you." Adam chuckled.

Trace was glad for an excuse to run away

from the teasing. He took off like a bullet, charging down the hill. "Utah, we're back!" Trace hollered. Another man with a handy gun, and Trace didn't want to startle anyone with a twitchy trigger finger.

Utah swung the door open.

"There's no danger. It was a Paiute man I call friend. I'll tell you about it later. Adam's just behind me, headed for the bunkhouse to pack up for the night. I'll be out as soon as I talk with Deb and Gwen."

Utah gave one hard nod of his head and swept past Trace without a word, holstering his gun as he walked away.

Deb faced him, wide-eyed. Gwen sat in her rocking chair in front of the fire. They both had their guns out and ready but were setting them aside as he came in.

"It was an Indian, an old friend of mine. He doesn't trust the whites, but he tolerates me on rare occasions. He's worried about that massacre being blamed on his people."

Both women nodded and visibly relaxed. "I'm gonna be gone a long while tomorrow, maybe even overnight, and maybe more than one night. So don't fret about me if I don't get home for a while."

"Where are you going?" Deb seemed overly curious. Trace wondered if that was the way of newspaper reporters.

"Today I went along the west side of Lake Tahoe, following the trail the killers took, but tomorrow I'm going up the east side. I'll stop in those settlements and in Carson City. I need to find any wagon trains still traveling and warn them, ask if anyone's seen those stolen horses and cattle. If there aren't any more trains, there still might be late travelers. I can tell the sheriff to put them on alert. Then I'll ride on around the north end of the lake and down the west side. There were a few settlements I missed today."

"And you think that might take days?" Deb asked. There was a funny note to her voice that Trace didn't recognize. Almost like she'd miss him. Well, if that wasn't what her tone meant, he decided he'd just believe it anyway, because he'd miss her, too.

"I want others watching for the outlaws, and I want to make sure folks know the danger that's out there. However long it takes, I'm going to stick with it until I make these low-down rats sorry they came back out of their hole."

Deb took a few long strides and grabbed his arm. "Came back out? You mean you think you know who they are? You mean they've done this before?"

"I know they've done this before. All the

signs I read say they're the men who killed my pa."

"They've been killing all this time? Didn't you say your pa died ten years ago?"

"Yep. And no, they didn't keep killing. The attacks broke off, and I started to believe the men who'd done 'em were all dead."

"What made you believe that?" Deb asked.

Trace decided she needed to know the truth. If he was going to think of a future with her, she'd best know everything . . . or most everything. "I believed it because I found another burned-out wagon train in the spring after my pa was killed. I recognized it as being attacked by the same men. And after that, I guarded that trail in secret, watching for them to strike again. And when they did —" he gathered all his strength and shoved the words out, and they came laced with all his anger and pain and grief — "I personally killed everyone I could draw a bead on."

Trace saw the horror on her face, the revulsion. Now she could do nothing but despise him. He'd ruined his chances with her almost before he'd gotten one. But they couldn't build a future on lies. He turned to leave.

"Trace, wait!" No doubt the reason she called out was to tell him he was as bad as those men who'd killed the folks on her wagon train. He couldn't bear to hear the words leave her mouth. He ignored her and left the cabin, slamming the door behind him. The picture he'd been forming of his future turned to ashes.

He headed for the barn, anywhere there was no one to talk to. He could never face her again. He'd live in his cave again. He'd hunt his food and cook over an open fire. He'd give care of the ranch to Adam and tell him to send a message next spring when Deb was finally gone.

He had to figure out a way to never go back.

"Trace Riley, you get back here!"

Deb charged out the door, swinging it shut hard behind her. It was a good thing the house was sturdy because she might've knocked it down.

Trace looked over his shoulder without stopping. She saw . . . it looked like . . . fear.

He kept striding away as if he planned to continue his escape.

She lifted her skirts, ran, and plowed right into him. They went tumbling.

He must not've run after all.

Landing hard on top of him, she rolled on

223

over and slid along the snowy ground on her back, then her belly, finally slamming against a snowdrift, which was frozen hard.

Trace crawled to her side on his hands and knees. "Are you all right, Deb? Speak to me."

He shook her by the shoulders. That made her aware a bit. She lay still, her eyes closed, stunned. "I'm fine." Not strictly the truth. "Just . . . the w-wind knocked out . . . of me. Give me a moment to catch my breath."

He didn't give her a moment. "I walked out, Deb, because I didn't want to hear what you must be thinking, not after I confessed my evil. But I was a coward to walk out. I'll give you your say. Then I'll leave and stay far away. The men can eat your food and bring you supplies and firewood. I'll stay away from you. I deserve to be cast out."

She heard such despair and such loneliness. Gathering her wits, she rested a hand on his forearm. "Trace, you're not going anywhere."

"I have to. I'm not fit company for you, Gwen, and the children. There were no more trains the fall my pa was killed, but the next spring I finally found my way back to that trail and came upon another burned-out wagon train. Those men had struck again. Instead of following the trail to a town, I picked a lookout and waited. When the next train came, I was ready. I slipped through the woods, finding men waiting to dry-gulch the travelers. I killed any man I could find. Where your train spent the night, and mine, that's the only stopping place for miles. Those men had plans to kill the pioneers in their sleep."

"You said you killed every one of them you could draw a bead on. But what you really did was guard the passage along that trail. You watched for the outlaws, and when you found them waiting to attack another train, you stopped them."

"I was full of anger and vengeance. 'Vengeance is mine saith the Lord.' Well, I hadn't given any thought to that verse, though I read the Bible through the first winter. And I might not have stopped even if I had understood it. I wanted the men who killed my pa to suffer, to die for their crimes. I'm a top marksman, Deb. I aimed to kill."

"Help me up."

Trace's hands were like velvet iron, the strength, the gentleness as he helped her sit upright. Then after a few moments, he lifted her to her feet. He held on until he was sure her knees wouldn't wobble, then stepped respectfully back.

"Now, Trace Riley —"

"You've called me by my first and last name two times. It don't seem like a good sign."

Shaking her head, she said, "I can understand the anger you carried around, but I can't judge as evil a man who protected innocent people from killers."

Trace shrugged one shoulder. "I reckon I enjoyed it too much."

She slapped him on the shoulder. "And when the attacks broke off, did you go around killing other people and enjoy that?"

Trace's dark brows slammed down. "Of course not."

"And why is that? Why do you say, 'of course not'?"

"I'm not a cold-blooded killer, Deb."

"I thought you just said you were."

Trace glared, then finally dropped his eyes to the ground, and kicked at the snow. "Don't make light of what I did. I found a Bible in one of the burned-out wagon trains — most of the books came from there, or I found them tossed alongside the trail when folks were lightening their loads. Lately I've bought a few. But that Bible survived the fire when my pa was killed."

"That explains its battered cover."

"Yep, I figured maybe God had spared it

just to give me a chance to read His Word. I could only read mighty slow at first, but I kept getting faster. I had four other books, so I spent the first winter reading them all through before spring came. I've read it through every winter since, and I'd catch a little more each time until I thought I started understanding all of it, which I see now is so foolish. I finally felt like 'vengeance is mine' was written with me in mind, or for men like me, but I was so angry and didn't let it stop me."

"And if you had understood those words, Trace? Would you have left the wagon trains unguarded? Is that what you think God would have wanted you to do?"

That was met with a long stretch of silence. "When I finally got to a town I heard rumors that the trail was haunted. That a ghost they'd named The Guardian stood watch over it. I didn't tell anyone it was me."

Finally, because she was getting purely cold, Deb said, "I don't hate you for what you did, Trace. If hate drove you and you feel it was an awful sin, then pray for forgiveness. Ask God to forgive you and learn to forgive yourself. And do it knowing that I hold no sin against you. That's not really what I came out here for."

"It's not?" Trace found his hat where it'd fallen off his head, put it back on, put his hand on her back and urged her back toward the cabin.

"No, I came out because I am going with you tomorrow. You need me. I'd hoped after today you'd know that. You'd realize that —"

"All right, you can come."

Deb stopped and whirled around to face him. "All right?" She was as stunned now as she'd been after the fall.

"Yes, after today I saw you were right. It made me wary not knowing who the men around me were. I wished you were there to tell me if you recognized voices. I would appreciate it if you'd come. I plan to ride straight to Carson City. Dismal is on south of us, and those men wouldn't have gone there, not without me knowing. The trail goes too close to my place. And besides they were headed north. You can help me talk to the sheriff. You can describe the man you saw and the voices you heard — it'd be better coming straight from the witness and not passed through me."

Deb stood speechless. She'd expected to have the fight of her life over this. And she hadn't intended to take no for an answer. Although she'd have to steal a horse from

Trace, and she didn't know how to saddle one, and she'd have to get past Utah and Adam. Still, she'd planned to go.

This sort of added to having her breath knocked out. "Well, umm . . . good. I'm glad we agree."

"Gwen will be all right, won't she?" A furrow formed between Trace's brows. "She'll have to care for the children and feed the men on her own. You both work mighty hard to get a meal on for us."

It was all Deb could do not to throw her arms around his neck. Honestly, he was just the sweetest man. Then she remembered his confession about killing and thought maybe *sweet* wasn't the exact right term.

"Gwen will be fine."

"We'll have to stay out overnight. I think we can get to Carson City and find rooms there. If we make good time, do our searching there, and move on past it we'll have to find some proper place for you to sleep."

"What time do we leave?"

"Before sunup. I'll knock on your door to wake you, then go saddle the horses while you dress. I've got food for the saddlebags."

"I'll bring along some more."

Nodding, Trace said, "That'll be fine, but we should be able to eat in Carson City so we don't need too much."

Deb determined she would be up and ready long before Trace. She wasn't going to do a single thing that slowed him down.

CHAPTER 18

Trace knocked quietly on the door in the darkness. Deb swung it open, dressed, a bag over her shoulder that Trace recognized from when he'd first come upon her. She carried a canteen in her other hand.

"I haven't saddled the horses yet."

"I won't get in your way, but Trace, when you ever get a spare moment, I'd like to learn to saddle a horse."

He wondered how long that'd take. She was a greenhorn. "Let's go. We'll save saddling lessons for another day."

They reached the barn, and Utah had both horses ready.

"I'd've done it, Utah."

"I know you would have, Trace. You're a man who tends his own horse. But this gives me a jump on the day's building."

He spoke as if Trace had done him a favor.

Trace boosted Deb up onto the saddle, then swung up on his own mount. Utah had picked well. Deb's horse was a gentle mare but no slacker. Trace wanted to make good time, and unless Deb wasn't up to the ride — hard to judge by the ride she'd taken on a horse with four riders — they'd make a fast trip of it.

Heading out an hour before first light, they hit the trail galloping. He glanced at Deb, who never claimed any top riding skills. "Let me know if you're having any troubles. We don't need to go at this pace."

"I'll let you know." Her determined expression and her firm jaw told Trace she'd die before she complained. He sure hoped it didn't come to that!

She had a viselike grip on the saddle horn, which was how greenhorns rode, but she was balanced well.

Trace planned to ride all the way to Carson City and to the north shore of Tahoe. He'd have slept on the trail, but with Deb along, they'd need a hotel. There was a decent little town at the north point.

Surely there'd be no more wagon trains. Even the latest travelers heading for the California Trail to Sacramento had come through by now. Only a fool would try to cross any later. But Trace had learned the hard way there were fools aplenty in the world. If he came across a wagon train, he'd warn them of the danger from the outlaws. He'd also warn them of the danger of rough weather. But he knew they'd press on regardless. By this point in the journey, they were low on supplies and money. They couldn't afford to lay up over the winter. He'd also make sure to check if a small group was splitting off from the bigger trains.

No one was reckless enough to attack a big wagon train — and the same thought of fools ran through Trace's head. Some of the trains stretched to a hundred covered wagons, and that meant lots of men and guns.

Reading tracks had told Trace it was three outlaws. But maybe there were others. Maybe only a few went for such a small train. He'd never seen an attack on a full-sized train — and he'd watched the trail for years, so he'd've seen it. Besides the sheer number of people, many of the men heading west were Civil War veterans and a tough salty lot who were ready, even eager, to aim and fire. Add to that the kind of men who'd attack and kill sleeping settlers were the worst kind of cowards. They'd never take on a big train.

Unless maybe they were desperate for money with winter coming on. Trace didn't put anything past such low-down skunks.

He'd leave word in Carson City so any late trains would be on alert. He'd see if anyone was traveling to Reno so they could pass the word, and he'd hope for someone heading for Virginia City. But a train this late, he doubted it.

Reno was the most common path. The California Trail, though there were several versions of it, split from the Oregon Trail and often passed right through Reno. Virginia City was a hard old ride west.

They settled into a steady gallop. These two horses were both strong, and neither Trace nor Deb carried much with them. They couldn't ride all the way to Carson City at this pace but they'd make good time.

"Let's give 'em a breather, Deb." Trace laughed as they slowed to a walk.

"What's funny?"

"I just realized those are the first words spoken between us in over an hour."

"Tell me what you've got planned for today, Trace."

"The first stop is Carson City. On the west side of Lake Tahoe there are several small settlements, but on the east side I'm mainly looking to spread the word about the massacre, make sure any lawmen know the Paiutes weren't involved, and warn any wagon trains."

"You've mentioned Lake Tahoe a number of times, but where is it?"

Trace's eyes flashed with pleasure. "I can show you. Not today, because the trail swings wide of it, but tomorrow I can pick a trail that'll put us in sight of it. It's the prettiest thing I've ever seen. A huge lake surrounded by mountains and trees. We rode along the west side on our way to my place. There's a lot of forest between us and that beautiful blue water. I'd love to be with you when you see it for the first time. The most beautiful thing in the world, I reckon, though I've heard tell that there's a canyon in Arizona Territory that's a wonder."

"The Grand Canyon. I've seen pictures but I haven't traveled much."

"The books I've read don't talk of such discoveries as the Grand Canyon. I've only heard stories. Anyhow, I can get you a look at Tahoe tomorrow. I want to ask around in Carson City, see if there've been attacks like this with similarities between the attack on the Scotts and the attack so many years ago on my own wagon train. Doing all that, well, it'll take most of the day, but I hope there's time to ride on. Tomorrow we'll round the lake and talk to any settlements I didn't get to on my ride yesterday. We'll be able to push on tomorrow night and sleep at home."

"Maybe they'll have the roof on the bunk-house done by then and you and your men can sleep in a warm house for the first time since I arrived and stole your home from you."

Trace grinned. "It ain't stealin' if I give it to you, woman."

Deb laughed quietly.

"Pushing hard to get the new cabin and the bunkhouse up is the best thing about you coming. I built that old cabin alone and I've kept it standing more with prayer than with any building skills. And so far my prayers haven't stopped the cold wind from blowing through the cracks."

"Well then, I'm very glad I could help by making all this backbreaking work for you." She sounded on the verge of laughing.

With a wide grin, he said, "I think we'd better get on. The horses are rested and the miles are long."

Deb kicked her horse into a gallop along-side Trace's. They rode through narrow trails and wide ones, trees thick around them and then openings into meadows. The ground was rugged, with mountains climb-ing up on their left and down on their right, with bare trees knocking in the cold breeze and stones scattered far and near, like giant rocks thrown about by the Lord himself.

They galloped on toward Carson City, and Trace realized he was in an overly good mood for a man searching for murdering thieves. The thought sobered him. How long was it going to take him to find the killers and bring them to justice?

Raddo strode down the streets of Carson City. There was a wagon train that'd pulled through right before he came to town. The folks would take at least five days to get to that deadly pass, so there was no use riding after them yet.

Instead, Raddo and his men would rest here two days, enjoy all the favors a bigger town offered, and then they'd ride hard.

This group was going on the main trail to Sacramento too, not turning off to head south. That Sacramento Trail had grown into the road with all the travel since they'd found the Comstock Lode. Raddo had pulled his own share of silver out of the ground before his mine played out.

So a busier trail increased the danger. But all Raddo could see was the cold winter ahead and the money to be had. If a man was going to strike it rich without digging in the ground, he had to take chances sometimes.

The wagon train was too large, he knew that, but he was desperate. Besides, it wasn't the biggest train he'd ever heard of at twenty-five wagons. He'd thought about finding a few more men, but he wanted all the money for himself. Well, himself and his saddle partners, if he ended up having to share.

He shrugged off his worries. There would be no travelers in the predawn hours. And Raddo and his men had scouted the trail; they'd picked out several prime spots where they could hide and wait for the train — getting in place ahead of time so they could be on hand for the raid. Meanwhile, they'd be on the lookout for sentries. And when they attacked, they'd work silently for as long as they could.

He nodded to himself. They were ready. Besides, it was so late in the season that these folks qualified as fools, so he, Meeks, and Dalt oughta be able to take 'em without much fuss.

CHAPTER 19

Deb and Trace reached Carson City by midafternoon.

Trace rode up to a livery stable. He stripped the leather, and Deb tried to help but was slowing him down. Once he'd seen to hay and a bait of oats, he said, "Now it's our turn to eat."

"We're in a hurry, Trace." Deb did her best not to limp. She didn't want to admit how painful dismounting was. She'd never ridden this long and hard before. The ride to Trace's place from the massacre didn't count because she'd gotten off and walked several times.

She wondered if he would've taken time to eat if she wasn't with him. "Let's just eat the jerky and biscuits I brought."

"Nope. We've got to talk to the sheriff and ask some questions of others. And the horses need a rest. We pushed them getting here."

"Are you all right?" He stepped up onto the boardwalk in front of the diner, then turned with worried eyes toward her.

She must've limped after all. "I'm fine." She forced her knees to lock while she nodded cheerfully. She hoped he didn't notice her clenched jaw.

He looked doubtful but swung the diner door open and let her go in ahead of him. "We ate a light breakfast on the trail. Now my belly's so empty it thinks my throat's been cut. We'll eat fast."

After a meal that was touched by hunger's magic seasoning, they went hunting the sheriff. They found his office, but he wasn't in. Carson City was the territorial capital and flush with money from the Comstock Lode, so it had a good-sized number of deputies. One of them knew where the sheriff was and pointed the way. After being questioned, the deputy also told them that a wagon train had just passed through town.

Leaving the jail, Trace said quietly to Deb, "We'll ride after them. We have time before they reach the dangerous mountain passes."

"You sound calm, but your eyes are dancing around like you're panicking."

"Well, I feel an almost frantic need to ride after those folks and warn them they might be in danger. But I've got a few things to finish here first."

They found Sheriff Moore coming out of the barbershop. He was a portly man with a tidy gray mustache and white hair barely visible below a battered Stetson. He wore a black leather vest with a silver star pinned over his heart.

The sheriff's eyes locked on Trace with only a quick glance at Deb. The man ambled toward him until he was close enough. "You folks lookin' for me?"

Trace jumped right in. "I've come to report a crime and warn of another that might be comin'."

The blue eyes hardened. "What happened?"

"One of the wagon trains was attacked. Folks got massacred. It was a smaller train that broke off from a larger one and then got waylaid. Near everyone was killed."

"Indians?"

"Nope."

Sheriff Moore nodded.

"Some survived the attack," Trace went on, but then he hesitated. Deb suspected he didn't want to say that she was one of the survivors. "Right now the men who done it think everyone in the wagon train was killed."

The sheriff frowned deep enough to turn

down the corners of his mustache. "I'm headed for the diner and coffee. Let's walk."

"We just ate," Trace said, "but we can sit with you and tell you our story."

Deb walked by Trace's side nearest the buildings.

Trace fell into step beside Sheriff Moore. "Maybe we should talk a bit before anyone overhears us. The outlaws drove off a small herd, horses and cows, and they might be trying to sell them. I never saw these murderers, so I can't trust the man at the next table right now. I have no notion of who the killers are except I can read signs."

Moore came to an abrupt halt. "You tracked 'em?"

Trace told all he knew as they walked slowly toward the diner.

"You can describe the tracks over coffee. Not much chance anyone will know what we're talking about. It's quiet in there this time of day anyhow."

"Why? It's gettin' on to time for an afternoon coffee break."

"Yep, but Charlie, who runs the place, is the worst cook in town, and he seems to take pride in that."

"How does he stay in business?"

The sheriff shrugged. "The place is cheap to run. Pretty sure he's feeding us whatever he shoots the night before. With deer that's okay — mostly — but he's served up some mighty odd stuff. I don't care what Charlie says, wolverine tastes just plain bad. Here's some advice. The coffee's barely drinkable, but it beats most everything else. And if you value your life, don't let him talk you into a piece of cake." The sheriff shuddered, then gave Trace an unexpected grin that made it easier to sit and drink burnt coffee and tell him all they knew.

"Where are these witnesses you spoke of?"

Deb hesitated. She knew Trace hadn't mentioned her because he wanted to protect her. She looked around the diner and it was empty. No one to overhear. Charlie didn't even seem to have stayed in the place. Chances were he himself went out for coffee.

"It's me."

Trace hissed and rested his hand on hers. "Deb, no."

She forged on. "That's why he brought me along. He said he'd pass on my description, but I convinced him it might be better firsthand, and besides, I might recognize one of them if he was in Carson City or anywhere along our trail."

"Being the only living witness sets you in the path of danger, miss." The sheriff tugged on the corner of his mustache and frowned.

"I know it." Trace looked annoyed. "That's why I didn't want her to identify herself. I just hoped she could look around and see if she recognized anyone."

"Can you describe them to me, miss?"

Deb did so to the best of her ability.

The sheriff said, "I've heard of attacks on wagon trains, but not for a long time. There were rumors that someone, or something, was a guardian of that trail. A few bodies were found and that fed the rumors and the attacks ended. This is a bad business, and I don't like to see it starting up again."

Deb held her breath and did her best to keep a blank expression on her face. A guardian of the trail? That's what Trace had done. Could a man be wanted for murder when he stopped a murder?

"I've heard of such things, too," Trace said. "If those outlaws are taking back up an old profession, then where have they been all this time? Did they move on and set up their ambushes somewhere else? They haven't paid for their crimes yet, and now they've taken up their ugly ways again."

The sheriff turned thoughtful. After a moment, he said, "I am sheriff of Carson City and I really don't go looking for trouble far and wide. I can be on the lookout here in town and these parts, but following the trail and protecting wagon trains that pass through here . . . well, once they're out of town, that's way outside my job."

Trace nodded. "I understand, Sheriff. I appreciate you doing all you can. We'll be on our way now. I'm going to ride on hard tonight and catch the wagon train that just rolled through Carson City."

They all stood to go, and the sheriff said something Deb didn't hear because she was a few paces ahead of Trace. She stepped outside, where a large rough-looking man knocked into her hard enough she'd've fallen if she didn't still have a firm hold of the door.

"You'd do well to look where you're going next time." The gruff man shouldered past her and hurried on.

She watched him walk away, a big man with a rude attitude. Sometimes big men, she knew, pushed those smaller around — it made them feel strong to barrel through any barriers with little care about what or who those barriers were. Something about him bothered Deb. Her eyes were drawn to him for some reason she couldn't quite understand. He glanced back at her, almost as if he could feel her stare. His cold eyes narrowed, but he turned forward again and forged on and around the corner of the building and out of sight.

She decided it was probably just his ill manners. It was such a contrast to the men at Trace's ranch who were so kind and generous to her and Gwen. Studying on it a bit, she realized he reminded her in some ways of some of the men back east who took advantage of her hard work and gave her father all the credit.

Trace stepped out of the diner and rested a hand on her shoulder. "Is something wrong?"

With a shake of her head, Deb said, "No, just almost ran into a man. So I stopped to let him pass. I'm looking at everyone with suspicious eyes, wondering if he might be the one I saw attack our wagon train. But that man's too tall, too heavy. The man I saw had a narrow face; he was skinny."

"You want to go after him, take another look?" Trace looked at her too long, as if he saw something in her expression that worried him. Then his eyes followed the boardwalk. "Where'd he go?"

"Around the corner of this building. No, it's not the man I saw. And we need to ride, don't we? The weather could go from chilly and light snow to a blizzard with snow a yard deep."

Finally, his hand on her lower back, he urged her forward. "We need to catch that wagon train and warn them, hopefully before we lose the light."

She shoved aside the strange feeling the big man had given her and shifted her attention to the ride ahead.

They were on horseback and galloping out of town within minutes.

Raddo clenched his fist in fury. He leaned against the corner of the building listening to the woman who had been watching him and realized someone had survived their attack. Not just survived, she'd seen Dalt. And now that wagon train they needed so bad was going to be warned and on edge.

Twenty-five wagons. It'd be the biggest group they'd ever tackled, more than double the next largest one. If he told Dalt and Meeks about the witness, they'd get stubborn and refuse to attack the train. Dalt out of a ruthless desire not to take too big a chance, and Meeks because he loved the killing but was a coward at heart. He liked to see men die under his guns, but he didn't want them to be awake for it.

And now here they'd planned on attacking in silence. Slitting as many throats as they could before anyone knew they were even there. Meeks had agreed, but if the train was warned and on edge, both men would refuse to do it.

Raddo considered for a long moment if they would be right. He should probably listen to them and call everything off. But a stubbornness welled up inside him. He didn't want to admit he couldn't handle bigger trains. He also knew he couldn't let that woman live. He'd never left a witness alive before.

The wind whistled through the narrow alley between the two buildings, and the chill reminded him of the one they'd called The Guardian.

Some called him a ghost. And if ever men might come back to haunt a place, it'd be a man murdered and left to burn and rot in the middle of a dead wagon train.

The Guardian was why Raddo had gone straight. Well, that and Luth striking it rich and helping all the men claim mines.

Raddo ground his teeth as he stomped off to find his much smaller band. Luth was a powerful man now, and he wouldn't like knowing Raddo had gone back to his old ways.

But Raddo wasn't wealthy, and that could be laid right at the feet of his big brother who'd claimed the most prosperous mines for himself and left Raddo with the dregs.

He didn't need to follow the woman he'd nearly run down. He knew they were heading out to warn the wagon train. He was tempted to act fast, gather the men, and go after her. They could stop her and her saddle partner from passing on their warning.

But were they too close to Carson City? A wagon train moved slowly. It wouldn't be a good distance from the sheriff yet, who had a reputation as a tough man who paid no attention to a crime committed long miles and many days down a trail, but would come hunting hard at a killing close to his town.

Raddo knew where to find Dalt and Meeks — in a saloon, right where Raddo had been heading when he'd had his lucky run-in with the woman.

Did they dare try and take her before she reached the wagon train? Or was it better to not let Dalt and Meeks know about this? They were already fretting about taking on such a big train. Now add a wagon train that'd been warned and was on alert?

They'd turn yellow and quit for sure if they tried to get the woman and failed.

He tossed different ideas around, not sure what to do. They did need to get out of town, though. If she'd described Dalt well enough, someone might point him out to the sheriff.

Dalt thought he should get more men, and maybe that was the safer bet. Raddo didn't like sharing, but he'd rather share than die.

Lots to decide, but one thing was for certain. That eyewitness couldn't be allowed to live. And the man who rode with her knew enough he needed to go, too.

It'd give them one less thing to worry about.

CHAPTER 20

Trace was worrying about Deb more every minute. Not a whimper out of her. Her spine was straight, but her knuckles were white, gripped on the saddle horn. He'd seen her head bob forward a couple of times for a second before she snapped upright again.

The woman was done in for a fact, and it was approaching dark in the short days of late October.

If he didn't find that wagon train mighty soon, he was going to have to call off their ride and find them a place to camp. And he was mighty sure she wouldn't like it. Something about properness, which he'd heard of in some of the books he'd read, but really had no idea what it meant exactly. He only knew Deb knew, and she seemed to give it some importance. He watched her, prepared to catch her if she fell off the horse. He could probably carry her until he found the wagon train. He wondered if that was proper enough for her. Well, she'd be asleep and maybe she'd never really figure out what had gone on.

And then as the last of the sun sank behind the mountain and the dusk faded to dark, he saw ahead several blazing fires that outlined a circle of covered wagons.

With a sigh of relief, he swung down off his horse. "Deb, c'mon down. We're near the train now." He eased her to the ground and held on, not sure her knees would wobble. "Hello, camp!"

She jumped at his shout and shook her head. He felt her steady herself.

Trace heard rifles cocking. It didn't bother him; he wouldn't respect men in the wilderness who weren't wary.

There was a right way and a wrong way to approach a wagon train. He didn't know how salty this bunch was, but he let them hear him and see him for as long as they wanted.

"Come on in slow," someone called.

The two of them walked in, leading their horses. Hands in plain sight, his pistol in his holster with the thong over the trigger, his rifle visible in the saddle's scabbard.

He reached the first man and asked, "Are you the wagon master?"

The burly man, with overlong dark hair and a beard shot full of gray, narrowed his eyes. Then after long seconds, he nodded his head. "You folks need a meal?"

"We'd appreciate it, sir." Trace offered his hand.

"Goff Eckley. Call me Goff. I'm the leader of this group. We're a friendly bunch." The man thrust his own hand forward.

Trace didn't believe it was all *that* friendly, though, considering five men had come out with the boss, and all had their guns to hand.

"I want to talk to you, pass on a warning." Trace's eyes slid along from man to man. "Are you the sentries and scouts? I reckon the whole train needs to know, but I'd prefer they hear it from you."

With a tip of his hat at Deb, Goff asked, "Would you like to join the women and get a meal, miss?"

"She stays with me. She's a survivor of a wagon train massacre, just a few days' ride from here on the south fork of the California Trail."

That got their attention.

All six men holstered their guns and stepped closer.

"Tell us what's going on." Goff crossed his arms tightly across his chest.

Trace made it a short, harsh story, sparing them nothing. Deb described the man she'd seen and the men she'd heard.

"We'll need to double the sentries." Goff looked at Trace. "I might have more questions. You folks go on and get a meal while we make some plans." He pointed to a fire visible between two wagons. "That's my fire. I've got plenty."

"We'd be obliged if we could stay the night too, Goff."

The man nodded. "I'd take you along as another sentry if I could talk you into it."

"I've gotta be moving. I'm hoping to find these men and have them in jail soon. Maybe before you even get to the trail through the Sierras where they prey on folks."

Goff nodded and turned, drawing his men into a tight circle.

"It's a lot bigger group than we had," Deb said. "Would those men dare to attack this large of a group?"

"It makes me sick to think they'd consider murder on this scale. But once they've begun killing, they may be cold-blooded enough to think five is the same as ten is the same as fifty."

Trace shook his head and guided Deb to the fire the trail boss had pointed to as his own. There was a good-sized pot of stew bubbling on the fire, and they helped themselves.

"They're a salty bunch." Trace looked back at the wagon train as they rode away from it. "They're gonna be ready for trouble."

"I worried they might not take us seriously." Deb rode at Trace's side the next morning. She ached in every muscle right to the bone, but she'd kept quiet about it and mounted up.

She looked back at the wagon train, just starting to roll. A wagon train managed about ten miles a day, while a rider on horseback could push to one hundred. She and Trace wouldn't make that because they had to stop along the way, but even so, they'd leave those folks far behind.

"I know a few of them didn't. They just don't believe a wagon train as big as theirs would be attacked. What more could we have done?"

Trace shook his head. "It helped that you told them what happened to you, Deb. I'm sorry you had to relive it."

"Do you ever get over it? The sounds of the killing and the ugliness of what you find after?"

"I still carry it around in my head."

"When you talked about 'a voice crying in the wilderness,' you were speaking about yourself, weren't you?"

Trace jerked one shoulder almost sheepishly. "That verse reminded me of myself, John the Baptist out in the wilderness, except of course he got folks to come out and listen to him, so he couldn't't've been all that far out in the wilderness. Not like me. But it fit, me out in the wilderness, and the crying, well, I was powerful unhappy about my situation, so that's how it struck me.

"But I was also struck by how John wasn't really alone out there because he had God with him. My pa was a believer, but we never went near a church or talked much about faith or owned a Bible. That Bible I found was an anchor to hold on to. It reminded me God was with me in the wilderness."

"I keep thinking our lives will quiet down some," Deb said. "And I'll be able to read in the evening, aloud to the children and to Gwen maybe. That would be a true pleasure."

Trace's lips quirked.

"What are you thinking?" she asked.

He smiled wider. "I was thinking maybe you oughta read to all of us. To me and the men, along with Gwen and the little ones."

"If the men ever quit working until all hours of the night, I'd be glad to. I'd enjoy it very much, except . . ."

She hesitated to say it, but it made sense.

"Except what?" Trace asked.

"It occurred to me that it'd probably be the most sensible thing for me to ride fast to fetch Gwen and the children, and join up with that wagon train back there. We'd get to California before winter after all."

She was surprised how hard that was to say. She should be relieved to get back on the trail. She would move out and let Trace have his house back. Yes, they'd talked of knowing each other better, but her plans were to stand on her own. And she wanted that. She was strong enough and it burned in her, the desire to prove to the whole world — even a world that would never know — that she had always been the one in charge.

"You can't go." Trace reached across from his horse and caught her reins. He pulled both animals to a stop.

That distracted her from her inner talk, goading herself into going with those folks.

"Why not?"

"It's too late in the season. That trail could snow shut right over your head." He angled his horse around so that he faced west and

257

she east. He could look right into her eyes this way.

"I'll tell them on the train to push hard."

"You might run right back into those outlaws like you did before. You and Gwen and the children could be killed."

"I'll be fine. You're The Guardian, remember?"

"Of course I remember I'm The Guardian."

"Now that you know the outlaws are active again, you will protect the wagon train, and me in it."

"I'm going to stop them if I can, but what if I fail?" He reached now for her hand, white-knuckled on the saddle horn.

"You won't."

"Well, then what about the children? What about their uncle? You wrote to him."

"I'll write him again and tell him where to come."

"What about . . . ?" Trace dropped her hand and dragged his hat off his head. He hung on to the brim as if the poor hat were making an escape. "What about me? I thought we were going to spend the winter . . ." He jerked one shoulder. "What about me?"

The hurt in his voice was her undoing, especially since, darn it, she didn't want to leave him, either. "What about my news-paper?"

Trace looked up, and his eyes were warm and kind. How could he consider himself cold-blooded when he was so decent?

"I'm wondering if you even really want to run a newspaper."

She scowled at him. "Of course I do."

"You've spoken often about how hard it was to do. I have no doubt you're able, but think of the jobs you had. Writing stories, selling ads, running the printing press, col-lecting on money owed you, paying out money you owed others. You had a paper route. You had to attend events and report on them. I'm sure you're good at it, but do you really enjoy it? Would you pick that to do for the rest of your life if it wasn't the only job you've ever had, the only work you know?"

Deb opened her mouth to yell at him. It was insulting. Of course she wanted to — wanted to — Her heart pounded so hard she could hear it. She wondered if he heard it.

He went on quietly, "It's in some ways as if the father who pushed you into that job at such a young age is still with you, still pushing. You don't have to run a newspaper if you don't want it, Deb. You can choose a life for yourself."

"Let's ride on."

Trace didn't let go of her reins right away.

"I need to think. Is it possible that what I've thought of as showing the world I did everything on my own is letting my father rule me from the grave?"

"You can have all the time you need to think, but don't fetch yourself a ride on that wagon train until your thinking's done. Springtime will be soon enough, surely." Trace released her reins, and they turned their horses so they were riding along again.

Nodding, Deb tried to hide her relief. She really didn't want to leave him, not so soon. "Yes, you're right. I can wait for spring."

Just saying the words lifted a weight off her heart.

"There'll be plenty of room for you. I expect by the time we quit this chasing around looking for outlaws, the bunkhouse will be finished. The trails will be snowed shut, and the men and I will have long idle hours after the evening meal. We could make a gathering out of reading most every night."

"I'd like that. Where are we going now?"

"Today we'll reach the north shore of Lake Tahoe. I'll take you up a narrow trail to see it. There's a likely spot to look down from one of the mountains that rim the lake. We can't dawdle, though. I hope to get home today yet."

"Let's pick up the pace then so we end up at home all the faster." Deb kicked her horse into a gallop, and she and Trace rode in silence for a long stretch.

Trace felt an itch at the back of his neck. For the first time he wished he'd brought Wolf along. But he'd taken him to Sacramento, and neither his dog nor the people there were one speck happy about it.

He saw Black's ears twitch. A twig snapped. Nope, not a twig. A gun being cocked.

Trace yanked on the reins and crashed Black into Deb's horse, veering them straight toward the woods. A bullet whistled so close, Trace could feel the heat of it.

"Kick your feet out of the stirrups!"

He felt more than saw Deb obey and launched himself off his horse. He tackled her off the back of hers, fell with her to the ground, and rolled hard up against a huge stone.

Another bullet split the air. Black reared. The mare whinnied, then both horses tore off at a full gallop. Trace used the horses' frantic bodies as a barrier and moved.

He shoved Deb down flat on her belly, then surged forward, crawling on his elbows and pulling her along with him. A bullet pinged off a boulder just inches above their heads.

Trace got them behind a man-high rock just as another bullet shredded the leaves over their heads, then more hit alongside the granite barrier.

Three guns firing. Three men. The number of murdering outlaws they were hunting. Somehow they'd caught up to the only witness.

"Trace —"

"Shhh!" Trace spoke barely louder than a breath. "Stay with me. Stay low."

He headed up the mountain, directly away from the boulder, and dodged between two trees that made an almost solid wall. He snaked along, hunkered down but moving. Deb kept up, silent but for her running footsteps. He could even tell she was trying to make her feet land quietly. She always did her best not to slow him down.

He heard the bullets firing back near the boulder. He heard shouts that weren't words he could make out, but they sounded like the gunmen were on the move. Thinking their prey was pinned down.

A game trail barely big enough for a

rattlesnake popped up in front of Trace. He turned at a right angle and plunged down the almost invisible path in the direction his horse had gone. Branches grabbed at them, evergreens clawing at their clothes. Trace did his best to shield Deb while racing on.

Black would come hunting Trace at some point. No idea about the mare, but horses were herd animals so she might stick with the stallion.

The bullets stopped. Trace heard quiet talk. Still no words were loud enough to make out, but the men were talking. They sounded like they'd reached the boulder. They'd made a run on that hiding place and saw no one there.

Any halfway-decent tracker would be hard on the trail Trace and Deb couldn't help but leave. He picked up the pace, stood straighter, sure now they'd gone deep enough into the woods not to be visible from where the outlaws were down on the trail.

How to stop leaving tracks? Trace studied the ground as they ran. The game trail he'd taken was so narrow they might just miss it.

"We've got to get some space between us and them," he whispered to Deb.

Connected only by their clinging hands, he felt her run faster.

Gunfire erupted behind them. Had they found the trail, or were they just blasting away at the area where they'd last seen their prey?

Driving forward, he watched for any opportunity to leave the trail in a way that wasn't clearly noticeable.

Then he saw a slash of white ahead and knew he was looking at a streak of pure stone. This was their chance. A good tracker would know where they left the trail, but the rock crossed this trail and headed in a white streak up and down the hill. There'd be no way to judge which way they'd chosen. And because only an idiot would go down, closer to where those men searched, he figured their pursuers would go up without hesitation.

So he went down.

It wasn't a smooth layer of stone, but it was wide enough that they weren't being whipped by tree branches every step. The rock branched out, and Trace didn't hesitate to follow, parallel again to the trail below, the direction they'd been heading before the men opened fire.

His sudden swerve tripped Deb.

He scrambled to hold her up, but she fell hard to her knees.

"I'm fine. Let's go!" She was on her feet

again, but he saw her knees bleeding, her dress torn, her jaw gritted against pain.

"No. Stop." His eyes darted around, searching for some place to hide her.

At the very thought of those men after them, of them finding her, his heart hardened into rage, and he decided he was done running.

It was time to stop and fight.

Time to stop being the prey and become the hunter. He swung her up in his arms and ran on, but now he was looking for something. A cave, a tight boulder with a little space behind it. Even a dense copse of trees.

"I can run, Trace."

"Hush, let me think." Did he dare hide her? Leave her defenseless?

A loud shout and a roar of gunfire. Not that close, but not far enough, either. They'd found the game trail. And if he wanted to waylay them, he needed to get into position fast.

There it was, a jumble of trees that looked like they'd been washed there by flooding spring runoff until they'd dammed up against each other and stopped. Years and years' worth of piled-up trees twice as high as his head, and just off this gashing white path of stone.

He ran for it, climbed right up, using the logs like stair steps. He never had to set a single boot on soil that'd leave a track.

He reached the top and looked down. A tiny gap behind the trees and the mountainside they'd skidded down. He hurried right down and set her on the ground.

"Trace."

"Shh! I'm going to see if we've lost them. I'm quick in the woods, Deb. They'll never see me." That's when he noticed her ever-present bag, slung over her head and under one arm. "Have you got your gun?"

She gave him a firm nod.

"Get your gun out and cock it now when they are out of hearing range." He sure hoped they were still out of range.

"Then don't make a sound." He squeezed her hand and realized how much he trusted her to be careful and how much he hated to leave her. He turned and sprinted back toward the men, killing hate eating at his heart.

It was a feeling he knew for a sin.

A feeling he hoped to overcome . . . someday. But he sure hadn't managed it today.

CHAPTER 21

He rushed along the white rocks, quiet, listening. It gave him grim satisfaction to know he was tracking them now. And they were running right for him.

Find the right spot. Pick off every mother's son of these vipers before they knew they were under attack.

Get back to where he'd had a choice with these rocks to go up or down.

Lie in wait.

A bullet fired. One of the men shouted something ugly. Trace wasn't sure what, but then the gunfire stopped.

Soon they came on, feet thudding like stampeding horses. He had time, just enough and not a moment too much.

He reached the spot where the white rock divided and stepped away from the rocks into the trees. His lungs pumped out rage and drew in pure fire. He was The Guardian again.

Hunkering down, he found a log in a good-enough spot and dropped to his knees. The trail was mostly covered by trees, but he could see enough. He could make out feet if they approached.

He rested his six-gun on the log and wished for his rifle. He was a dead shot at any distance with that. Good enough with the pistol, yet he could pick these men off faster and more surely with his rifle.

Breathing too loud. He didn't fight it, deciding they were still far enough away and he needed to catch his breath the best he could. It'd help keep his hands steady. There'd be plenty of time to go dead silent later.

The voice of one crying in the wilderness.

That came to him as if blown on the wind.

He faltered in his righteous hate.

Shaking his head violently, he went back to his cold, deadly intent. These men were murderers. Trace wanted justice. He wanted to save lives. God was on Trace's side.

The voice of one crying in the wilderness.

Footsteps finally sounded and told him all he needed to know. They'd reached the white rocks. They'd be visible in seconds.

A battle raged inside him as if his very soul were being torn in two directions. Fighting the quiet conscience, he leveled the gun. Those words echoed within.

"I don't like this." A slow drawl stopped the man's feet. "We're running blind."

The voice dropped, the murmurs too quiet. A long moment beat as if it were Trace's own heart as he wrestled with his conscience.

Was God telling him to let them go and leave the wagon train at risk? Leave the men who'd killed Ronnie's parents running free?

The tread of hurrying feet faded away, heading back the way the men had come.

It sickened him. He could have shifted his position, gone after them, opened fire. The cowards would have run, and Trace could have picked them off one by one.

Even now he could hunt them. But it was as if the hand of God pressed him into this kneeling position.

Maybe he could see their faces. He'd be another witness. He could at least measure his description against Deb's to make sure these were the same three men.

He could move then. He holstered his gun. He wouldn't use it unless he was faced with a gunman ready to attack.

He steadily covered the ground between him and the outlaws. Slipping up, nearer, nearer.

Only a curve separated them now. Trace

left the trail. He didn't think the men knew he was here and he wanted to remain concealed. If he got the chance, he'd take a prisoner. Not kill anyone who wasn't aiming at him, but he'd be glad to haul one of them back to Carson City under arrest. Even more than one. Let the sheriff look at old wanted posters and ask these men some hard questions.

He felt the difference in his gut, from vengeance to justice, and he was grateful now to the still, small voice that had stopped him from opening fire.

He'd see them in a few more steps. He eased forward and saw them walking away through thick bushes and leaves. A snake-thin man. One a bit taller, still thin as a rail, but he moved like a coiled muscle. It reminded Trace too of the wild longhorns he'd rounded up. Dangerous critters. Kill you first chance they got. The third man was big and burly. Gray hair showed under his wide-brimmed hat. None of these varmints were kids. They might've been around ten years ago.

"Let's go back and see about thinnin' out those wagon trains." The high-pitched voice Deb had mentioned. Trace wasn't sure which man was speaking, but he thought it was Snake Man. "We don't have to wait until we attack. We can take a few of the tougher men out tonight."

His muscles stiffened. If this was their plan, Trace would have to act now.

"Stupid fool. If y'all hurt even one of 'em" — Trace was sure this was the big man speaking — "they'll be callin' the law, and everyone'll be rarin' to kill, standing on razor's edge. We won't have a lick of a chance."

Listening for their every word, Trace drew nearer, completely silent.

Longhorn said, "I'm out. I'm done. This is the devil's own bargain."

"You skeered you're gonna get in trouble, Dalt?"

They'd called him Dalt. Trace had a name now.

"Nope, I'm plumb skeered," Dalt said, "that I've fallen in with a pack of half-wits. You know I'd kill every man, woman, and child if it meant I'd come away rich, but I ain't interested in a fight I can't win. Anyhow, Luth'll kill you when he finds out you're at this."

"I can handle him, so leave that be. Be thinkin' of the money in those wagons. It's a prosperous bunch. Lots of stock, too. Enough we'll live high through a cold winter." The big man sounded coaxing now.

Appealing to the man's greed.

"I think we can do it." Greed was winning out. "But not if you attack now. If that's the plan, I'm hittin' the trail."

"We won't. We'll watch 'em. Learn where they post sentries, learn who's tough and who sleeps on watch. You'll stay then?" the big man asked gruffly.

"I could use a stake." The man turned, and Trace saw half his face. For just a second the man's eyes swept past him and Trace froze. There were plenty of trees between them, with Trace in deep shadow. But if he could see that man, it was possible the man could see him.

The man looked forward without reacting, and Trace dared to breathe again. This had to be the man Deb saw. Dalt was his name. Trace itched to look through wanted posters. The sheriff had suggested it to Deb, but Trace hadn't wanted to take the time. Now that they both knew what to look for, maybe they should go back.

"What about that witness?" Dalt asked. "Those two folks spreading the word about us?"

"We've got 'em on the run now. We can catch up to them later. They've done their damage. Let's go see just how savvy these movers are before we worry more about those two."

If he could just see a little more, see the faces of the other two men. He rounded a big oak and walked straight into full view of a huge grizzly bear not ten feet away. It should've been in hibernation, but if it hadn't eaten enough and gotten fat enough, hunger might've driven him to stay awake. It might drive him to eat a man.

Trace froze. His hand went to his pistol and knew that was a ridiculous defense against this monster. The grizzly rose to his hind legs and roared. He swung a paw and cracked a young tree in half.

One of the men on the trail, the one with the high-pitched voice, said, "That's a grizz. Let's get outta here."

The sound of running feet on the trail faded while Trace took one step back, then another. Feeling his way, fumbling for the big oak he'd just stepped around, he was tempted to duck behind it, but it was too close. He needed distance before he made any sudden moves. He kept opening space. Trace judged the bear to be near nine feet tall. And if he was skinny from hunger, it didn't show with that thick brown hair. The grizz flexed paws the size of dinner plates, its claws bared. He roared until Trace was shaking in his boots.

Bracing himself for the charge, Trace continued back. Fifteen feet, then twenty, then thirty. Then his desperate eyes noticed another oak tree a few feet to his left. He jumped behind it. Then he spun around, keeping the tree between him and the grizzly, and ran for his life.

Listening for the roar of a charging bear, Trace thought only of space, of getting out of this with his hide in one piece.

And then he thought of Deb, hidden away, left far behind. If something happened to him, what would become of her?

But the bear wasn't coming. Trace was mostly sure. The outlaws were on the trail heading straight away from the direction he was going, with no plans to kill today, but soon enough.

Now he headed for the trail. Once there, even the tiny game trail would make for better traveling. His normal speed was driven higher by the close call with the bear and his fear for Deb.

It felt like running home.

CHAPTER 22

Deb knew the sound of those feet.

She'd been on edge, paying attention to every sound, every bird tweet, listening for crackling twigs, branches rustling against each other. Praying with all her might.

But she didn't even hesitate to lower her gun, uncock it, tuck it into her bag, and start climbing.

"You all right, Deb?"

And he was warning her that he was coming, so there'd be no accidental shooting. Also letting her know he was out of earshot of the outlaws.

"I'm fine." Her head popped up at the top of the pile of trees. She couldn't help but smile when she saw him. "I didn't hear any gunfire."

"I heard them, but I never got close enough to even take a shot." He cleared his throat, "Not that I was going to take a shot anyway . . . if I didn't have to."

Deb climbed down so fast, Trace didn't have a chance to come up and help her. She wanted to show him she was no burden. Also, she was glad not to be alone anymore.

"When you left you were furious, Trace. You look better now."

"I am. God had a little talk with me about hate and revenge."

Startled, Deb looked at him as he caught her arm and started them walking along the white stone. "The men aren't following us. I overheard them say they were going to stake out the wagon train but not attack until the trail that goes over the Sierra Nevadas, so we have a few days to plan. Let's get down there and search for our horses. Oh, and I tangled with a grizzly, just a little."

"Tangled with a grizzly?" Deb had heard of the giant bears but she'd yet to see one. They were known for their ferocious temper. "Just a little?"

"Yep, the bear got in between us just enough to get the outlaws moving back toward the wagon train and me heading back to you. They never knew I was there — the men. The bear spotted me sure enough." With a disgusted tone, Trace added, "I wanted to at least get a look at them. I hoped to maybe get the drop on them, or separate them somehow and take a prisoner."

"You against three men?"

Trace was leading her, and for a second he glanced back and gave her a shrug. "I'd've been careful. I'd've waited until I could do it without gettin' myself killed." He pointed ahead. "There's a fork in this game trail that'll take us downhill."

Deb couldn't make out the trail they were on, let alone notice a fork in it.

"We'll hopefully pick up our horses and ride on to Ringo. We'll get a meal there and ask around if anyone's seen those men. Ringo hasn't got a sheriff last I was there."

Trace veered off downhill. "I got a look at one of the outlaws. I think he's the same one you saw." He told Deb everything the men had said. "I also heard two names. The one we both saw was called Dalt. They also mentioned someone named Luth, but it was someone they were talking about, not one of the three. Lawmen travel the area. Lots of lawlessness due to silver. Maybe we'll see a marshal along the trail, and we can ask him if Dalt and Luth are wanted men. We've got time because those varmints are hanging back for now."

Deb could see a trail, sort of, if she used her imagination. The evergreen branches still scratched at her, and the bare branches reached out and clawed like skeletal fingers. The scrub brush and young trees caught at her ankles. Yet she wore a heavy coat and warm wool stockings, so mostly she hurried along unharmed.

Feeling a little giddy from having Trace come back, and knowing those men were far away, Deb said, "Can I ask a question?"

"Sure."

"How did God talk to you?"

That earned her a look back and a big smile. "I left here killing mad, Deb."

"I noticed," she said dryly.

That got another smile out of him, but he didn't slow his pace. "I told you I went hunting men like this, those who massacred my own wagon train, and I kept at it for a couple of years. I thought I'd either driven them off or killed them all. But these men are working so much like the others did, they have to be the same men."

"When did you come out here exactly?"

Trace shrugged without missing a step on the steep downward slope. "It's been ten years."

"It's 1867, Trace. Two years after you got here is when the Comstock Lode really went wild. Are you sure you killed so many men you drove them off, or did they just go to mining or start doing silver heists and robbing miners instead of pioneers?"

Trace stopped so suddenly she stumbled into him, and only his steady strength kept them from tumbling to the ground.

"I've never thought of that." He caught both her upper arms and looked into her eyes with what seemed to her like hope.

"Do you really know how many men you killed? Did you see their bodies?"

"Uh . . ." He looked through her, into the past. "I-I remember I was frustrated how few bodies there were."

Deb hugged him, imagining how angry he was, how vengeful, how scared and sad.

He caught her close and held tight. "There were some, Deb. Don't go thinking this was all just me shooting wild. Sometimes when I knew I'd hit something, I'd get there and find blood, but I'm a crack shot. I hit what I aim at. I could tell they'd been killed and carried off. They'd want to carry off their dead to keep anyone from recognizing a body and connecting him to a gang of outlaws."

"Killed — are you sure? Or wounded?"

Shaking his head, Trace let go of her and headed on down. "I need to think."

"All right, but you never really told me about God speaking to you."

"Well, Deb, He didn't speak out loud or

nuthin'. He didn't sound like thunder comin' out of a cloud. What happened was, I remembered that verse we talked about."

"You mean *'the voice of one crying in the wilderness'*?"

"Yep, that's been a verse I've loved for a long time. It's made me feel less alone from the first time I read it. And that popped into my head. It just reminded me I'm a God-fearing man. A Bible-believing man. I ain't never quite gotten to where I can turn the other cheek. I especially can't turn it when I see someone else being hurt. I think God wants the strong to protect the weak, doesn't He?"

Deb didn't answer. She'd read her Bible well, but maybe not quite as well as Trace.

"Anyway, that verse went through my head, and I couldn't pull the trigger. Then I didn't really have to choose because those men never came into my view. Almost like the hand of God blocked their way or entered their thoughts to make them fear heading into unknown country with some-one maybe waiting for them.

"I might've gone ahead and done some-thing terrible, shot them from cover. Just mowed them down, like the worst, most sin-ful part of myself."

"And put an end to their murderous attacks?"

Trace said, "Yep, that was riding me hard. But I didn't do it. I did go after them, though. Like I said, I hoped I could've seen their faces or maybe even captured one or more of them. The grizzly was just *there,* right in front of me. I stopped. The outlaws heard the roar and took to runnin'. If that wasn't a sign from God to stop being so angry, I don't know what was."

Deb wondered if, instead, it was God saving his life because he'd have been in terrible danger if he'd caught up with the three evil men.

But whether that bear was a sign or not, she was glad Trace seemed to have let loose of his fury.

"There's the trail we ran off of. Those men were heading away from us, but let's still take care." Trace's voice dropped to a whisper. He stepped out only a few inches into the trail when she heard him laugh quietly and a whistle broke the air.

"Our horses, both of them, about a hundred yards away and coming fast." He stayed at the edge of the woods and held Deb back, no doubt worried the outlaws might be coming.

Then she saw past the thin layer of trees

and Trace's wide shoulders, and his black mustang trotted up to him. Trace wasted no time plunking her on her own saddle. "Get going." He slapped her mare, and they were gone. The mare seemed eager to move fast.

His horse galloped right behind her. She pushed her horse as best she could. Trace should've had the lead, but she could sense he was holding back, setting himself in place to shield her if anyone closed from behind and opened fire. And unlike that game trail, Deb could see this one well enough. It was a road cut into a level strip surrounded by trees and mountains sloping up on both sides. No way to get lost here.

Deb didn't say anything. Instead, she bent low and urged every bit of speed she could out of the willing horse. Trace would never let her shield him, so all she could do was put as much space as possible between herself and the threat of those men.

They rode to Glenbrook, where Trace asked his questions and learned nothing more, and then they rode north to Ringo. It wasn't late enough to stop. Trace chafed because he could ride no farther for the day.

Yes, he needed to ask questions. It wouldn't take the rest of the day, but it wouldn't be proper to ride on out of town with the next boardinghouse or hotel too far for them to reach until long after dark — especially because he needed to stop in several small settlements along the way — and none of those settlements had places in which to sleep over.

He eyed Bolling's Boardinghouse in the midafternoon sun. It looked tidy, with two full stories. The second floor had a row of six windows. A line of horses was tied out front. "We need to get rooms."

"It's quite early to stop, isn't it?"

Trace didn't want to go into proper and sleeping and how late was too late. Desperation gave him an idea. "Remember how I said I'd show you Lake Tahoe?"

"Do we have time for that?" Deb rode up to the boardinghouse and swung down as Trace tied his horse to the hitching post.

The way Trace saw it, they had nothing but time. "Let's see about rooms and then ride up the trail. There's a great view at the top of a trail just west of town. We won't ride all the way down to the shore, but there's a beautiful overlook close by."

Deb arched a brow at him. "You've seemed to be in a great hurry, Trace. Suddenly we have time for sight-seeing?"

He didn't mind a smart, logical-thinking woman, but right now it was a nuisance.

"Yep, we do."

An explanation only gave her more ideas for questions. He headed inside, and she came along quietly.

The boardinghouse had two rooms available. "You'll need to pay now," said the innkeeper. "I've had folks such as yourselves passing through change their minds and ride on without paying. Then I miss out on rent because I refuse other travelers."

After paying Mr. Bolling, Trace said, "We're riding up to look at Lake Tahoe."

The innkeeper's face lightened. "I've traveled far and away, youngsters, but I will tell you, short of that huge canyon down in Arizona Territory, I've never seen a prettier sight than Lake Tahoe. And there's no nicer view than the one right up the trail. Have a good ride. It's getting late in the season for it, but you should make it there with no trouble." The man gave them directions. "Above the tree line it gets a little steep. The horses can manage if they're mountain-bred stock, but I usually tie mine off and walk the rest of the way to the top. There's a second trail that leads to a big old mansion on the lake, but the owner's unfriendly. Don't go that way."

He took what little they had packed that Trace didn't insist on keeping with him and waved them off with a smile.

Outside, Deb muttered, "No trouble? Hah, spoken like a man who isn't going himself and already has his money."

Trace chuckled and would've boosted Deb onto her horse, but she swung up before he could get to her.

CHAPTER 23

They rode the trail the old man had recommended and were soon swallowed up in the trees, climbing. The trail was rugged, rocky, and surrounded by a thick forest. They'd been winding their way up, down, or sideways all day. No level ground anywhere.

"It's so quiet here," Deb said beneath a canopy of leafless oaks. "It's like we're in a church."

"A lot of the birds have flown south. Animals are starting to hibernate." *Except for that one grizzly.* "Or even if they don't hibernate, they spend long hours asleep in caves and burrows."

Trace was always sharply aware of the woods around him — particularly right now, for killer bears — but he admitted that Deb was a powerful distraction.

They reached a large pine tree that had fallen across the trail, like an ancient sign demanding they halt. They could've made it around — their horses would have gone on — but this was the spot the old man had recommended they leave the horses behind.

Dismounting, they began walking, Trace holding Deb's hand. There was snow and ice all around them. The trail was mostly rough and stony, keeping them from slipping. They managed to make decent time without falling. But small slicks of ice and a drift here and there made walking tricky.

Trace saw the mountaintop looming before them and knew in a few more paces they'd round the last outcropping of stone and view the lake below. He took Deb's hand more securely. He glanced at her and wanted to say the lake was the prettiest thing he'd ever seen, but here was Deb. Lake Tahoe paled in comparison.

Then they stepped around that last boulder.

She gasped.

Though he'd beheld the lake many times, Trace gasped right along with her. It was a powerful sight.

"I've never seen anything like it," Deb murmured. "Surely it must be the most beautiful site on earth. The lake itself is so high up here in the mountains. And look at the white peaks and the forests surrounding them, all reflecting on the water. It's spectacular. How is there such a huge lake up here?"

Trace removed his hat, raked his hair back with a gloved hand, and settled the Stetson back on his head. "I always wonder the same thing. Seems like it oughta just flow down the mountainside. It must be trapped somehow. There are gushers of water coming in." He pointed at several spraying out of the rocky heights around the lake. Others trickled down gently. "Some are natural springs, but there's lots of snowmelt and rainfall, too. And I've heard tell there is only one river flowing out, the Truckee. I reckon it just comes in as fast as it goes."

Without tearing her eyes from the view, Deb reached out and took Trace's hand. "This is so wonderful. Thank you for taking the time to show me this, Trace."

Long minutes passed in silence. Deb stared at the lake as if it were a drink and she'd been thirsty most of her life.

They stood in the buffeting wind, looking down on the water, white-rimmed with ice, reflecting the dazzling sky, mostly white with clouds. But the sky opened, and the sun shone down. The lake reflected the stunning pure blue. Then more clouds scudded across and turned Tahoe white again. There was snow in the air, mostly tiny crystals rather than flakes.

"It's so cold, but I can hardly bear to stop looking."

Trace, his heart pounding from the beauty and the woman he shared it with, wrapped his arm around her shoulders and pulled her close. Keeping her warm, they lingered and watched.

"This is one of the most perfect moments of my life." Her eyes, bright as the sky, blue as the lake, glowed as she turned from the view and looked at him. "And it's thanks to you. Everything that's happened since I met you has been a revelation. You've taught me how fine a man can be. I've had to do some growing up to understand that. My father left me with a poor image of men. I've harbored that in my heart. But because I've met you, I now understand that not all men are like him."

Trace smiled and said, "Deb, I never dreamed my life could be so much finer than what I've lived for the last few years. The beginning was harsh, but since I got settled, had hired men, found people I could talk to, I've thought my life was busy and full and happy. But I had no idea how much better it could be until you came along."

"Any woman would have meant just as much to you, Trace."

"No." He shook his head in firm denial. "That's not true. Gwen is wonderful, an angel with the children, and a good, strong, fine and decent woman. But nothing stirs in me for her, except maybe the affection I'd have for a . . . sister." *Or a sister-in-law.* He wasn't quite ready to say that out loud. "It's only you, Deb, and it'll always be you. If you stay with me, it'll be the greatest blessing God could give me. If you go, I'll miss you forever."

Deb's mouth gaped open. Her hands clung to his. Which he appreciated a lot more than . . . say, if she took off running.

Plunging on, almost sick with fear, he said, "Marry me, Deb. Please give me this chance at such great happiness. I promise I'll devote my life to —"

Deb tore one hand free of his and pressed her gloved fingertips to his mouth.

He stopped talking, and his heart sank. He braced himself to hear *no.*

"Yes," she said.

And now his smile broke like the Nevada sun. His heart leapt with the joyful energy of the rivulets cascading down the mountain to Lake Tahoe.

"Trace, I just said, only moments ago, that this was one of the most perfect moments of my life, and now you've made it even more wonderful. You told me we'd spend the winter getting to know each other, and I should be thinking of you, deciding if we'd suit. And even this morning, I was thinking I needed to move on, begin the life I have planned. But when you asked me if I really wanted to run a newspaper, well, I've already given that a lot of thought. I don't need a newspaper. And I don't need the winter. I can think of nothing but you. I would be the luckiest woman in the world to have such a fine man as my husband."

It was only pure grit that kept him from collapsing with relief. Instead, he dragged her into his arms and kissed her.

The cold was forgotten. The warmth of her embrace and their love for each other burned through him as her arms came around his neck.

The beauty of their kiss and the beauty of the lake wound around him, creating a moment as precious as any he could have imagined. It was a moment to inspire a man for the rest of his life.

"Are you done with your woman, Trace?" Tavibo stepped out from behind the rock that sheltered them.

Deb screamed.

Trace caught her in midair as she jumped

back. He pictured her falling off the high ledge all the way down to the lake. A bad end to his proposal.

"It's all right, Deb. He's a friend. Tavibo is a Paiute and a good man. I've known him for years."

"Friend?" Deb asked, her voice trembling, but no more screaming. "I'm sorry. I — my — I'm sorry."

Tavibo nodded as if to accept the apology.

Holding her tight, because he'd have his hands full getting down there and fishing her out before she chilled clear to a chunk of ice, he asked, "Is there trouble? Why are you so far from your winter village?"

"The Paiutes watch the comings and goings of those we know, and many we do not know. We saw you ride away from your land with your woman."

"I'm not his woman."

Trace squeezed her tight. "Yes, you are."

She tilted her head as if she'd never thought of it before, but now that she did, she said, "You're right. I am your woman."

Trace liked that.

"I saw you leave home. It is not a time for travel, so I wondered if you sought the men who killed all those from the wagon train. I had news of that and wanted to tell you, but I waited until you were well off the trail so I could be sure to talk to you alone." His dark eyes shifted to Deb. "I've come to tell you I heard talk among those who trade with your people — that the wagon train that burned was found and the crime was blamed on Paiutes."

Trace clenched his jaw. "I talked to a lawman in Carson City, and he said it was the first he'd heard of the massacre. Who found the train? Who passed on the gossip?"

"Maybe the men who did it started the talk?" Tavibo's black eyes narrowed. "Better to blame others right from the beginning."

"There's another train going through that pass. We caught up with them last night and warned them. I'm going to watch over the path it takes. I've got several days because the wagons move so slowly."

"The Guardian rides again, huh?"

"Can your people help me?" Trace asked. "These folks aren't taking the trail that's had trouble before. But I got close enough to hear the outlaws plan an attack. Because it's new to me, I don't know the good lookouts. I don't know the most likely place for these men to lie in wait. They've had weeks to scout and find the best spots. If we had many eyes on that trail, the outlaws wouldn't have a chance."

His expression grim, Tavibo shook his

head. "I am sorry, my good friend. Our Paiute village is headed south even now. They want to put many miles between them and the next attack. And they are making sure others see them on their migration so there will be evidence to protect them — that is, if the whites accept their own eyes as proof against a Native man."

"Not even you can stay?"

"No, I let them go ahead so I could warn you of the talk, but I will ride hard now to catch up with them. I am sorry, but that is all I can do, and I think you know it's necessary."

"It is, and I do understand why. Thank you for passing this on."

"I must ride now. It is our only hope to protect our people." Tavibo looked at Deb and bowed. "Trace is a fine man. He will do well by you."

As silently as he came, Tavibo walked back into the woods. Even watching him go, Trace lost sight of him within seconds.

Trace turned to Deb. "I hope you'll get a chance to know him better. You'll like him. He taught me a lot of what I know about life in the West — though I'd already learned some on my own."

"If he's your friend, Trace, then he's mine as well. Now let's get back to town and out of the cold."

The sun lowered, and the wind picked up and drove the clouds away as they rode to Ringo. They talked quietly of the future, holding hands when the trail was wide enough to allow it.

As they entered town, Deb noticed, tucked behind the boardinghouse, a little building of raw wood that was so new it hadn't seasoned yet, with a roughly fashioned cross above the front door. A man wearing a parson's collar stood at the open door, sweeping dust out onto the stoop — a small landing on top of three steps. He closed the door as he stepped out and went to work making sure the stoop was swept clean, too.

Trace pointed to the building. "Let's get married, Deb." He flashed a smile that she could never look at enough.

"Right now?" She thought of Gwen and wished she could be here. But how? If they went home, they'd have to go somewhere to find a preacher, and with winter coming, that might be dangerous. And not all settlements even had a parson living among them.

Besides, she wanted to be married right now, this moment. Trace hadn't spoken of love, but his words echoed with deep affection. She wondered if the words were in him and if she would ever hear them. And just because he hadn't said the words, did it matter, when she was sure of his feelings toward her and that he held her in such warm regard?

"Right now," he replied. He sounded so confident, she set aside her regret about Gwen. Trace was her family now, just as surely as her sister was.

"Yes, Trace. Let's get married."

They rode to the rustic church, and the parson straightened from his sweeping to greet them. Though it was cold outside, he wore only a white shirt and black vest with his black pants. He was a stocky man, balding, with round glasses.

"We'd like to get married, Parson," Trace said.

Deb nearly gasped to hear him tell someone else the news. The idea was still so new to her.

Holding the broom in one hand, the parson adjusted his glasses with the other, and a smile that seemed to surround them spread across his face. "I'm Parson Stossmeier. I love performing wedding ceremonies. Hitch your horses and come on in. It's too cold out here anyway. You can get out of the wind inside the church. I'll run next door and fetch my coat, Bible, and prayer book. And I'll bring back my wife to stand as witness."

Trace led Deb inside the church, which was only slightly warmer.

Shivering from the long, cold ride, and from excitement and nerves, she wished they could light the potbellied stove that sat in one corner. But they'd be done and gone before it even began to warm the place. It was probably only lit for Sunday services.

"Deb," Trace said and took her hand, "thank you for saying yes. I'm going to promise, along with my vows to God, to do my best to make you happy all your life." He lifted her hand and pulled off her glove. "I have no ring or any idea where I'd find such. I only know a man gives a woman a ring because I read it in one of my books. I'm sure there isn't a ring in Ringo." He chuckled. "That sounds funny." He kissed the back of her finger, right where a ring should be. "But I promise to buy you a ring just as soon as I find one."

"Hush now," she said. "We won't worry about such nonsense as a ring. Not when you've already given me so much. The beautiful home we will live in. So many things." She fought the urge to start listing the things she was thankful for. She'd said it so many times. And she didn't want this marriage to be out of gratitude only. She didn't say yes because she wanted his protection, or anything else he could give her. She simply wanted to pledge her life to him . . . because she loved him.

He leaned very close, so close she didn't feel cold anymore.

The church door swung open, and Parson Stossmeier strode in smiling, wearing a coat, his cheeks pink from the chill. Right behind him followed a lady only a bit shorter and a bit rounder.

She was grinning, too. Wearing a heavy wool coat and a bonnet lined with sheepskin, the lady clapped her hands together and held them under her chin. "I'm Mrs. Stossmeier. Here to witness your vows. A wedding — how wonderful."

It *was* wonderful. The parson spoke their vows with good cheer. Trace and Deb repeated them before God. Afterward, the parson's wife gave them both a big hug and invited them to share the evening meal with her and her husband.

As kind as this couple was, Deb desperately wanted to be with her new husband right now. But she hesitated to say so. It seemed rude.

"I appreciate that very much, ma'am," Trace said, sliding his arm around Deb's waist, "but the boardinghouse will provide dinner, and I'd as soon spend the evening alone with my wife."

"And well you should." Mrs. Stossmeier beamed with approval. "It's a night for romance. Thank you for including us in your happy occasion."

CHAPTER 24

Trace held Deb's hand as they led the horses to the livery stable where they stripped off leather and some supplies. They left the horses and saddles behind, taking with them their bedrolls and saddlebags. Then they started walking toward the boardinghouse.

He stayed so close to Deb, it wasn't proper . . . not that he was sure. He had no notion of what was proper or not now that they were married. But he suspected even married folks ought to put a bit more space between themselves when out in public.

It didn't make him let her go. And she didn't push him away as they walked through the softly falling snow. They went inside and were warm for the first time in so long, Trace shivered. Deb looked up at him and smiled and shivered, too.

Trace led her to the innkeeper. "We just got hitched, sir. I paid for two rooms, but

I . . . uh, that is, we need only one now." He shivered again, and cold weather had nothing to do with it this time.

Mr. Bolling gave them a generous smile. "Not to worry. If I'd turned renters away I might feel different — but probably not. I'm happy to refund your money." He plucked a key off a row of nails behind him. "It's just a few minutes until Ma rings the supper bell. I'll show you to your room, then get the baggage you left and bring them to you. You've got a few minutes to take off your coats and wash up." He pointed to the hallway that ran alongside the stairway. "Dining room is down thataway. We've got a good crowd tonight, so Ma made plenty."

Keeping up a running chatter about where things were and such, he led them up the stairs and down a short hallway to a corner room. He unlocked the door and then handed them the key, saying he'd be back shortly.

Trace peeked into the room as the man walked away, then closed the door behind them. "It's a nice-sized room," he said to his new bride. "That fella's being mighty kind to us."

Trace shed his gloves, coat, and hat and hung them on a row of pegs near the door. Deb did the same. There was a basin and a pitcher of water in the room, and they took the time to wash away a long day's travel.

The innkeeper returned with their few bags just as they'd finished cleaning up. "It's a night for love. Come on down and eat, and if you don't stay long, Ma and I'll not be surprised." He walked out chuckling.

Trace closed the door and turned to pull Deb into his arms. "I just want a few minutes to let it sink in that you're really my wife." He sighed, leaned down, and rested his forehead against hers.

He heard the faintest breath of a laugh from her. "It is surprising, isn't it?" Deb wrapped her arms around his waist. They stood there together, quietly, at peace with the world.

Then Trace lifted his head just far enough to see her eyes. He moved forward and kissed her. His arms tightened while hers rose to encircle his neck.

He pulled her closer. Tilted his head and deepened the kiss. One of her hands slid from around his neck and rested, palm open, on his cheek. Her thumb brushed his lips.

The dinner bell rang.

Groaning quietly, Trace broke off the kiss. "All day long I haven't given you a minute to do more than chew jerky. I don't want to share a moment's time with anyone else, but I suppose we'd better go eat."

Grinning, Deb nodded. "I'd forgotten about food, but you're right."

The bell rang again, almost as if with the one ringing it knew they'd need a good nudge.

Pulling away and taking her hand, Trace led Deb out and down the stairs. Though the food smelled delicious, nothing called to him like holding his new wife.

Trace had a sudden thought about the night to come that had never entered his head when she'd been in the room with him. He missed a stair and had to grab the hand railing to keep from tumbling all the way down to the first floor. It was a relief he hadn't managed to drag her down the stairs with him, head over heels.

Deb caught hold of him. "Are you all right? What made you trip like that?"

He wasn't all right, yet he didn't know how to bring it up — what it was he'd been thinking about when he stumbled just now. But then they were downstairs and in the dining room, other folks around them. Some had already gone in to take their seats at the table.

"I'll tell you later," Trace said.

He probably had to confess, but how

could he? He had no idea what exactly went on between a husband and wife on their wedding night. Maybe no one knew such things and had to discover them on their own. And Trace feared his being alone so much had stunted a big part of his education.

Of course, he lived on a cattle ranch so he had some idea. But without the hooves and such, he was afraid it was different for men and women.

He didn't see how she'd know, either.

If they'd just stayed in the room, gone on the way they'd been going, he'd've never thought of it and they'd've been all right . . . at least he hoped so.

Now, instead of being eager for the night to go on, he was terrified. He decided to eat real slow.

Deb picked at her food. She wanted to ask for seconds, just to slow things down, but her stomach was in knots and her throat bone-dry. She could barely swallow the food she had.

Her ma had died before there'd been time for a talk about . . . married things. And anyway, Ma hadn't cared much for Pa and probably quietly prayed neither of her girls would ever get saddled with a husband.

That was just a suspicion Deb had. No such words had been spoken.

She practiced ways of telling her husband she'd like more time.

We really don't know each other well, Trace. I'd like more privacy before married . . . events pass between us. Privacy like they'd get while sharing Trace's cabin with Gwen and two small children?

Could we just check to see if the innkeeper still has two rooms available?

Despite her best efforts to separate her meal of chicken and dumplings into bites of one drop per spoonful, Deb's plate was eventually empty. She'd even lingered over a piece of pie. All the other guests had left the dining room, and the innkeeper's wife had glanced in on them rather nervously twice now, no doubt hoping to clear their table.

Trace scraped his chair back so suddenly, Deb jumped. She stared at him as he nearly knocked it over and almost fell.

He stood and gave her an overly bright smile. "I'm finished."

The way he said it sounded a little like the crack of doom. He had to mean with his meal, but something about his extremely, almost madly happy expression made her wonder if the words meant something else.

Like perhaps he was finished delaying the inevitable.

She cleared her throat and wiped her mouth. "Yes," she said and stood.

Trace offered her his hand.

Grimly determined to do her wifely duty, she let him lead her out of the dining room. She didn't know why he was in such an all-fired hurry.

Deb slowly roused from what seemed like the deepest, most restful sleep of her life. Before she opened her eyes, she was aware that something seemed wrong. When she opened her eyes she knew it was the room.

Had Trace and his men built yet another house?

Then she realized she wasn't in bed alone.

She looked down and saw a strong arm draped over her belly and felt the solid form of someone lying beside her.

And it all came back in a rush.

Married.

She had gotten married yesterday to Trace. She was now, good heavens, Deb Riley. She'd changed her name.

Snuggled close against Trace, she knew she'd changed a lot of things.

"You awake, wife?" Trace asked, his voice raspy from sleep and warm with affection.

She couldn't believe she could feel so close to another human being.

"I am, husband." She heard a quiet chuckle.

"We've got a lot of stops to make today, people to talk to, many miles to travel, and a mighty big announcement to make to your sister."

"You're right." They rose to get on with the day.

Deb went to the window to see if the deep snow had finally come.

"Trace" — all her cheerful calm vanished — "get over here." Instantly at her side, Deb said to him, "Look at that pair of oxen."

The big Holsteins disappeared down a trail into the forest.

Trace was gone, dragging on his clothes. Deb did the same, then pulled on her boots and laced them up quick as chain lightning. She left the room only a few steps behind him.

He didn't tell her to stay behind and it was just as well, because she wasn't letting him go after those oxen alone.

Sprinting out the front door of the hotel, she charged after Trace, dashing as only he could toward the livery. A man stepped out of the stable as Trace ran in, and they crashed into each other hard enough they both ended up on the ground. By the time Deb got there, Trace was on his feet again, the other man standing before him, gun drawn.

Had he run into a man quick to draw and shoot? Deb got to Trace's side, but before she could say a word, she saw the silver star on the man's vest. A lawman. Heaving a sigh of relief, she opened her mouth to talk, but Trace beat her to it.

"I'm sorry, sir. I'm running because I just saw a man driving a pair of oxen I know are stolen. Those cattle came from the wagon train my wife rode west on. The men who attacked them left a lot of folks dead. If we can catch him, we —"

"Hold up there." The snap in the lawman's voice brought complete silence. He still had his gun out too, though it was pointed at the ground now. "Are you talkin' about those black-and-white oxen that just left town?"

"You saw them? Good. Do you know — ?"

"Quiet!" The lawman had black eyes and looked to be in a mood to match them. "I know the man who just left town. I passed him as I rode in. Name of Paddy Candle. I've known him for years. He just bought those oxen. They're an unusual team, huge critters and a matching pair. I asked him about 'em and have no reason to believe Paddy would lie to me. I'd put his word above a stranger's any day."

"Well, we don't mean to accuse an old friend of yours of nuthin', Sheriff," Trace said.

"I'm a US Marshal. Marshal Bates."

"Trace Riley. And this is my wife, Deb. If he lives around here and has for years, then finding him will be easy. If you trust him, that's good enough for me. But he had to buy that team somewhere, and like you said, they're an unusual pair. We need to talk to him. We need to —"

This time Marshal Bates cut Trace off with a single hand gesture and a cold glare.

Trace glanced at Deb, and she could see he wasn't going to just quit talking.

"I know Candle well. He's an honest man, but he's not a man who suffers fools. I agree that team is odd enough we need to find out where he bought 'em. He'll talk to me alone, but he's a man who won't be pushed and is spoiling for a fight. If you show up, all upset, he'll never tell you nuthin' and enjoy watching you work yourselves up. You tell me what's going on. I'll handle Paddy alone. Then I'll bring back any information I get from him."

Trace pulled in a slow deep breath. Deb

saw him fight his need to hurry. He said, "We ran out of our boardinghouse without breakfast when we saw that team. Come on back with us and share a meal, and we'll tell you everything. We've got a story of a massacre, robbery, and it looks like there are plans for more of it. We'd appreciate your help, Marshal."

Bates nodded in terse agreement.

Trace gestured for Deb to go ahead back to the boardinghouse. They weren't really being slowed down much. They'd left what supplies they had in the room, and they normally would have eaten anyway. Those oxen had just sped their morning up. But now Marshal Bates would handle that, and they'd have a second lawman helping them find the killers.

After they'd told him the whole story, Bates said, "I know at least Dalt, that's Dalton Callow. Last I heard he was in prison in California. I was working California then, so we knew he was an outlaw. He's a mean one. I always knew he could've been a murderer. Must've served his time and got out. I don't know any of his saddle partners. I'll start hunting and see if anyone around here's seen him, and who Callow runs with."

Trace thanked the marshal for his help,

then added, "We heard the name Luth, too. Anyone around here answer to that name?"

"I'll have to think on that. If the real name's Luther, is it the man's first or last name?" He shook his head. "I can't think of anyone named that right off. But I've got your description, and I'll be digging around."

"We'll go back to that wagon train now, warn them. They can get some men together and scout the hills. These outlaws are there, waiting and watching."

"You know how late it is in the season. And they're fully warned. Better for them to head on through and keep moving. When they get to that stretch over the Sierra Nevadas, that's when they need to be scouting the hills. Those three men after them may not even stay nearby. If I were them I'd push on to the trail and find overlooks and well-placed cover and get ready. I will make sure and talk to them and warn them they need to move on through on that trail, not lay up for the night. But you're not going back. With yourself on edge and all those pioneers out there, there's bound to be shooting trouble and the wrong folks are gonna get killed."

Trace's jaw tightened at the lawman's words. "Fine, Marshal. Then we'll go on as we planned, and on our way along the west side of Tahoe I'll check in at all the settlements. My ranch is on past the end of South Tahoe so it's right on our way."

Marshal Bates huffed. "Best you just leave it be, kid."

Trace's eyes narrowed, and Deb held her breath. She didn't know if the marshal was a good lawman or not, and as much as chasing bad men wasn't her preferred activity, it chafed her to leave this to the gruff, bad-tempered old coot.

"Are you sure you wouldn't like some help?" Trace asked. "You're going after those Holsteins. You're going out to the wagon train. You're going to check in at the settlements. And it's all gonna be in the next few days because this is all going to happen fast."

"You let me worry about how I do my job." The marshal looked mad enough to start arresting anyone in his sight.

"All right. We'll leave it, Marshal, for now. But we're not going to forget these men. See that you don't, either."

The man's black eyes went cold as death, but he gave a hard, fast nod of his head. "You can be sure I won't. I'll go talk to Candle now, and I'll warn the wagon train. Then I'm going to ride out to that wagon train massacre site, and I'll spread the word at those settlements."

"And it wasn't the Paiutes." Trace clearly didn't like leaving the hunt to someone else, not one bit. But Deb could see he was looking at trouble if he got crossways of the marshal. "It's not their crime, but there are a few things staged to look like it is."

Nodding, Bates got up and headed out.

Trace said to Deb, "Let's go home."

She wished that meant they could be done with all this forever and ride home for the whole winter. But she sincerely doubted it was going to be that easy.

CHAPTER 25

Trace felt a twist of both relief and frustration when they rode into his ranch yard late that night in the cold and dark.

The frustration was easy to explain. He should've stayed on the trail of those men. They were dangerous and shouldn't be allowed to run around loose. He'd come close to turning around a dozen times. This felt like that first day when he'd taken Deb and Gwen and the children home instead of going after those vermin.

But how could he keep hunting after what the marshal had said? He had no choice now, just as he hadn't then. Even so, those men were still roaming free.

He should've stood and fought the day before he met the marshal. He should have dodged that grizzly and gone on after them.

No, he didn't think it was wise to take on three full-grown men without any help except a woman. Granted, a tough woman

— or at least a spunky one — yet he didn't think she had any real skill with that gun. But by the great horn spoon, she had it with her.

So maybe better to say a woman willing to try and be tough.

Still, he could've gone after them in the woods, or gone back to the wagon train instead of coming home. He should have demanded the marshal get a posse together. He should have set out hunting. He'd gotten so close when he might've attacked just hard enough to break up their gang, drive them away, and maybe leave their herd a whole lot thinner. Instead he'd turned aside from the chase.

As stubborn as the marshal was about doing his job himself, and taking offense at Trace's offer to help, he doubted the man would form a posse. And the outlaws were mighty good at sneaking, not a bit afraid to back-shoot a man. In fact, they seemed to like it.

So it was easy to understand his being frustrated.

The relief, however, surprised him. He hadn't known he liked his home quite this much. He suspected he liked it a whole lot more now that he was married to Deb.

"There's smoke coming out of the bunkhouse chimney, Trace." Deb sounded deeply impressed, also very tired. "They got it done, and they've moved in."

"I'm glad. Everyone's got solid walls and a tight roof against the winter." Trace chuckled for a moment.

"So much work and done so fast and with such a good spirit." Deb rode for the barn, Trace right on her heels.

"You go on in, Deb. I'll put your horse up."

"As if I'm one speck more weary than you."

Trace figured it to be well past midnight. He had no pocket watch, and he could've judged decent by the moon, only the night was overcast, with snow coming down and whipping wind in his face and down the back of his neck.

Stripping leather off his horse, he found fresh hay already pitched into Black's manger. His men had planned for him. So he went to help Deb and met her emerging from her horse's stall.

"I got the saddle and bridle off." She sounded prouder than a mama cougar dragging supper home for her cubs.

Trace went in quick to make sure it was all done, then came right back out, leaving her mare happily munching hay. "We made it home." He was so tired, his mind wasn't thinking much past the present moment. He just walked right up to his wife and pulled her into a hug.

With a mild huff of amusement, Deb said, "It's so nice to know a warm bed is waiting for us."

The way she said it gave him a little more energy to get on with settling in for the night. He rested one palm gently on her face and, touching irresistibly silky skin, leaned down to kiss her. "You are the finest kind of woman, Deb. I am so blessed to have you for my wife."

Her light blue eyes, washed gray in the darkness, shimmered. She looked at him so close he felt like she was peering right into his soul.

"I'd have to say the same about you, Trace. The finest man I've ever known." She gave him her warmest smile. "Let's go in. Gwen will be in a room with both youngsters, so we can go right to bed."

Deb was turning to walk out of the barn when Trace caught her arm. He had a strange expression on his face. Worry maybe? Nervousness? Or he might just be overly tired.

"What is it?" she asked.

"Do you think . . . that is, will Gwen . . .

should we — ?" He cleared his throat. "I should probably sleep in the bunkhouse this first night."

The jolt in her heart surprised her. "You don't want to sleep with me?"

Trace drew her into his arms again and kissed her. When he eased back this time, he said, "I can hardly stand the thought of being away from you. Last night, just having someone to hold . . . I have always been a lonely man, Deb. Less so in recent years, but having you for my wife has made me realize just how much I've missed in not knowing the presence of a woman in my life. Being close to you, I feel like a hole in my heart is healing, a hole I didn't even know was there."

"I don't want to be away from you either, Trace. I think it will do no harm for you to stay with me. We'll make sure and explain things to Gwen right away. I'm usually up early with the children and see her for a bit. I'll have time then to keep her from being overly surprised. Come on in with me."

"I would like that very much." He took her hand, not even trying to keep the smile off his face, and walked with her toward the house. The night full of wind and snow, his lips still warm from their kiss, his heart full to overflowing.

She gave him a sideways glance and a quick smile.

He was so dazed about getting to join her, he only noticed Wolf when the dog caught him around the pant leg. Almost like Wolf was trying to guide him to the correct place to sleep.

Well, Wolf didn't know what was what.

Trace followed Deb right into the house. Wolf disappeared into the night before Trace could try to coax him inside. For the first time ever, Trace was warm enough he could almost understand how the critter felt about sleeping on a snowdrift.

Deb considered waking Gwen to tell her the big news. But once in the warm cabin, she was so tired and so deeply chilled, the thought of a celebration was overwhelming.

And there probably would be a celebration. Gwen would be excited for her older sister. There might be some jumping and squealing and giggling — not just by Gwen, either. And that might wake the children up.

And then . . . well, all in all, Deb decided it was best just to sneak in and go to sleep and put all that off until morning. So she didn't make a sound when she led Trace to the bedroom.

Trace.

Her husband.

Straight to the bedroom!

God bless us all, how drastically things have changed.

A glance inside told her the room was empty. Deb had been sharing with Ronnie. But she'd expected Gwen to take the little guy with her to the bedroom she shared with Maddie Sue while Deb was gone.

The young'uns had slept with them since the wagon train had set out. Between the limited space and the cold in Trace's old cabin, it'd seemed wise to continue the arrangement.

This cabin was very well built. Utah had laid split-log floors in the room while she was away. Not a single one of them squeaked, but that might be because Deb was floating a few inches off the floor.

She was tired enough and cold enough and feeling blessed enough that she expected to fall asleep fast and deep in her husband's arms.

She was right about the deep part, but wrong about fast. Trace had other ideas.

Gwen's scream sent Trace stumbling backward into the bedroom. Looking for protection, he glanced back to see Deb spring up from the covers, get twisted in them, fall off the bed, kick the blankets away and dash forward until she slammed right into his back.

"What are you doing in that bedroom with my . . . my . . . my . . . ?" Gwen ran away.

Maddie Sue cried from the bedroom, and seconds later Ronnie chimed in.

Deb ducked around him and headed for the crying little ones, but Gwen blocked her way. Trace was glad Deb was between him and Gwen because she came charging into the room holding a huge knife, one Trace didn't remember owning.

"Gwen, what's wrong?" Deb stepped forward. Trace caught her and held her right in front of him.

"I think she's noticed there's a man in her house," Trace said, firmly behind his bodyguard of a wife.

A moment of dead silence reigned. Well, dead silence except for the howling children and Gwen's heaving breath.

Throwing her hands wide, Deb laughed. "We got married. Trace and I got married while we were in town."

"M-m-married?" Gwen's eyes went from Deb to Trace to the butcher knife. She whisked it behind her back as if afraid he might get the wrong idea.

Or rather get the right idea.

"It's all right, Gwen. I'm proud to have a sister that'd stab a man to protect Deb." He leaned sideways and forward to catch Deb's eye. "We'd be mighty glad to stab someone for you, wouldn't we?"

Deb narrowed her eyes at him. "Let's try to stab as few people as humanly possible."

"Agreed."

The front door slammed open, and Utah charged in, gun drawn. His eyes zipped from one person to the next. "Who screamed?"

Adam was a pace behind him, still tugging on his coat.

Deb spoke up again. "Trace and I got married. We just told Gwen, and she's happy for us."

Utah arched a brow. "That big old knife doesn't say *happy,* not to me."

Gwen marched over to the kitchen table and slapped the knife down with a clatter. Her cheeks pinked up as she said crisply, "I saw a man in the house. I thought it best to arm myself first and talk later."

"Wise thinkin', Miss Gwen." Adam tipped his hat.

Deb rushed into the bedroom and brought out the two sobbing children, one on each hip. Trace took the little boy. Maddie Sue wrapped her arms around Deb's neck, her legs tight on her waist.

Utah grinned. "Congratulations, you two youngsters. I'm glad we got the house done in time for you to have a decent place for yourselves. I plan to start on the barn today. I keep thinking the snow will stop us, but until it does, I'm gonna keep at it."

Trace nodded and said, "Thanks. Sorry to cause such a ruckus." He looked at Deb, who smiled back at him. "And the house looks real nice, Utah." He stopped and let out a sigh. "I haven't seen my cattle for days — I'd better ride out and be a rancher for once."

"The barn's the largest building we'll put up," Utah went on. "So we'll be at chopping trees for a while. A couple of days, probably. Honestly I'm figuring we'll be lucky if we get this one up before the weather hits in earnest. I want to be ready so we can put it up fast. A half-standing building would knock over too easy if the winter shuts us down."

Gwen broke an egg into a bowl with a rather violent crack. Trace exchanged another look with Deb.

"Give me Ronnie and finish getting yourself dressed, Trace. I'll get to work on breakfast, and Gwen and I can take turns dressing for the day."

Gwen gasped, looked down at her night-gown, then swiveled to look in horror at the men. She dropped the second egg, shell and all, into the bowl and ran into her room. She slammed the door much too hard.

Deb decided her sister had a point and took both children with her into her room to dress, as well. Good heavens, the men had been right there.

Being married certainly addled a woman's mind.

As she quickly pulled on her clothes and told the children a very brief version of what getting married meant, she heard the men speaking in muffled voices outside the room. The kitchen door opened and closed, and a few moments later, Trace came into her room.

He was in his longhandles, and come to think of it, at least one of the other men had been, too.

It was not a proper beginning to the day.

And then it got worse.

CHAPTER 26

"I won't be back until this is over, Deb." Trace packed food into a satchel. His bedroll was beside the satchel, all of it on the kitchen table. He finished with the food and then wrapped the satchel in his blanket, all set to tie on the back of Black. Wolf was coming, too.

He heard an odd sound and looked up, expecting to find a wounded cougar in the kitchen with him.

It was his wife. Standing between him and the front door. And from the look on her face, he'd've been better off with the cougar.

Gwen lifted both children by wrapping her arms around their bellies and heading to her bedroom. The door shut with a loud crack. He heard Maddie Sue say, "Why are we in here? Why is Deb yelling at Trace?"

Then a shushing noise from Gwen. Strange. Why were they in there? And Deb wasn't yelling.

"What's the matter?" He rushed to Deb's side, expecting to find she'd stepped on a nail or something.

"You're leaving?" She was speaking in a really high — and loud — voice. He'd never heard that exact tone before. "We've been married for two days and you're leaving?"

He'd said that, hadn't he? Just now. Then he thought he might know the problem. "Don't worry, I'm coming back." He'd already said that, too.

What was she thinking? That he was moving away? That he didn't like being married? That he was thinking of hunting for gold in San Francisco?

Women were so confusing.

"And just when will that be?"

Good, now he could reassure her. "I'll be back as soon as I find the outlaws and haul them to jail or kill them."

There was that sound again. He glanced down. She was standing solid on her two feet, so it couldn't be a nail.

"What's the matter?" He'd asked that before, but no answer had been forthcoming. At least not one he could make any sense of.

"Do you think that *maybe* you should have told me about this?" She spoke in an odd way, slowly, one word at a time. He was pretty sure her teeth were clenched.

"I'm telling you right now, Deb." He should have told her before. He was listening, learning.

She drew in a deep breath. She flexed her hands, and it was only then that he noticed she'd made them into fists.

"I mean, leaving the ranch, heading out on a mission that might just get you *killed*. Seems to me like the sort of thing a married couple should discuss. Not a simple announcement that you're leaving and you'll be back once you've either captured or killed three brutal murderers, all by yourself. As if you *weren't* leaving on a life-or-death trip and might never see me again."

Well, he didn't plan on dying, but then who did? "We've talked about me guarding that trail. I'm The Guardian. I know we talked about that. How could this come as a surprise?" He paused to study her. "But it has. I expected you to know what I had to do, and you didn't. So I am sorry. And now, would you like to sit down and talk about it? About why I think I have to go and protect those people?"

As he said it, he felt his temper stir a little.

He'd talk her through his plans, slowly, give her lots of unimportant details. Of course, he hadn't really thought of the details. Pack food, head for the trail. What other details were there?

He caught her arm and guided her to the table and tugged on her overly stiff knees to get her to sit down. He dragged a chair around to sit in front of her.

"I never for a second thought of this as something that would get me killed. I'm not reckless, and I won't face down three armed men. I'm smarter than that." Yep, temper again. She was insulting him, though she might not quite realize it.

"I want to get there ahead of the wagon train so I can scout the area. Given time, I'll find the likely spots where the dry-gulching cowards will hole up. The best overlooks on a trail are easy to see. Then I'll find shelter for myself of some kind. I'll be out over several nights because, by my reckoning, the wagon train won't be coming through the most dangerous stretch of the trail for at least three more days, maybe as many as five, but I think three 'cause they'll be pushing hard. They need to get through the last bad stretch before the weather turns bad. The outlaws will get there ahead of them and find their hiding spots. I'll be waiting for them when they arrive."

There, he'd said a powerful lot of words

right there. That'd make her happy.

"I am furious, Trace."

Or maybe it wouldn't. He listened real close so he could figure out what had upset her. None of the men had said a thing when he'd told them he was going, except Adam had teased him about hiding out because he didn't want to help build the barn, and Utah had offered to come along.

He couldn't believe they might get that barn built this fall. He'd never dreamed —

"I married you just two days ago."

Oops, he'd meant to listen . . . had she been talking long?

"Now without so much as a by your leave, without talking one word of this over with me —"

How could she not know he had to go? Surely that'd been as plain as the nose on her face. Of course he was going. Did the woman have no common sense?

"— you make a decision to leave that might end in your *death.* You might never come home."

"I'm really good at guarding a trail, Deb, and sneakin' up on men in the wild. I move quiet as a ghost. Wolf and Black are knowing critters, and nothing can sneak up on them without their knowin' it, and they'll be going with me. No man will hear me.

No man will attack me. If I have to run, no man can catch me."

"Can you outrun a bullet, Trace?"

The woman had a sharp tongue, and that was that.

"It's honestly an easy way to catch these bushwhackers. They'll split up and watch the trail. They'll be separated, and I can get them one at a time, tie 'em up tight and, before you know it, I'll have 'em slung over their horses, and I'll parade 'em right to Ringo and hand 'em over to the marshal. They'll never be able to hurt anyone again. And since I saw them, you won't even need to testify."

Of course, Deb had been the one to see them in the *act* of murder, so he'd best not make any promises. "Or if you do need to testify, I'll ride home and fetch you." He smiled and hoped that was enough. His throat was startin' to hurt from all this yammering.

She surged to her feet and jammed her hands on her hips. Trace stood to face her. He was a newcomer to this husband business, but he was pretty sure that wasn't the way a woman stands when she's cheered up and the talkin' is over. Then her arms dropped, and the angry expression faded from her face. She launched herself right into his arms.

He held on to her tight and forgot figuring her out. It was way more fun to hold a live, warm woman in his arms.

"Trace, I know we're new at being married, and I'm not going to try and convince you not to do what you think needs doing. You're a good and honorable man, and that's one of the best things about you. But . . . if only you would talk to me, I'd like to know what's going on. When you left the first time you barely said where you were going. Now you're doing it again. I want to know."

Trace paused, wondering just what he should say now. Had they discussed it enough? "Uh, Deb, you know . . ." He glanced at the bedroom and lowered his voice. "You know I'm The Guardian, don't you?" Why whisper? Gwen had probably already heard them.

"Yes, of course."

"So you know I've done this before." Trace grasped her upper arms.

"That's not it. But it does comfort me to know you're skilled at these things. But you need to talk it over with me. And you would if you trusted me."

"I trust you more than anyone I've ever known, Deb. I'm used to going my own way and, well, just thinking everyone else knows what needs to be done so it's a waste of time talking it over. I'll learn to discuss plans with you." Trace leaned down and kissed her. "I'm going to be careful, Deb. I've never had such a worthy reason to get home."

Deb nodded. "Get on your way. I appreciate knowing enough to aim my prayers where they're needed most."

He left the cabin and sorted through what'd just happened. All he could figure really was the simple fact that women were strange creatures.

Deb watched until Trace disappeared around a bend in the trail. Men were strange and that was that. She said dryly, "You can come out now, Gwen."

She knew well and good that her little sister was listening. Or maybe Deb just knew that, in similar circumstances, she sure would be.

The door pushed open immediately, and Gwen carried both children out. "He wasn't even going to tell you where he was going?"

"Nope. You heard every word he was going to speak."

"Men are strange."

"I've had the same thought myself." Deb

didn't think Gwen went far enough. "They're also knotheads."

"And he's The Guardian?" Gwen looked at the door as if she could see through it to judge Trace a bit differently.

Deb got on with her cooking. "Have you heard of The Guardian?"

"A few words here and there from the men. Do you think they all know it's Trace?"

Deb lifted her shoulders helplessly and shifted her attention to a pile of turnips. "I have no idea, and we can't ask because then they'd know when Trace might not want them to."

"So what exactly is The Guardian?" Gwen sounded lost.

"I have so much to tell you. A lot more went on other than just a wedding ceremony. Let's get on with feeding these hungry men. The ones who do stay around deserve a good meal." She sounded a little snippy. With her husband off saving lives, the big half-wit, she really should be more gracious about it.

"What made you decide to marry Trace, anyway?"

That redirected her thoughts, and she was glad something did. She paused for a moment to remember his touch and his beautiful words. She also remembered that there'd been no talk of love. Which she'd so hoped for. She was sure he did love her . . . she hoped. But would she ever hear the words? The little scene they'd just gone through proved the man wasn't overly thoughtful to a woman's more delicate sensibilities. And when he protected her and fed her and built her a cabin, she didn't think she had a bit of business fussing about it. Of course, she hadn't said the words to him, either. She'd wanted him to say them first.

She didn't tell Gwen everything. It felt too personal and intimate, both the proposal and for certain what came after the wedding, the time they spent together in the night.

But there *was* something that made for a wonderful story. "Trace took me riding to an overlook of a huge lake. He called it Lake Tahoe."

"A lake? Up here?"

"Yes, the most beautiful thing I've ever seen. Honestly more beautiful than anything I've ever imagined. And while we stood there, he asked me to marry him. He made simple words sound as majestic and inspiring as that view."

Deb went on to describe the wonder of Tahoe as best she could. She thought about giving up her dream of running a newspaper. It hadn't been hard to do. Not when a man she loved offered her a home and marriage. But running a newspaper was different than writing. She could still do that. She knew newspapermen back home and one man from a magazine — and a few librarians who would send her more names. She could write about Lake Tahoe, describe its grandeur — such things were all the rage in magazines. If she sold her article, she might think of more to write. Were there stories to tell about the Comstock Lode? How about the pioneers and wagon trains? She could write about her own journey out here. Maybe she could earn enough to make Trace's life a bit more comfortable, although truly, with this new house and all the helpful men, Deb's life had never been more comfortable.

She told Gwen of the beauty she'd seen and the idea she'd had about writing. They spent the morning caring for the rambunctious children and cooking and talking about marriage and the oncoming winter.

After the men had eaten and headed out, Gwen said, "I'm going to put the children down for a nap. They fall asleep faster if I lie down with them, so it could be a while."

Deb hung up a dishcloth and moved to wipe the table clean. "You go on, and if you fall asleep too, there'll be no harm in it. We've got the roast on for supper and no more chores for hours. I might sit down and try to read one of Trace's books."

"You deserve a little time off your feet." Gwen carried Ronnie and led Maddie Sue by the hand into the bedroom she now shared with them.

Deb went to the box they'd brought over from the old cabin. Trace and his cowhands had been too busy for reading. They'd been working late into the cold nights to get the barn under cover before the winter set in. She bent over the heavy box and removed its lid, then lifted out the Bible. She'd start there. Though a believer, Deb admitted she hadn't spent enough time with the Holy Scripture. She'd been run ragged by the newspaper.

She laid it aside to replace the box lid just as a board creaked behind her. One of the children had left the room. Smiling, Deb straightened to turn and see who'd escaped.

Before she could look behind her, a callused hand slapped hard over her mouth.

An arm like a vise clamped around her waist and pinned her arms to her sides. Lifted clean off her feet, she was whirled around and carried right outside the wide-open door. Squeaking and thrashing, she tried to gain someone's attention.

While the man wasn't large, he was strong enough that she couldn't even feel him straining himself as he carried her. He never stopped moving. He strode straight for the trees while she kicked and wrenched her arms to get free.

There were two horses waiting, grazing. Another man came out of the woods, smiling wickedly at her. The man who had her leapt onto a horse, dragging her along, and nudged the horse with his knees. Without saying a word, they rode out of the small clearing away from the cabin.

The other man came up close, and reaching across from his horse, he quickly bound her hands in front of her. The horses never stopped walking.

Still not a word was spoken. They didn't do a thing to draw attention to themselves.

Terrified, she realized how calm they were behaving about everything. How silent. The horse's gallop might've sounded an alarm. He hadn't had to untie the well-trained horse or let Deb loose more than a second. They moved for long minutes while she twisted and fought. Furious, desperate, she bit the hand of the man who had her. Hard. He made a ruthless move that nearly jerked her teeth out, then shoved her chin up and held her jaw and mouth shut tight.

Finally, the distance must've been enough because the man holding her leaned forward, and his words were more hiss than a whisper. "You do that again and I'll knock you cold. I may do it anyway. You're a heap of trouble."

She twisted her head, and he let her. He sneered as she saw who had her.

The recognition blazed in her eyes. The only man she'd seen at the wagon train massacre. A filthy, brutal murderer had her in his grip.

"Know me, don'tcha? I reckon you're mighty scared. Well, I need you alive for now, and I'll do my best to keep you that way, because we're using you for bait to draw that man of yours out so we can kill him. He doesn't know I saw him in those woods when the grizzly startled us, but I did. And we followed the two of you all the way home. Havin' the two of you out of the way'll make it a lot easier to attack another train. You just sit tight. The only thing I need from you is screaming — which you'll do when the time is right. I don't need that for hours yet."

"Shut her up, Dalt," the second man said with cold cruelty. "She's gonna twist loose if we ain't careful."

Another move with the hand cut off her breath.

She fought the grip. He tightened it. There was no way to find even the smallest hint of air through her mouth or nose. The world began to narrow and her lungs heaved, fighting to inhale. She fought his grip with everything she had, and then her strength faded as her lungs starved. The narrow world went dark, and her last thoughts were of Trace and how, instead of being silently hurt because he didn't tell her he loved her, she wished she'd told him. What difference would it have made whether he'd said it back or not? At least he'd've known.

God, deliver me. Give me the sense and strength to know what you want me to do, and when.

She realized her wild, silent prayer was, in its own way, the voice of one crying in the wilderness.

That was her last thought before the world turned pitch-black.

CHAPTER 27

God, please protect Deb while I'm away.

Trace was flooded with a powerful need to pray. And he did pray that he could catch these men without killing and without being killed. But suddenly that wasn't enough. He was called to a prayer that was . . . deeper. He prayed for his wife left at home. He wasn't sure why God put it on his heart, but it was a pleasure to pray for her, so he did as he galloped toward the trail through the Sierra Nevada Mountains.

When he was close he, Black, and Wolf faded into the woods. He knew of a cave in this area that wasn't usually a spot to hibernate. Finding it, he went in prepared to back out and search on if it was inhabited. A fight with a bear or a mountain lion was bound to be noisy, and Trace was aiming to be as silent as fog.

This cave was the very dickens to get into. Trace had to move several heavy stones, which he'd added to over the years to help keep it blocked. But he'd found a bear in here a couple of times.

The cave was unoccupied, so he led his horse in, stripped the leather off him, and gave him some oats. Wolf dashed away, and Trace figured he was hunting his own meal. Trace ate a quick meal himself, no fire. The smoke would probably disperse, and it was windy enough the smell of cooking food wouldn't be noticeable, but Trace was in no mood to be careless.

When he was ready to go on, he regretted leaving Black. That animal was a lot of help. But the tracks of a shod horse would be so much harder to hide than Trace's own. And Wolf, well, those were wolf tracks. A wolf out here was no big surprise.

Trace brought out a blanket that he'd bought special and sewed into shape some years ago. White. He pulled it on, knowing he'd be nearly invisible against the snow, then emerged cautiously from his cave.

The cold stirred Gwen. She'd hoped to doze off with the children; she'd put in some long days while Deb had been off getting married.

But why was it so chilly in here?

Slipping as gracefully and silently as possible out of the bed where she was resting, nearly pinned between two sleeping children, she got to her feet, held her breath that neither would wake up, and went out into the kitchen. She closed the door with painstaking silence as she left the bedroom. One step and she saw the door wide open.

Rushing to close it, she nearly skidded to a stop before she got there. A Bible lay open, facedown on the floor. Pages were bent, folded, and maybe torn.

"Deb!" Dashing to the front door, Gwen shouted, "Deb, where are you?"

She ran out without a coat or, she realized, shoes, toward where the barn was going up. Hammers pounded. An ax rang out in the woods. The new barn was out of sight, nearer the canyon where Trace penned his cattle.

"Help me! Something's happened to Deb!"

The noise ended instantly. Feet moving fast. Gwen was terrified, but she nearly wept to think these men were here and coming to help.

Utah appeared first. "What happened?"

Adam was only seconds behind.

"Deb's gone." Gwen's feet went out from under her as she tried to stop.

Utah caught her and kept her upright. He

set her on her feet again. "Gone? Did she go after Trace?"

"She'd have told me. Did she take a horse?"

Adam ran for the barn to check.

"She didn't go anywhere willingly. Not with the door left open."

Adam was back in seconds. "She didn't ride out of here."

"I came out from putting the little ones down for their nap and the door was standing wide open. A Bible was on the floor, all askew. My sister would never treat a Bible like that. Someone must've taken her."

Utah asked no more questions. He hurried for the front door of the house. "Stay back."

Gwen was only vaguely aware of how cold her stockinged feet were.

Utah crouched but not for long. "Someone, a man, carried her out of here, not long ago. He headed into those trees over there."

Rushing for the spot he'd pointed out, he pushed into the woods. "A horse was standing here. Whoever had her let her stand for just a second because her prints are here in only one spot."

Spinning to face Adam, Utah barked, "Saddle two horses!"

Adam headed for the barn at a sprint.

Utah turned to Gwen. "We shouldn't leave you, but we have to go after her." He looked almost torn in half. "Get inside. Lock the door and keep a gun close to hand. Be on guard." He paced after the tracks.

Adam returned leading the horses, each with a bedroll tied behind the saddle.

Gwen swallowed a sob as she dashed into the house. She noticed one of the firmly closed shutters was broken. There was a little corner cracked off. She bent to study it. The man who'd taken Deb had been watching them. Waiting for his chance.

And he'd found it.

Once outside, Trace made every move in silence. He hoped he'd beat everyone here, the outlaws and the wagon train, but he'd work as if he were surrounded by enemies.

He quietly stacked stones over the cave entrance so that a hard-to-get-into cave became impossible to get into. His horse wouldn't be able to get out, either.

Then he started along a path parallel to the trail the wagon train would travel on, Wolf at his side, except when he trotted off to sniff around. Shrouded in the white cloak, Trace studied the position he was in, eyed the trail below, considered and discarded many places where a bushwhacker might hide and fire from cover.

It was done a step at a time, sometimes an inch at a time, heading up and down slopes, looking for the perfect nest for a viper to hide in.

Careful to conceal every footprint he left behind, he inched along, picking several prime spots where a coward might wait to attack.

The white of the snow, even in the heavy woods, made it possible to work as the sun lowered and the shadows deepened. And through all his work the pressure built to pray for Deb. Trace couldn't figure out why it rode him so hard, but when the good Lord put a burden on his heart, he listened.

The long, cold day and constant climbing wore him down, yet worry for the wagon train drove him onward. And his constant urge to pray for Deb kept his mind sharp. He wasn't going to quit until he'd seen all he needed to. There'd be time for a few hours of sleep, because he probably had at least another full day before the wagon train passed this stretch. And common sense told Trace he should go back to the cave and get that sleep.

Those varmints can't attack a wagon train that isn't here.

Night caught up to him, but Trace didn't

stop.

"Bring her over here." Raddo looked up from where he sat by a fire, behind a near mountain of fallen trees left from years of avalanches and rockslides that must've leveled the whole mountainside above it.

The sheltering stack of fallen logs was solid, with an overhang so extended it dipped until it nearly closed into a room. Raddo had used this as a hideout back in the days when he rode with Luth's gang. He could've lived here too, if he wasn't figurin' another avalanche might come along sooner or later.

He watched with grim satisfaction as Dalt lowered the woman off his horse. She was gagged and bound tight, both hands and feet. She must've made a nuisance of herself, and Dalt wasn't one to put up with undue noise or fighting.

She was limp when he dismounted, but her head shook and she struggled against her bonds, so maybe Dalt had put her to sleep, or maybe she'd fallen asleep herself.

Dalt shoved her under the sagging trees and let her drop to the ground.

"Untie her." Raddo noticed a line of claw marks on Dalt's cheek. Yep, she'd been trouble.

Since Dalt was already leading his horse away, Meeks came up to obey the order. Raddo saw the deep creases in her arms and legs and his mood turned sour. "We need this woman in one piece. We need her to stand and walk and talk."

Meeks paused in loosening the ropes to look over his shoulder to where Dalt had been. He was out of sight, picketing the horse in a hidden notch in the mountain. "Dalt has a mean streak."

Nodding, Raddo said, "That suits me just fine most times. I got one myself and so do you. But if this woman's ropes cut off her circulation too long, we might have a real hard time getting out of her what we need."

Meeks had her untied now, and because they were a long way from any help and facing a bitter cold night, he had no doubt he could keep her under control without much trouble. Besides, where was she gonna run to?

"Take the gag off, too. Let her scream if she's of a mind to. If her man is out huntin' us near the trail that wagon train'll go, then he's far enough off he can't hear her."

"Gotta figure there are men back at the ranch Dalt stole her from who are huntin'," Meeks said, loosening the gag.

The woman moaned. Her arms flopped

to her sides as if they were numb and nearly dead. She gasped in pain as she forced her hands to rub her wrists. Her legs twitched enough that Raddo figured she still had some blood flowing. She'd be fine.

Dalt came back into the shelter in time to hear Meeks talking of being pursued. "The men from the ranch'll come a-runnin'. There's another woman and two little ones in the house. But I set a false trail. They'll be riding the wrong way. She can scream all she wants."

He went to his bedroll and dug out a tin cup and helped himself to the pot of coffee nestled at the edge of the fire.

A cruel smile curled Dalt's lips. "She was a whole lotta trouble for me." He rubbed the raw scratches on his face. "I let her get a hand loose when I was adjusting her ropes, and she took her shot. And then I took one. I'd as soon make her scream a little."

Raddo watched as the woman sat up slowly. She studied each of their faces. Maybe checking to see if any of them had the look a merciful man might. Raddo knew his men. A more merciless lot had never gathered.

"We're moving quiet from this step on,"

Utah said to Adam.

With a nod, Adam slowed his horse.

Everything in him was driving him to hurry, but instead Utah was even more mindful of where his horse stepped so as not to crack more twigs than was necessary.

Then he came to an area blown clear along a long, flat stretch of rock. Not a track to be seen for a dozen yards. He knew which way he'd've gone just by common sense, in the direction of the trail that wagon train'd be on. But that was a careless way to track. This trail had been hidden by a knowing man, and after tracks left by a fast getaway, Utah had been slow in picking out the direction he'd ridden. There'd been more than one false trail left, too.

He held up a hand to stop Adam, then dismounted and tied his horse to a low branch. There was even a hardy clump or two of tall dried grass showing, so the horse could eat for a minute. Adam alit and did the same thing.

"Have a care on this trail."

"How far ahead are they with her?" Adam's voice had a note of panic to it, and Utah didn't blame him — she'd been in those men's clutches for a long time now. Too long. No woman would be safe under their power.

"The time is driving me loco too, Adam, but we've gotta be sure we're going the right way." Utah set to work. Adam watched for a long minute, then studied the trail on another side of the flat stretch of stone.

He should rest. Trace had tomorrow to hunt if his figuring was right. And it'd be better to study the trail in the full light.

The moon was about to rise when he finished one side of the trail. But instead of heading back, he slipped across the trail and climbed up to the other side of it. Wolf sniffed along with him and sometimes the critter vanished. Trace knew the dog could take better care of himself than Trace could, so he didn't worry much. If there was any movement to be seen, Wolf would be back fast to warn him and fight beside him if need be.

Another stretch of hours passed, and Trace had a good picture in his head. In fact, if these outlaws were half smart — and he suspected they were more than half — then Trace knew of about ten places that were perfect for what they had in mind. The only ten places.

He looked down on the trail. He stood right above a wide grassy stretch. Along its whole length, there was no more likely spot for the wagon train to circle for the night. It was so obvious that he hoped the wagon master would be too savvy to pick it. But if Trace was right, the spot where he stood would be the prime place for an outlaw bent on a dawn ambush to lie in wait.

He darted across the trail and felt an itch on his neck with every stride.

He reached the cave and climbed in to see how Black was doing. There was feed and shelter and water. The horse had it easier than Trace.

Wolf leapt through the small opening in the cave. He skidded onto his haunches to stop in front of Trace, then barked and clamped his mouth over Trace's wrist. He didn't bite, but he held on and pulled.

Trace followed along. "What's the matter, boy? I'm ready to sleep."

Wolf dragged him a few more paces before letting go. He then turned, barked, and dove out of the cave opening with one leap. He barked and growled and leapt back in again.

Trace had known Wolf for a long time. He kicked the rocks away from the cave's entrance and saddled Black in record time. Wolf dashed out. Trace pushed Black as hard as he dared down the side of the rugged mountain slope. Wolf slowed from time to time so that Trace could keep him in sight. All thoughts of sleep were quickly forgotten.

Deb wished she could sleep so she could maybe forget what had happened for a few merciful hours. But she didn't dare. She'd need to be alert, because she had a plan, and the timing of it could very likely be the difference between life and death. For too long she'd been waiting for her moment, but it just would not come.

Every time she closed her eyes, her mind was flooded with images of what could happen to her while these men held her captive. She was scared to death. She hurt something awful, especially her wrists and ankles. She'd been dragged around, hit a couple of times, and was so terrified she could barely breathe in and out.

Sleep would be a welcome escape.

The men were all in bed, not worried enough to even tie her up or post a guard for the night. And they'd used their names and made no effort to hide their faces. Deb had no doubt that their plans did not include her surviving whatever it was they were up to.

That made it worth her effort to try to run, even if at the risk of her own life.

Deb needed to slip away, but she'd heard

these men plotting. Raddo seemed to be the leader — and he was the man she'd almost run into in Carson City. Meeks was the one with the high-pitched voice. Dalt was the one who'd grabbed her and treated her so roughly.

They'd laughed about what would happen to her if she tried to escape, and they'd said things that made her think they knew exactly where Trace was. They were a long distance from him, and if she ran off, they'd just track her down and drag her back. They'd made that threat several times.

But she would go despite that. Her wrists and ankles were feeling like they would work if she tried to use them.

Listening, she heard snoring. All three of them. There was no sign they were just pretending. She'd slip out quietly, but instead of running for her life, she would hide. She'd be careful of leaving tracks, find a place to hole up for a while. They couldn't track her if she wasn't moving — she hoped, anyway. She'd find a place fast and then wait in silence until help came.

She flexed her legs and her ankles to test the pain. It was bad, but not so much she couldn't work through it.

Looking around at the strange overhang, she could be outside through a gap right behind her with only a few steps. She'd need to place her feet carefully. The moon was near full.

She'd seen Trace brush out tracks and step on rocks and logs when possible. Instead of running, she'd pick a deep shadow, stay still in utter silence. They'd have to trip over her to find her.

It was time. The snoring might not remain so deep for much longer. Their noise would cover hers. Gathering herself, she said a quick prayer, then was up and out in three soundless steps.

She listened again, heard no shouts or sounds of pursuit. A glance around showed a thick log. She hopped up, realizing she was fortunate to have boots on but sorry they made a tiny scraping sound against the log. Fighting each sound and hurrying each step, she walked the length of the log and saw where it crossed another one. She set out in a new direction.

A stone, swept clean by the wind, made a perfect next step. She finally saw what she wanted. A massive tree lying on its side, its roots forming a small cave. Almost too small. No one who wasn't desperate would consider it a hiding place. She thought the men might just rush right past it.

With a prayer for protection, for God to

close the eyes of her pursuers, and for help to come soon, she silently slipped into the cave made of roots.

CHAPTER 28

Utah held up his hand. Adam halted.

The kid was the perfect partner in this search. They were almost reading each other's minds, communicating in utter silence.

They were on foot, leading their horses. It felt as if they were crawling along while fear for Deb ate a hole in Utah's belly and drove him to hurry. But he fought down the urge. If he'd been hurrying, he'd have missed the turnoff and followed the false trail.

He turned from the obvious direction and followed well-hidden tracks. Well hidden, but not quite enough.

Picking out each step for as much as a hundred yards in the dark, twisting forest, finally he saw it. Utah smiled and held up a hand again. He tied his horse to a tree and stepped close enough to Adam so they could speak. Utah's voice was quiet as a breath of wind.

"He quit hiding his tracks. Movin' fast. Thinks he's fooled us, lost us. I'm bettin' he's close to his camp. Leave the horse."

A nod of agreement and Adam tied off his horse, then pulled his rifle from the scabbard on his saddle.

Utah moved slowly and quietly, gun in his holster, rifle strapped on his back. The search was over.

"She's gone!" Raddo thrashed to his feet.

Deb heard every step as he charged out from the overhang. One man laughed; both were right behind him.

"Love chasin' down a woman." Meeks was the lowest of them all in Deb's judgment. And that made him mighty low.

Deb breathed slowly through her mouth. They'd have to hear her heart beating if listening was how they found her.

"Split up!" Raddo's shout sent the men running away. While he came directly toward her. Not trying, not for a second, to cover the noise. He was so confident he could find her, he wouldn't even sneak.

As he drew near, she fought down the urge to break from her scant cover and run. She had watched Trace move through the woods with such assurance, and she realized that was exactly what Raddo wanted — to flush her out. That's why he was so noisy. He couldn't find her. She knew it. The place she'd chosen to secrete herself was so tiny, the merest bow in the heart of the tree roots.

If she could just stay still. She filled her mind with prayers for protection and courage, calm and wisdom. She couldn't fight these men and win. And she couldn't outrun them. Common sense kept her from considering either.

Raddo drew nearer. He wasn't walking on the logs; instead he stomped along, hollering, jeering. The path he was on, as far as Deb could tell by listening, was going to take him right past the mouth of this little concave in the tree roots.

Closer — yelling things so vile if she didn't show herself, that she was tempted to surrender in the hopes of avoiding his fiendish plans.

Closer — a step at a time. She could hear him muttering, trampling along with no more grace than a buffalo. Shouting her name. Shouting his threats.

Closer still. Now he was right in front of her. He stopped. She could have reached out and tugged on his pant leg. Except then she'd have to boil her fingers to get the awful feeling off her hand.

"Have you seen her?" He shouted loud

enough to shake snow down out of the trees.

One of his men shouted back. He was too close for too long. He'd see her or hear her or just plain sense that she was close.

Finally, one step, then another, and he walked past. That was no reason to move, but she felt like she should. The other men were in hearing distance, though moving away from her. They'd gone three directions. Surely if she went the fourth . . .

Utah heard a shout far to his right. Too far away to make out the words. Then came a return shout, about the same distance to his left. He turned to Adam and pointed left. Adam nodded quickly, and Utah realized he could see. The pitch-black night had turned to deep gray.

Darkness covered so much. Utah had hoped to get very close in secret. Now they were running out of time.

Adam vanished into the woods one way while Utah started another, then heard a twig snap only feet from him. Utah froze. There wasn't another sound. He drew his gun, braced himself, and held his breath.

Wolf had barked a few times and growled more. But now he'd gone silent, slowed down, and put his nose to the ground. Trace knew right where he was: a long way from home in a place that had nothing to do with a wagon train.

Maybe the outlaw gang was holding back. Maybe they'd done their scouting and judged when the train would come, and for now they were holed up. But they hadn't counted on Wolf.

Trace found a heavy copse of trees, dismounted, and tied Black to them. Everything was on foot from now on. He slipped along, fast and silent as a ghost. He'd done plenty of it before.

Wolf waited, then went on, then waited again. No one in this fight had the advantages of a critter like Trace had. Black would've been good too, but the horse had no sense about stepping on twigs.

He moved on, his eyes alert in all directions. Keeping Wolf within sight.

Then he heard something, so little, the sound maybe of cloth rubbing on bark. Freezing, he looked around and saw nothing. But something, or someone, was definitely there.

This time she was doing it. She was running. It was time to get away from here.

Deb gathered herself to jump out of the jumble of roots and run the fourth way, the direction none of the men had gone.

And leave footprints with every step.

That stopped her cold.

Grimly afraid she should have gone, she yelled inside her head for being a coward. Yes, her hiding place was good, but she realized that the dark was turning to dawn. And her hiding place was only as good as the dark.

A gunshot fired in the woods. Someone shrieked, but Deb couldn't tell who. Her guess was Meeks. Another gunshot, this one sounding different from the first, fired over and over. It came from right where she'd heard the cry of what sounded like pain. But Meeks was a foul man. If that had been him crying out, it could have been with animal savagery. Because he'd shot someone.

Briefly she hoped it was one of his own men. Out there in the dark, such a thing could happen.

Though God had guided her to this place of temporary safety, she was rather pessimistic that things would be solved so easily. She braced herself for Raddo to come storming back, right past her. He didn't come.

Another shout. This one wasn't Meeks. Was it Dalt? It sounded a distance from where the gunshots had sounded, but she couldn't be sure in the dense woods.

Then she heard a step, very nearly silent. Raddo sneaking back. An overwhelming panic washed over her, and she couldn't stay still. She tensed her muscles to leap up and run, when someone slapped a hand over her mouth and held her in his grip.

"Stay still."

The panic gave way to tears.

Trace. Trace had found her. That was his footstep. Raddo hadn't come back, or he'd headed directly to help his gang.

Seconds passed. Trace eased his hand from her mouth and then kissed her. She flung her arms around his neck and wept while she held him tight.

He'd come. She was so in love with him, and she'd tell him just as soon as she didn't have to remain utterly silent.

"Deb, are you here?" Utah whispered.

The tears came faster. They'd all come to save her. And they'd done a fine job of it, too.

Trace ended the kiss and pressed her face against his chest. She felt surrounded and protected and supported in every way.

"I've got her, Utah," Trace said quietly. "There's a third man."

"The boss of the gang is still around." Deb

still clung to her precious husband. "When I ran, they went in three directions. Raddo went past me."

Utah came into view. "I'll get after him."

"What was the gunfire?" Trace asked.

"Adam ran into one of 'em. They both came up with a fire iron. There was no choice, and Adam won the fight. But he looked mighty sick."

Deb thought Utah looked a little sick himself.

"I got one tied up, out cold. I didn't have to shoot, but it was a near thing," Utah continued. "He came up on me so quiet, and he didn't know I was there until it was too late for him."

Trace slipped off his coat and slung it around Deb's shoulders before she could protest, and then with the heat of his body warming it, she couldn't stand to give it back. Still, she tried.

"No, Trace. I was near the campfire with those men. You've been out in the cold all day and night."

"I've got a cloak on my horse. I'll put it on."

"We'd better find Adam," Utah said, "and pick up the man I caught. With one man still runnin' loose, I don't want Adam bushwhacked."

They found Adam, who'd rounded up all three of the outlaws' horses.

"Where's the other one?" Adam asked as he threw the first outlaw over a saddle.

"He must've just kept going. Just abandoned his partners. He couldn't have known how much trouble they were in." Deb shook her head and realized the dawn was full upon them now. But the day was gray, and fat flakes began drifting down.

"That heavy snow we've been worried about, looks like it's coming," Trace said. "Unless we want an outlaw living with us all winter, we'd better head for home, drop Deb off, and get these men to Carson City."

They set out. Found where Utah left his man tied up and loaded him up, too.

"That one they call Meeks." Deb pointed to the dead man.

"I saw Meeks when I followed them on foot and had a run-in with that grizzly."

"And Dalt is what I heard for the other — he's the one who came to the cabin and kidnapped me, and he's the one I saw at the massacre. The marshal in Ringo called him Dalton Callow." Deb looked at the two men in disgust. "The other calls himself Raddo. He's the boss, the one who abandoned his men."

"His first reaction was to run like a yellow

dog," Adam said.

"Well, no surprise he's a coward," Trace added. "We've known that about all of 'em from the first. Now, let's head back for the ranch. Gwen'll be scared."

"What about the wagon train, Trace?" Adam asked.

"He ain't gonna attack it alone. They're safe now. I'll bet they push hard through that trail with this snow coming down. They'll run through the night if they have to. These varmints would've had a hard time attacking twenty-five wagons with everyone wide awake. I'm going to get home, then haul these men to jail. Carson City is closer than Ringo. I'd like to give 'em to the marshal, but I need to turn them in and get back before the winter closes in around us. It'll be a running trip."

"I saw Raddo in Carson City," Deb said. She walked close to Trace. "Remember I said that a man ran into me and was rude? That was him. So I can describe him now. When Dalt brought me to their hideout, I heard all their names and heard them threaten me and you, Trace. And they bragged about their monstrous plans for the wagon train. I can tell the sheriff all about it as a witness."

"You'd better come along then. We're

leaving as soon as we get home. We'll ride hard and hopefully get back late tonight."

Trace went after Black and soon caught back up with them. Then they got to the horses Utah and Adam had left behind.

"How did you find me, Trace? Utah and Adam followed the tracks, but how did you get here?"

"Wolf led me right to this place. He was on a scent."

"Wolf is here?" Deb hadn't seen him.

Trace nodded. "Yep. He'll turn up any minute."

CHAPTER 29

Wolf turned up about ten minutes after they got home. The wolf-dog was carrying a patch of blood-smeared denim cloth in his mouth.

Trace stared at his dog awhile. "I reckon he caught up with Raddo."

"He definitely had pants on that looked like that." Deb gave Wolf a closer look. "If he didn't kill him, he must've scared him into a flat-out run."

"Probably treed him until Wolf got bored."

"Maybe that'll run him off for good. With no men for his gang, and the sheriff in Carson City with a name and description, he'll have to quit the country."

"Yep," Trace said. "It don't sit right to let him go, but I've barely got time to turn his men over and get back home. He ain't likely to cause trouble for a while, not with Wolf's fang marks planted in his backside."

Gwen had turned her worry into a need

to bake. There was pie and fresh-baked bread, and she'd cooked a stew heavy with meat and vegetables. Though it was break-fast time, they were all starving and shaking with the cold. The meal nearly fixed them, though a few hours' sleep would've done even more. But there was no time for that now.

Adam returned to building the barn. He declared they could have the roof on before the snow made that impossible.

Trace, Deb, and Utah rode hard for Carson City and turned over the men with plenty of questions to answer from the sheriff. They headed home in a snow so heavy Trace worried if they'd make it.

He might have to carry Deb for the last few miles.

She was afraid Trace might have to carry her the last few miles. The snow was now chest-deep on her horse. It was fluffy and that helped them forge on. Her horse's head hung low. Her feet were numb to the point of scaring her.

Beside her, Black was holding up better than the shorter mare she rode, but even that mighty horse was slowing down and breathing hard. To add a rider to the brave horse was cruel, and Deb refused to ask for help.

Finally home came in sight. Deb might've cried with relief, but the tears froze before they could fall so she didn't count it as crying.

"Let's get you inside, Deb." Trace rode straight for the cabin. He swung down and lifted her off. She didn't even try to stand.

"You're so strong, Trace," she whispered against his chest.

"I've had some practice with these winters."

Deb only distantly noticed Utah riding toward the barn, leading two horses. God bless these men who were caring for her. Then she was inside.

"Gwen, drag the rocker close to the fire." Trace's voice was as weary as she felt. But he was carrying her.

Gwen had Maddie Sue clinging to her ankles and Ronnie in her arm, propped on one hip. She rushed to Deb. Gwen did any doctoring they needed for the family.

"I've got a huge pot of chicken soup ready. That'll warm your insides." Gwen's voice was so laced with worry, Deb had to wonder how she looked.

"I'm worried about her feet; they might be frozen," Trace said. He set Deb in the chair, then grabbed kindling from the woodbox and went to build up the already-roaring fire.

Gwen knelt at Deb's feet and began pulling off her black lace-up boots. They were caked with snow, her stockings too. She did it all with Ronnie in her arms and Maddie Sue clinging to her.

Deb sighed when she felt the flames. Trace finished with the fire and knelt in front of her. Looking up with an uncomfortable expression, he said, "Let me have Ronnie. I'll go get her a pair of dry stockings."

Gwen nodded. Deb felt his awkwardness and appreciated that he didn't undress her, even though a husband could certainly do such a thing.

Trace left the room.

Gwen helped Deb off with her woolen stockings. Snow fell off in chunks as they peeled away.

With a gasp, Gwen picked up one foot and began rubbing it briskly between her hands. "Your feet are splotched with white, Deb."

Trace came back, saw Deb's condition and, moving fast, gave Ronnie back to Gwen, knelt in front of Deb, unbuttoned his shirt and undershirt and took the foot Gwen was working on, lifted the other, and pressed them both against his bare chest.

Shuddering, Deb felt the first prickle of pain.

Gwen brought a blanket.

"Do they hurt?" Trace asked, wrapping the blanket around her ankles.

"Yes."

"That's good." He massaged the tops of her feet as the bottoms rested against his chest. "They're not badly frozen."

They were starting to burn by the time the men trooped in, each carrying an arm-load of wood.

Deb squirmed to be caught so under-dressed, but the men ignored her, and Trace held on tight.

"Riders coming in, Trace," Utah said. He unloaded his armfuls of firewood into the box.

Trace's head came up, alert, braced for trouble. "Not one man alone?"

Deb pulled her feet free and rushed to the window. Her feet were still icy cold but worked just fine. She peered outside. Two riders, wrapped in coats and scarves, hats pulled low, approached the house in the deep snow.

"And neither of 'em has a bandage on his hind end?" Utah asked.

Trace laughed, but there wasn't much humor in it. He eased Deb aside. "Can't really see his hind end with all those wraps."

"Neither of them is Raddo," Deb said. "They aren't stout enough to be him. And anyway, where would he have gotten a horse so quickly?"

He could have stolen it. And he could've found someone else who rode the outlaw trail.

"Raddo's never come at anyone directly. He's a coward. Neither of these men is him," Trace said, watching every move they made.

"No reason to think this is trouble." He turned back to face the room. "Gwen, take the children to your room. Deb, go to our room and get wrapped up better. Shoes on. Pay attention to your feet if they start hurting overmuch."

"If they're just travelers, invite them to dinner. Poor things." Gwen swept both children up in her arms like a seasoned child wrangler and ducked into her room, shutting the door firmly.

Deb was only a step behind, dressing quickly and warmly.

Trace swung the door open. "Welcome," he said.

"Can we see to our horses?"

Trace's voice was as cold as the weather.

"Let's see if you're stayin' first."

Utah and Adam were alert, guns holstered but ready. They'd gone to opposite corners of the room so they had good angles on the men.

One man stepped inside, eyes alert. He wore a cavalry hat and a long woolen coat that looked to be part of a uniform. Army maybe.

One look in those sharp eyes and Trace knew this was a tough character. "Where you headed, stranger?"

The man had a severe expression. "We're on our way to right here. This is Trace Riley's ranch, ain't it?"

Touching the brim of his hat, Trace said, "That's me."

The man, for all his toughness, heaved a sigh of relief. "We made it. Thank heavens, the snow's getting powerful deep. This is my sister, Penny Scott, and my name's Cameron."

Trace's eyes shifted to the other rider and realized it was a woman. Dressed like a man but with female eyes, which was about all he could see of her face.

"Little Ronnie is named for you," Deb said quietly as she emerged from her room.

Trace glanced back. He'd hoped she would stay in the room longer. But if this was Cameron Scott, there was no reason to believe there was danger lurking about.

"I'm sorry about your brother and his wife," Deb went on. "But the children are in fine health. I rode out west with your family. The children and I survived the wagon train massacre. I'll tell you everything that happened over supper."

"There'll be no time for talking. We've got to get the children and go before the snow buries all the trails."

"Get them and go? You mean right now?" Deb's eyes widened in horror, though Trace also saw grief. She was as much in love with those children as he was.

"Yep, we're going to have to rush. This is my first Nevada winter, though I rode the area with the cavalry some. Go get the youngsters."

"You can't take them," Deb said.

Scott scowled at her. "Of course we can."

To Trace he had the look of a man more used to giving orders than taking them. Some kind of officer, no doubt.

Deb turned to Trace with pleading eyes. He'd have taken her side no matter what, but his reasons were more practical. "Scott, I don't know how far you have to go, but a couple of adults might be able to fight their way over the trails for a while, but you'll kill those little ones."

Scott quit glaring and turned to look straight through the wall, thinking about what he'd just ridden through. Trace held his peace because Scott looked like a sensible man, and Trace had spoken no more than the truth.

When there was no word of agreement coming from him, Trace said, "They'll be fine here with us for the winter. Come back for them in the spring."

Scott's shoulders sagged. "You're right. I might be able to make it home — Penny too, who's as tough as they come — but not the children."

Penny spoke up for the first time, her voice deep for a woman. "We're not leaving them, Riley. If they can't go, then we'll stay. Where do we sleep until spring?"

Trace hadn't considered that. He really didn't want two more people in his cabin. It was already full with five people. It'd be mighty crowded for seven, and he was plumb sick and tired of building houses for all and sundry.

"I'm not leaving my daughter and nephew behind." Scott's expression was stubborn, like it'd take a stick of dynamite to get rid of him. "I've been away from them for too long already. If they can't go, then we'll stay. We both homesteaded. We'll build a lean-to cabin on the property line so we can prove up. I left a small herd in a corral out of the wind where they'll find water and food enough. What other things we have, well, there's likely too much snow for anyone to get to it and steal our things. We don't have to worry about being gone."

"I'll put your horses up," Adam said. "You folks get warm." He left the cabin. He'd never gotten his coat off after he came in with the firewood.

Utah, Trace noticed, stayed off to the side. He looked more relaxed now but still alert. And he had a little smirk on his face.

Utah said, "Trace, I reckon you and Scott here oughta spend the winter in the bunkhouse with us cowpokes."

"I want to stay near my children," Scott protested.

At the same instant, Trace said, "I want to stay with my wife."

"Guess I'd better get a fire going in the bunkhouse." Utah's smirk turned into a chuckle. "Gonna be an interesting winter." He spun on his heel and walked out.

CHAPTER 30

Deb hurried forward and took the woman's arm. "Come to the fire. Trace and I are just in from a ride to Carson City, and I am still half frozen."

The woman went with her, but she wasn't shivering, nor did she seem likely to tear her shoes off and roast her toes by the fire.

"Sit in the rocker and just rest awhile." Deb helped her shed her coat and other outer garments.

Penny gave her a confused look. "I'll stand, thank you."

"Cameron, come by the fire." Penny stretched out her hands to warm them. "Mrs. Riley, would you please bring the children out so that Scott can see Maddie Sue. I lived with Abe and Delia until Cam and I headed west — that was before Ronnie was born. I doubt Maddie Sue remembers me, but I remember her and have pined to see her again and also meet little Ronnie."

Cameron's expression turned grim. "There's no chance Maddie Sue'll remember me. She knew me for only a few weeks after the war."

Deb couldn't help but feel bad for the poor man. She hung up Penny's coat, scarf, hat, and gloves on a peg by the front door, then hurried to Gwen's bedroom door and knocked. "Come on out, Gwen. Maddie Sue's pa is here."

A gasp from behind the door told Deb her sister hadn't understood what they'd been talking about until now. The door remained closed.

Deb knew exactly how Gwen felt.

Finally, slowly, the door inched open. Deb waited patiently.

At last Deb could see Gwen, and see the way she clung to the children, one on each hip, looking as if opening that door was breaking her heart. Gwen slowly stepped out to where she could see the newcomers.

Penny smiled. Even with her windburned cheeks and bedraggled brown hair, the smile transformed her face to a very pretty one. "Maddie Sue, it's your aunt Penny. Do you remember me?"

Maddie Sue frowned and looked at Penny with wary eyes.

"Maddie Sue, it's Pa." Cam smiled and

rushed forward. He reached out and she screamed. She turned her face away and clung to Gwen, screaming as if a longhorn was charging her.

Although truth be told, she'd probably be more comfortable with longhorns.

Cam tugged at her. Maddie Sue's screams grew louder.

Little Ronnie howled in sympathy and nearly crawled over Gwen as if to hang on to her back where he could better hide from this scary man.

"Mr. Scott, please let her go," Gwen said. She tried to sound calm, but a thread of desperation underlined it. "You're scaring her."

Cam didn't seem to hear Gwen. He was too intent on trying to hold his daughter.

Deb could only imagine how much he'd missed his child.

Trace came up and clamped a hard hand on Cam's shoulder and dragged him back.

Cam whirled around, a fist clenched. "Let me go. I haven't seen her in . . . in . . ."

"You're scaring her to death. Just calm down. Let her get to know you a bit first."

Deb braced herself for Cam to throw that fist.

Cam's chest heaved, breathing too fast. Deb could see the fight for control. He was furious, but more than that, she could see he was devastated, brokenhearted.

"I have a daughter who doesn't even know who I am. I'm nothing but a frightening stranger to her." Cam ran his hands over his face, thick with beard stubble, his hair overlong and uncombed.

"I don't blame her for being terrified of me." Cam's head dropped so his chin rested on his chest. "I abandoned her."

The screaming kept up. Both children were clinging to Gwen, their faces red and streaked with tears.

With his shoulders slumped, Cam turned away and found where he'd shed his coat. He grabbed it and, dragging it on, headed for the door. "I'll go see if I can help outside." He left the house, swinging the door shut.

Deb couldn't even hear over Maddie Sue, whose face was pressed against Gwen's chest, howling louder than the loneliest wolf.

Epilogue

Deb crawled into bed with Trace. Dragging the covers up over both of them, Trace whispered, "I thought I was going to end up in the bunkhouse with all the other men."

Deb threw her arms tight around him. "I was afraid you might. You know there's not much room in this house anymore."

Groaning, Trace rolled onto his back and drew Deb along so that her head rested on his chest and her arm surrounded his waist. "No one in a hundred miles is tough enough to get me to give up holding you in the night."

Deb giggled, and Trace covered her mouth and hissed, "You be quiet. There are too many ears close by."

Wriggling away from his hand, she said, "Listening to Maddie Sue and Ronnie cry so hard reminded me of a voice crying in the wilderness. Maybe you're too tough to cry. And I'm certain you're too tough to admit it if you did."

"Darn right I am." Trace kissed her on the neck in a way that made her giggle again, but she was going to have her say.

"But fighting this snow, Trace, how did you survive it? From Missouri? You couldn't have had any idea what you were facing."

"Not really, but Pa had talked of stocking up food for the winter. And we'd lived up on a mountainside in Tennessee, so we got some snow there. But you're right — I wasn't ready at all. It was only hard work and a whole lot of prayers that got me through."

"Well, your experience saved lives when you guarded that trail. It also saved my life along with Gwen's and the children's. And it provided you with a wife. And this home is going to help poor Cam get to know his children."

"They didn't even get near him at supper. They were almost as scared of Penny. They act like Gwen is their mother. They love you too, but it's her they go to."

"Yep." Deb rested her head comfortably against his shoulder. "But I don't mind that at all. They love us both, though I'm glad they picked one of us for a special attachment. That seemed better for them, yet I don't know how they're going to act when Cam and Penny try to take them away."

"I know how I'm going to act." Trace kissed her before she could ask what he meant. He went on, "I'm going to jump up and down and cheer at the thought of having all those people gone out of my house."

She laughed again, but much more quietly this time, and Trace silenced her with his lips. "I love you, Deb."

Deb gasped and pulled back. "You do?"

In the dark, she could see Trace's brow furrow. "Well, a'course I do. It'd be a foolish man who'd have such a wife as you and not count his blessings every day and love her with all his heart. I never dreamed such a wonderful thing could happen to me. Didn't you know I love you?"

When he put it that way, she almost felt like she'd done wrong. "The thing is, you never said you loved me. I didn't know if a man would speak of such a thing, and I was afraid I'd never hear those words from you."

"You like me saying it?"

"I like it very much. My father never spoke kind words to my mother or to Gwen and me. The words are so nice to hear. I wish you'd just say it about every night at bedtime. It gives me a warm and happy feeling to hear it. And it makes it easy for me to say it back. *I love you,* Trace. With all my heart." She snuggled closer. "I have a husband. Imagine that."

"I don't think we need to imagine a thing." Trace snuck in another kiss. "Not while I'm holding you in my arms."

She giggled once more, only this time he seemed serious about her being quiet, because he set himself to keeping her mouth busy for a long while.

ABOUT THE AUTHOR

Mary Connealy writes romantic comedies about cowboys. She's the author of the TROUBLE IN TEXAS, WILD AT HEART, and CIMARRON LEGACY series, as well as several other acclaimed series. Mary has been nominated for a Christy Award, was a finalist for a RITA Award, and is a two-time winner of the Carol Award. She lives on a ranch in eastern Nebraska with her very own romantic cowboy hero. They have four grown daughters — Joslyn, married to Matt; Wendy; Shelly, married to Aaron; and Katy, married to Max — and four precious grandchildren. Learn more about Mary and her books at:

maryconnealy.com
facebook.com/maryconnealy
seekerville.blogspot.com
petticoatsandpistols.com

The employees of Thorndike Press hope you have enjoyed this Large Print book. All our Thorndike, Wheeler, and Kennebec Large Print titles are designed for easy reading, and all our books are made to last. Other Thorndike Press Large Print books are available at your library, through selected bookstores, or directly from us.

For information about titles, please call:
(800) 223-1244

or visit our website at:
gale.com/thorndike

To share your comments, please write:
Publisher
Thorndike Press
10 Water St., Suite 310
Waterville, ME 04901